Me & My Girls

Published by Street Knowledge Publishing

www.streetknowledgepublishing.com

Me & My Girls

A Novel by Leondrei Prince

Me & My Girls ®

Published by
Joseph Jones: Street Knowledge Publishing.
Wilmington, Delaware
Email: jj@streetknowledgepublishing.com

ISBN 0-9746199-1-4

For sales inquiries, commentary, book orders or
author's, appearances please visit our website at
www.streetknowledgepublishing.com.

This book is dedicated to Ms. Natae Hollis Owens and Mr. Trans Dwayne Owens
You two are missed everyday by the family. Much love for you from your big cousin Leondrei Prince.

Special Acknowledgment

A letter for my brother: Mr. Jermaine (Marlow) Wright.

How and where do I begin a letter that has no starting point, and no ending? I don't know, but I'm going to try. Marlow, Mar told me the other day that you was really hurting about not seeing your name in my first book, *Bloody Money*, I sincerely do apologize and if you read the acknowledgments over again you'll see that I forgot Radee, Rayya, and Gammy. It was simply a mistake, that's no excuse though. So again, I apologize.

Marlow, you know how I am. I'm very emotional when it comes to the people I love and I can't take too much hurt, so what I do is I try to forget. But how can I when a part of my soul is gone? You're that part of me that's gone over some bullshit! I'm hurting because of it man! I cry almost every motherfuckin' day thinking about how they got you in some muthafuckin' cage for some shit you didn't even do; it's crazy! But you know what? As I'm writing this, I do feel the selfishness I'm displaying. I'm only thinking about my feelings, when it's yours I should be thinking about the most. So brother I promise to tighten up.

Marlow, do you know that ever since you been gone I cannot get it together? I'm still doing the same shit; fucking up! That's where you used to come in. You were the will power and I was the brain. Yo man, I miss you! See this is the shit I'm talking about, I'm crying now. Look man, I'm out here meeting people, big people in high places, and I'm on my grind trying to get you home, even though it may not seem like it, but I am. Marlow, again I apologize and my selfishness is ending today.

Love you
Nigga!

Your lil
brother, Leondrei Prince
(P.S.) Baby boy I'mma get you out of there, watch!

Love Ya!

Acknowledgments

First and foremost I'm going to say I bare witness that there is no God but Allah, and I bare witness that Muhammad is his messenger and servant. I want to apologize to my brother and sister Mr. Radee Prince and Ms. Rayya Prince for missing them in the first book. (Sorry) but y'all know y'all's brother is half crazy. To my daughter Ms. Khalia J. Thomas, your dad is going to get it together one day, love ya! To my grandmother (Gammy) hey baby girl, you're 80 plus and still kicking ☺, please stay for 80 more, love ya! ☺ To Ms. April (Munch) Fennell, hey sis! Give my love to my nephews Ken-Ken and Amir for me, and since my ex-wife is acting so stupid, please tell my kids I love 'em and give 'em a kiss for me. (Thanks!)

To my sisters: Jamia (Tanya) Redden, Gina Redden, Dee Redden, Azia Redden, Orrin Redden, Robin Redden, and Theresa (Sabiyah) Redden-Chambers (for life!) and you too Lamby Redden. Ms. Dawn M. Broton.

To my brothers: Willie Brothers, Kenny (Love) Davis, "R.I.P" LeShawn Stokes, Calvin Redden, Mark Redden, Kevin Redden, Tyrone Bruton, Aaron Bruton, and Raymond Bruton (Rico), (Hey baby!!)

I know we all have something in common by sharing the same daddy, but I have a father Muhammad Salaam whom I love dearly, and it wouldn't be right if I didn't let that be known, or shout out my brothers and sisters! To my beautiful lil sis Ms. Camilia Salaam, you're at Penn State baby; break some records! Ms. Hafeeza (HaHa) Salaam hey baby, keep singing! To my brothers Talib Salaam, Balaal Salaam, and Sied Salaam, love y'all.

To all my nieces and nephews, I love you all but it's just too many to name! To my daughters, Ms. Kiesha and Ieshia Jenkins, hey y'all! Love ya! Tracy too!

I shouted out nearly the whole city in my last book, so if I miss you this time, please don't run up on me with the: "Why my name wasn't in the book, shit." Damn, it's only a book. You shouldn't need the recognition of a shout out in this little city because you should already be known. Now, for my shout outs!

Again, this book is for the Red Brick City! Long live (Riverside, Bucket, 2-6)! Whass'up y'all! Y'alls boy banged out another street classic! To my peeps: Michael (Dog) Lindsey, Paul (Sponge) Clark, Animal Cub, Dro-Heathen, Repo, Naphie, the entire M.U.C.C family. To my brother-in-law Teddy (Yeddy Bear), hey baby! Cousin Frog, I need you baby! That's our little joke! Cousin Too Sweet (Turtle) one of the funniest men alive! Young Grams a.k.a. (Boog), Chino, my baby boy Pete Rock, congrats on the seed boy! Little B a.k.a. Brian Camile, whass'up lil brother! Block Captin (Fredd Fox), Len Brown, and Plug, whass'up. Cousin Tasha (Tasty) Clark, Kia Clark, Aunt Vickie, Hey baby, your nephew did it again! Cousin Monie, hey babe! To my sista, Ms. Ursla Hagler, after all these years of being the shit you're still the shit. ☺ Tell them to talk about that! To my cover girls, hey y'all! Ms. Sherise, Angel, and Tammy. Tune up y'all's acting because the play is coming soon. To my big cousin, Kevin (Big Daddy) Moore love you cuz, and slow down on your pimpin' (Ha! Ha!). To my boy Slash (Wardell) and family, I love y'all.

To my partner, Mr. Joseph (Joe-Joe) Jones. Bare with me baby. I know I give you gray hairs, but I also make us plenty of money! Let's flip it and bounce it all the way to Hollywood! We ain't going to let no money tear us apart like it did those before us! To Michael (Lil-Gene) Johnson and his wife Ms. Shelly Johnson, I love y'all. Oh do y'all remember who hooked y'all up? Well I'm still waiting on my (Thanks!). To A-6 media, whass'up Kenny?

To my cousin Mr. Robert C. Cottman, C.E.O of Flatline Records, whass'up boy! Let's get this "Bloody Money" movie done! I'm tired of bullshitting! To the entire Flatline family: crazy shouts to my boy "Streetz" yo cuz, your name fits you like no other! To the Boah Mil, Cannon, Neko, lil Var 23rd St., keep putting out good hood music!

To my Hilltop family, my second home! Cousin Tuck a.k.a. (Big Thug), Tommy Jr. B-More, Cheeze, Shock, E-Money Baggs, Var, E.S., Alfie, Jermaine, Jersey, Shack, Rell, Chico, The Twins-both sets, C.P. Craig Parker (P. Mungler) cousin April, hey girl, cousin Iesh! Cousin Gil, Jihad (Jay), Fam, Bruce and Brian, Easy, Chuckie, T-Otis-Hey baby! And to my lil sister Ms. Marriahya Stevens! Yeah, I know I spelled the name wrong, but I ain't forget you, did I? To your girl Latise too! To my baby Tamira (Marge) Stevens! Be easy ok. You are too sexy of a woman to be trippin and going crazy! Don't lose out on opportunities because of a piss poor attitude!

To my boy, Slash lil brother, Slash cousin and every body else, Mr. Jerome (Doo-Doo) "The Beast" Perkins you are loved by few, hated by many, but respected by all! Love you Boah! Cousin Eric (Butter Rico) Lloyd hold ya head baby, we miss you like a mutha-fucka! Cousin Artie, Leonard, Markie (Clobber), Damon (Lil Cos). To my boy Dwayne (Flite) Washington, sorry I missed you in the first one!

To my brother from another mother: Mr. William (Datta Boy) Smith. Fuck what you heard, we're always going to be the shit! Nigga'z ain't got nuffin' on us, we get ourselves, so let's tighten up!! Toy-stay strong, and stand by your man girl, the best days are yet to come. I just wish mines had your strength! To Thug and The Queen (Shooby). Hey y'all! Snoody (2-g's). S-Dog, hey baby!

To my brother and other half: Mr. Jermaine (J.D. Hogg) Dollard. I know you get upset with me at times, but you of all people should know that I'm a ninth inning player, fourth quarter soldier, and overtime specialist! It's only the beginning of my madness! Nigga, I'm about to be rich! And I'm not talking about that being my name either! Hey Aunt Cookie and Sandy! I love y'all. Aunt Shelia, Carla, and Vonnie love y'all too!

To my fellow writers: Ms. Kashamba Williams, *Blinded*, hey sista! We are definitely putting Delaware on the map! Mark Anthony, *Paper Chasers*, Tonya Nuez, *Flowers Bed*, Ms. Ebony Stroman, *The Hood*, Mr. Winston Chapman *Caught Up* and to everyone else it's just too many to name. Oh, my boy Shannon, *B-More Careful*, Holmes whass'up? To my home bookstores: "Mejah Books" Tri-State mall and Hanif's on South St., Philly. Y'all have been such a help to me. Hey mom Emilyn, and Aunt Marlyn DeGaines love y'all! To Culture Plus Distributors, A&B Distributors, and Lushena Books Distributors in Chicago, Ill., thanks to all of y'all for carrying my work and getting me known to the world. To all the bookstores that support black authors! To my boy Marcus at Nubian bookstore, in Greenbriar Mall, Atlanta, GA. Ms. Fanta Books, South DeKalb Mall, Atlanta, GA. Thanks a lot for helping me out when I needed y'all most!

To the A.T.L. (Atlanta!): I know I wasn't born there, but I'm damn sure coming home! To my very special friend, my Georgia Peach, Ms. Janell "Unique" Brant, I owe you girl, and thanks for pushing those books! I'll see you soon! Mr. Amir Ali, Sondra Tolson-Ali, Cee-Cee, and Marquise, love y'all. To my boy Kurtis, Chi-Town's finest! Hey folk! To my big brother's "Ooo-Wee" and "Junior" the ATL's finest, hands down! Thanks for accepting us with open arms. This time's, it's on us! To my boy lil Kenny & Sid down in the (Bluff), keep trappin' folk! To my lil sis India Lewis, hey girl,

I'm on my way home soon, I just have to find the house I want! Love ya!

Last but not least, to Delaware and all the sets, I got mad love for ya! To my boy Deon (Young) whass'up baby? As for the haters, yeah, y'all know who y'all are! The one's who smile in Lee-Mudds face, and eats his flesh out when he's gone, check dis out: You receive no gain, I'm a house hold name, from Florida to Maine so stop hatin' it stunts your growth! Now talk about that! (Ha! Ha! Ha!)

Peace

I'm Out!!

(P.S) Strawberry Cream Cheese Bagels, it's past Nov. 16th, why haven't I heard from you yet? Whass'up with that major proposal that could land you a job for life? (Smile) That's a riddle to a friend of mine so don't rack your brains trying to figure it out everybody.

(P.S.S.) Another thing, if I forgot your name and you feel as though it should be in here, maybe it's just that I'm making some changes in my life, and you might be a part of the change. Did I say it right Minyon? (Smile)

Me & My Girls

Chapter One

Tish could hear her son Tymeere crying as she lie awake in bed. "Thank God it's Friday." She said to herself, as she glanced at the digital clock that read 5:45 A.M. "I'll be so glad when I graduate this year, I don't know what I'mma do?" She continued, before going to tend to her son. Tish got up, walked over to the crib and picked up her child. Using her index finger, she ran it across the edge of his diaper and he was wet. Tish laid Tymeere down at the foot of the bed and within seconds, before he could even roll over, she was back with a new diaper and baby wipes. "Hey stink butt don't you think it's about time for you to start asking for the potty?" She said playfully and poked a finger at his nose. When he smiled, Tish's stomach turned, and she literally almost threw-up because that's how much he resembled his father Saafie. Saafie was a small time drug dealer around the projects when they first met, but now he and his boy Tyaire ran the city. Tish couldn't stand him now, but she remembered the day they met like it was yesterday.

"Come here girl." A voice called; as Tish passed the corner she hated passing so much. This particular corner was where people did everything from shoot dice to sell drugs and it just so happened to be on the same route she had to take when walking home from her bus stop. Tish looked into the crowd of boys on the corner and tried to put a face with the voice, but to no avail. "I really don't need to know who it is anyway if he's standing over there." She said to herself and kept stepping.

"Oh, you ain't going to stop?" She heard the voice say again, but this time she saw who it was.

1

"It's him! That cute boy I always see when I walk to the corner store." She thought as he made his way over to her.

"I wasn't until I saw it was you." She answered.

"Whass your name?" The cute boy asked.

"My name is Tish. Whass yours?"

"Saafie." And from that very moment Tish knew Saafie would be the one to steal her virginity.

On that note, Tish snapped back to reality from her daydream and fastened Tymeere's diaper.

"Fuck your Daddy! We are goin' to be fine all by ourselves." Tish said to Tymeere as he laid him on his side, and propped his bottle up on the pillow. Tish looked up and the clock read 6:15 A.M., so she ran off to the shower. She put on her shower cap and lathered up with Dove Body Wash, and stood under the hot spicket for what seemed to be like 10 minutes, but when she saw the clock she panicked.

"Damn, I only got 15 minutes to get me and him dressed." She said.

Tish sat on the foot of her bed staring into the full-length mirror that covered her bedroom door and lotion up. Tish was tall, around 6 feet and built like a goddess. If you didn't know her, you'd never know she was a mother because her body showed no traces. Many people said she resembled Tyra Banks, but she didn't think so, she thought more along the lines of a taller Lisa Raye. Tish stood up and stepped into her matching pink polka-dot thong and bra set and looked at herself in the mirror.

"Shit, Saafie don't know what he's missing." She said to herself, as she continued to get dressed.

When she finished getting dressed, she couldn't do nuffin' but shake her head. The powder blue Roca-Wear sweat suit fit her curves to a tee, and her white Nike's set it all off, as her hair hung shoulder length.

"A mutha-fucka can't say I ain't sharp!" She told herself as she walked down the hallway to her mother's room.

"Mom" She said, as she knocked on the door instead of just walking straight in. The thought of what happened just two days ago made her smile with embarrassment, as she saw her Mom and Mr. Joe getting it in.

"What?" Her Mom said.

"Can I come in?" Tish asked.

"Yeah, now what's the problem?" Her mom said.

"Can you please take Meere-Meere to daycare for me?" Tish asked.

"Where's his no good ass daddy?" Her mom said.

"He has to go to court today, so he can't come." Tish said.

"It's always some'em! I'll do it, but this is the last time I take care of his so-called daddy's responsibility." Tish's mom said.

"Whatever!" Tish said, and left the room with a slam of door. "I'll be so glad when I get my own shit!"

"What you say? Don't get fucked up!" Ms. Carla, the older version of Tish, said.

Ms. Carla Wallace, a single mother of one and grandmother to another, sat up in bed and grabbed her robe from the whickered chair directly at her right. A sense of pride overcame her as she realized she managed to instill moral values in her only child and build an open and honest friendship with her at the same time. She remembered ever so clearly the news that literally broke her to her knees when Tish said, "Momma, I'm pregnant." Even though the news was unexpected, Ms. Carla understood, and was proud that Tish could be so honest. When she was pregnant, she couldn't muster up the strength to tell her own parents, so hearing and seeing Tish tell her, she knew not only did she have a good daughter, but she also had a best friend.

*   *   *   *   *   *   *

"Beep-Beep" The horn sounded.

"Here I come, damn!" Tish said from her bedroom window.

"Come on Bitch, you always late!" Tasheena yelled from the passenger's side window.

"What you say girl?" Ms. Carla yelled back out of her window.

"Nuffin', Ms. Carla, Oooo I'm so sorry." Tasheena said embarrassingly.

"Hey Rayon, I knew your mouth wasn't that nasty." Ms. Carla said, knowing it could probably be, if not worse.

"Nope Mom Carla and never was." Rayon shot back.

"Bye Mom." Tish said as she locked the door behind her.

"Bye baby." Ms. Carla said and almost forgot about some key items. "Where are all of his things at?"

"Downstairs on the couch." Tish said and slid in the backseat of Tasheena's car. "Damn y'all, she gets on my nerves! I got to get my own shit and fast." Tish said to Tasheena and Rayon.

"Bitch stop crying! I know what you need early this morning," Tasheena said.

"Me too!" Rayon added, as they high-fived and said in unison "A blunt Bitch!" as they all fell out laughing.

"Well it looks like you two bitches already had one," Tish said.

"We wish, but bitch we only got 5 dollars we can spend. The rest of the money is for some gas and munchies." Tasheena said.

"I know that's right." Rayon added.

"Well who got it? Y'all wanna go see Ol' School on 2-4 or the young boys down on 27th street?" Tish asked.

"Let's go see the young boys 'cause we can work them. Ol' School ain't havin' it!" Tasheena said.

"Who you tellin'," Tish and Rayon said at the same time.

Rayon pulled her Honda Accord away from the curb in front of 2718 Bower Street and headed to 27th street. Tish looked around at the place she called home for her 18 years and was glad to be leaving the eye soaring slums, even if it was only to be going to school.

"Tasheena, do you feel the same way about this shit?" Tish asked.

"About what shit?"

"About the projects, like it ain't no way out of these muthafucka's"

"Hell no bitch, we ain't going to be here forever, we too damn sharp for dat shit. If anything, a nigga going' to get us up outta here."

"Bitch that's your problem now. Deon done spoiled you and now since y'all ain't together, you just think a nigga posed to take care of you, huh?

"No, I ain't say dat. I'm just saying you can stay on the piss pot, but I'm not. I refuse to stay a project kid." Tasheena said.

"I heard dat," Rayon intervened.

"Bitch what you know about the projects and you live way out in the suburbs?" Tasheena shot back.

"Bitch I be in them around y'all so much, I might as well be from them! Put it this way, I know it ain't no place to want to be." She said as she crossed Market Street.

27th and West Street in Wilmington was a known drug spot for marijuana. Rayon pulled her car up to Fat Cat's corner store and parked, to avoid looking so obvious about buying weed because it was hot. Not hot weather wise, but hot as far as the police were concerned. It seemed as though they frequented the block every five minutes.

"Who's getting out to get it?" Rayon asked, the suburban side of her starting to kick in. "cause I don't like it up here like dat," She finished.

"Bitch, you just scared." Tasheena said.

"Look just give me the money and I'll go get it." Tish said.

Tish strutted up the block like she was the baddest bitch in town and her tall stacked body shook in all the right places. It was too early in the morning for the block to be jammed packed, but for the couple of young boys that were out there, they got an eye full.

"Damn she phat as a mu'fucka!" One of them said.

"Yeah, she phat, but that's Saafie's baby's mom" The other one said.

"Oh shit! It is? She still phat dough."

"Whass' up y'all?" Tish said as she walked up on them. "Who got da dro?" She asked.

"Ain't no dro, but I got some blueberry," The first to speak said.

"Well I ain't got no blueberry money." Tish replied then heard someone call her name.

"Damn, did you have to call my whole government?" She said when she saw it was Tyaire.

"Girl shut up." He said smiling. "What'chu doing out here?"

"I'm trying to get some weed so we can get smoked before we go to school."

"Who's we? Is the babe Rayon with you?" Tyaire asked.

"Yeah she wit me, but she ain't thinking about you." Tish said.

"Yeah dats what your mouth says. Tell her I said whass'up. She know I been tryin' to smash dat for years."

"Yeah that's just why you haven't smashed it 'cause she know that's all you want to do," Tish said sarcastically, then continued, "Now who got da weed out here?"

"Here you can have my lil' personal sack," He said and pulled it from his back pocket.

"Damn cuz! I thought you was coming right back," Deon said.

"Deon, is that you?" Tish asked surprised, but more confused than anything.

"Oh shit! Hey sis, how you doin'?"

"I'm doing fine, how about you?" Deon said.

"I'm alright, I'm not like I used to be, but I'm alright," He said, yet his eyes told a very different story.

Deon looked bad! His hair wasn't cut and sharply lined like it usually was and his clothes weren't even right. His Timbs were leaning over and dirty and Tish just shook her head. She felt bad for Deon because he became like so many young boys in da hood, doped out. He literally looked like he gave up. She remembered when Deon was the "Man" and when he and Tasheena were hot and heavy. In fact, he was the one who put Saafie and Tyaire on in the game, now it seemed as though he was on the verge of begging Tyaire for some'em.

7

"Deon if you ever need me, call me ok? You still got my number right" Tish asked.

"Yeah I got it," He answered with watery eyes. The pain Deon felt inside was almost too much bare, but he managed to fight back the tears. "Yo Tish, I love you sis. He said.

"I love you too Deon," Tish replied and hugged him tightly.

"Tell Tasheena I miss her and I love her to death."

"I will." Tasheena vowed.

"Don't forget to tell Rayon what I said," Tyaire interrupted.

"Whatever" Tish replied not paying him any attention and he knew it too.

Because of the situation that just occurred between Tish and Deon, he understood the cold shoulder. He also silently wished that his boy Deon could get it together and leave that dope alone. When Tish got back in the car, her whole demeanor had changed and her girls knew it. They waited until they pulled away from the corner store before asking her the reason for her strange mood.

"Nuffin." Tish said.

"Oh shit girl! Ain't dat the vice car?"

"Ooo yeah! Hurry up, roll down the window girl. Tyaire!" Tish called. "5-0 coming around the corner." And with Deon on his heels, Tyaire sprinted through the alley.

"Girl that looked like Deon." Tasheena said knowing it was him. She had heard some rumors about how he was getting high, but never actually saw him doing it, so she drew her own conclusions. "Whatever he's doing," she thought on more than one occasion, "must be more important than me."

8

"It was him girl and he looks a sight. I told him he really needs to get it together, 'cause he's too good of peoples to be goin' out like that." Tish said.

"For real?" Tasheena asked, "What did he look like?"

"His hair was woofin' and his Timbs were ran over, but it didn't look like he lost a whole bunch of weight or nuffin." She answered.

"Oh," was all Tasheena said as she split the blunt to roll the weed. She would have done anything to get her mind off of Deon because she loved him and hearing of his condition only made things worse. She wished like Hell she could help him, but she remembered clearly what her aunt had said about addiction because her uncle was addicted. "Baby don't worry about Deon, he will be fine. He just has to hit rock bottom." So she figured that rock bottom hadn't come yet.

"Bitch you ain't done twisting the weed yet?" Tish asked from the back seat.

"Yeah, give me a lighter."

*   *   *   *   *   *   *

Howard High School, HCC, as it was known, was one of the only school's blacks were allowed to attend back in the in the 1930's through the 1950's. Now it was more like a popular career center known for its high fashion dress code and popular basketball teams. Howard was the school of choice for anyone wanting or trying to get noticed as someone of importance. People were willing to spend whatever on clothing, jewelry, and shoes and kept themselves manicured, pedicured, trimmed, dyed and blow-dried in hopes of being placed on the school's most popular list. You could be or become whatever you wanted at Howard, if you were willing, but if you weren't careful and forgot the most important reason for being there, to get an education, you could find yourself on the long list of dropouts.

Rayon pulled into HCC's parking lot and parked directly in the nurse's spot.

"Bitch you can't park here." Tasheena said.

"Girl I ain't thinking about these people. The only thing they can do is call my tags in over the intercom system and make me move it, that's when I usually go ride around and tell them I couldn't find a parking spot."

"Bitch you so petty."

"Ain't I though" Rayon said sarcastically.

"Look bitch, I'm high, and we almost late so I'll get wit' y'all later." Tish said.

"When?"

"Around lunch time," and she grabbed her bookbag and left.

Tish stopped in the ladies room and splashed some water on her face to make sure she looked presentable just in case she so happened to bump into Trans, her new boyfriend. And just like she figured, Trans was waiting at her locker, like he did every morning, in his usual pose, with his foot up on the wall.

"Hey Beauty," He said gingerly and gave her a warm hug and squeeze on the ass.

"Hey Boo," She replied and stood on her tiptoes to give him a kiss.

Trans was tall, 6'6 to be exact, but the way he wore his clothes made him look like he was about 6'3. His tall stature, dark, chocolate skin, dimpled cheeks, white teeth, and temple tapered, baby Afro made him what the ladies called "the shit." Not only was he sharp as hell, but also he was also the most

talked about high school ball player in the country since
LeBron "King" James and Tish loved him.

"You know I got some good news to tell you right?"
Trans said.

"What news?" Tish asked.

"I just signed my letter of consent to UCLA" Trans
said.

"For real?"

"Yeah I'm for real and you can go out there with me to
visit next month."

"I can't go."

"You can, I already arranged it. I told them if my girl
couldn't come, than neither can I." Trans said. Tish could do
nothing but blush. Trans always did sweet shit like that and
that's what distinguished him from Saafie.

"Well I guess I can then, huh?" She answered then the
bell rung. "You better get to practice, right?"

"Yeah, the team has no classes today 'cause of the big
game tonight up at Chester High. I know you coming, right?"

"I don't know baby? You know I ain't never see you
play before except once and y'all lost, so I don't know. I might
jinx you or some'em."

"Baby, I want you to come. How some'em that look as
good as you be a jinx."

"Boy shut-up!" She blushed again. "Damn, he always
knows what to say," She thought as he walked her to her
cosmetology class.

Tish stepped through the door five minutes late, as
usual, and Ms. Johnson didn't pay it one mind. Tish was her
favorite student and the only one who actually worked at a real
salon. When Tish saw Ms. Johnson she couldn't do anything
but smile because she knew Ms. Johnson saw right through

her. Tish didn't have to explain one thing, on the grounds that more than once she was caught necking in the hallway with Trans by Ms. Johnson.

"Good morning Ms. Tish and how are you today?" Ms. Johnson asked.

"I'm fine."

"Why are your eyes all chinky," Ms. Johnson asked knowing the reason. She just wanted to make Tish squirm a little bit; let her know that she was slipping.

"Um, um, no reason, why?"

"I'm just lettin' you know other people see you better than you see ya'self, remember that," And Tish smiled. Ms. Johnson was her girl.

"Whass up?"

"Ain't nuffin', just tired of this damn class girl. It's too much, but girl this is where the money is at."

"Who you tellin'? You know I know as much money as I be making down at Che-Che's shop."

"Huh? Girl what style are you getting ready to give that mannequin?" Renee a girl in her class asked.

"Probably a lil' Bob or some'em. I'm just going to go light enough to keep Ms. Johnson straight, feel me?"

"I feel you. Oh by the way, how's my lil' boyfriend doin'?"

"Who Tymeere?"

"Yeah girl, who else. You know I'm waiting on his lil' behind. Shit when I'm 35 he'll be 21," Renee teased.

"He's alright. Bad as hell though. Done grew two more teeth and is tryin' to bite everything and everybody that picks him up."

"Awww, y'all better leave my baby alone."

"Damn!" Tish thought as Renee walked away. "Dat bitch will talk a bitch head off!" But before she could clear the thoughts from her head she was back.

"Oh, I almost forgot. Are you going to the game tonight? Girl it's sold out and everything, they said ESPN was shooting it live on TV tonight."

"Yeah I'm going. You know I ain't goin' to miss my personal Michael Jordan play in the biggest game of his life." Tish said making sure she rubbed it in at Renee. She knew deep down inside Renee had tried to fuck him a few months ago, but she felt they were both lying when they said nothing happened.

"I heard dat," Renee said and got the hint.

*   *   *   *   *   *   *

Trans bopped into the gym ten minutes late and not even dressed for practice. Coach Stormy blew his whistle and called a team huddle the moment he saw Trans. "Trans come here now!" He demanded.

"Who you talking to like that? My own pops don't even talk to me like that cuz!" Trans snapped taking it harder than he usually would 'cause he was on the spot.

"I'm talking to you!" Coach Stormy didn't back down. "Just because you signed your letter to attend UCLA, this morning don't make you exempt from being a part of this team! You need to be here like everyone else, who do you think you are?"

"Trans Owens."

"Well Mr. Owens, you won't start tonight!" Coach snapped. "Now everybody get back to practice!" He finished and walked away leaving Trans stunned.

*   *   *   *   *   *   *

13

Chapter Two

"Order in the court! Order in the court!" The judge spoke as he rapped his gavel on the table, trying to silence the murmur that overcame the courtroom when the jury returned unexpectedly fast.

"Has the jury reached a verdict?" He continued as the foreman of the twelve jurors stood up. "Yes we have your honor." The foreperson said.

Saafie looked over at his attorney puzzled, and then over his shoulder to his boss, Pretty E. Pretty E looked at him with a smile and a wink of reassurance. This was the same reaction the courtroom had last year when him and Dog were on trial for more than a 15 brick indictment. Frankie, The Don, had done another favor for Pretty E, and paid the jury off in Saafie's case.

"On counts one and two for drug possession and intent to distribute and counts one and two for weapons possession, we the jury find the defendant NOT GUILTY of all charges." The courtroom erupted. Every police and vice officer present felt a slap in the face as Saafie stood and hugged his attorney. "I told you baby boy everything was going to be fine," Pretty E said. Then before he stepped off, he looked over at Saafie and said, "Call me."

Pumpkin stood dead center at the swinging gate in the courtroom, which separated the spectators from the actual trial itself. Saafie stepped through the wooden gate and received the kiss and hug of a lifetime from his main girl.

"Hey baby!" Pumpkin said and puckered up.

"Hey." Saafie said disillusioned.

Saafie was still in awe every time he saw Pumpkin, but as he held her, he quickly discovered why she had that effect

14

on him. Pumpkin was B-A-D, and as she stood before him in
her Prada skirt set with the matching shoes and handbag, he
literally shook with excitement. He knew from the moment he
saw her he had to have her, and he went right at her. See
Pumpkin was from South Bridge Projects, no better than Tish,
but she was different. Pumpkin had to struggle to take care of
her three little brothers and little sister while her mom smoked
crack and drank Crystal Palace gin. In fact, when he met her,
she was at the bus stop in a Burger King uniform headed to
work. He had loved her from that moment, just off her
strength alone and made a vow that he was one day going to
get them out of the projects.

    "I'm so glad you're coming home with me," Pumpkin
said. "But baby if you wasn't, I was prepared," She finished
and retrieved a $1,500 money order from her purse.

    "See baby, that's why I love you. You don't just think
about you." Saafie said.

    "Of course not, that's why when I get off of work
tonight I got some'em even more special for you." She said in a
real sexually provocative way in his ear. "Now come on, I have
to go to work. I told 'em I'd be there by twelve."

    "O.K." Saafie said.

    Saafie drove his convertible XJ8 Jaguar smoothly down
King St. with his baby in tow. He looked at the clock on the
dashboard and noticed that it was only a quarter of eleven,
plenty of time for a quickie. "Baby," he said excitedly, then
touched her thigh. "Wanna get a quickie?" Pumpkin looked at
the clock and the thought crossed her mind, but she quickly
changed it when she saw her job, the bank on 4th and Walnut.

    "Nah baby, I have to take a rain check." She answered.
"I got you tonight," She said and sucked his ear lobe as he
pulled up to her job.

15

"Come on baaaby," He whined.

"Nope," She said full of energy and pecked his cheek, as she got out of the car. Saafie didn't pull straight off, he watched as Pumpkin swung her hips provocatively and then disappeared through the revolving door. "Damn, I should call her back," he thought and grabbed at his crotch at the thoughts of just how good his baby's loving was. After pondering the thought and being snapped back to reality by the long toot of the horn, he pulled off.

Saafie made a left off of 4th St. onto Walnut St. and made a right on 9th. The jag rode so smoothly that he never felt a bump beneath him and as he rode down the street, he fed off of the envious looks he received. He only blew at a couple niggas from C.B.W., he knew, but for the rest, he smiled a sinister smile. He remembered the days all too fondly when people would tease him about being mixed, but now he was up. It was his turn to get back because half of these niggas out here were broke. On that note, he headed up Rt. 202 towards Faulk Rd. where his two-story duplex sat.

Saafie pulled the Jag into the driveway and pressed the automatic garage door opener that was clipped onto the sun visor. He parked in the two-car garage directly next to his new H-2 Hummer and for the first time really looked at it since it came home from the shop getting 24-inch shoes and a new system. "I'm pulling dat out today." He said proudly as he went through the door leading into his home. No sooner than he stepped foot on the wall to wall blood red carpet, Pumpkin's twin Szhit-zu's, Lady and Tramp, greeted him. "Hey puppies," he said gingerly to the little ones as they wagged their tails excitedly and spun around in circles. "Damn, I gotta get my baby this operation," he thought sadly about Pumpkin not being able to have kids. Just thinking about the look on that sorry nigga's face when he said, "Remember Pumpkin nigga" mad Saafie feel a certain kind of way. He had kept those feelings he had buried, especially since he had murdered that nigga that night, but it was different now. It was really starting to get to Pumpkin, and he saw it every time he had Tymeere with him. Saafie reached down and patted the two hairy dogs on the head and made his way through the spacious home. The all-white mesh furniture, matching lamp, and end tables set the carpet off, as well as the paintings that hung on the walls throughout the house. Saafie stood next to the fireplace and looked up at his favorite poster, and like always felt good again. It was the one where Muhammad Ali stood dead center in the ring, arm folded to his chest, mouth open, and towering over a battered Sonny Liston.

"Ali-Ali-Ali," he chanted as he walked down the hallway towards his bedroom.

Saafie hit the switch on the wall and the beautiful 150-gallon fish tank built in to it, lit up like an aquarium. The huge piranhas swam back and forth aimlessly like they had chips on their shoulders and the algae eaters stayed stuck to the glass. Saafie reached into the small portable refrigerator that sat beneath the tank and grabbed two huge rats wrapped in wax paper. The moment he lifted the lids on the tank, the fish sat stark still facing the open tank. Before the first rat could even hit the water, one of the huge piranhas leaped from the tank. Saafie dropped the second rat and sat on the edge of his bed enjoying the frenzy. As he watched blood ooze and mix in with the now cloudy water, he made a sinister chuckle and thought; "This will happen to any nigga who tries to cross me" and then the phone rang.

"Hey nigga! Congratulations prick!" Tyaire shouted from the other end.

17

"Yeah nigga and fuck you too pussy!" Saafie shot back in their normal playful mode.

"Nah, whass'up though cousin? You know they got your shit on the twelve o'clock news."

"Yeah I know, them mu'fucka's was in the courtroom."

"Word?" Tyaire said.

"Yeah. Whass'up wit'chu, what you doin?"

"Nuffin."

"Why don't you ride down to Howard with me right quick, so I can go see Tish and see if I gotta pick up my son or not." Saafie said.

"Alright, come get me. I'm at the detail shop getting my car done."

"Oh, you know I went and got the H-2 from up in Philly last night. This mutha-fucka is sitting so pretty, I don't want to drive the mutha-fucka!"

"Say word."

"Word nigga! You'll see it. I'm on my way."

"Awight." Tyaire said.

*   *   *   *   *   *   *

Change clothes and go…
You know I stay-
Fresh to Death
Brought it from da projects
And I'mma take it to the top of the globe
Change Clothes
Jay-Z *The Black Album*

"Ya dude is back, May Bach coupe is back, tell the whole world the truth is back!" Saafie sung along as Jay-Z's Black Album pounded through the Hummer's new Alpine system. Tyaire cringed up his face and stepped out the detail shop singing the hook, "Sexy, Sexy," when the black truck pulled up.

"Got damn baby boy, you know I'm jealous right?" Tyaire said as the Sprewell's spun endlessly.

"For what nigga?" Saafie asked.

"'Cause my shit ain't done yet, that's why nigga!" Tyaire responded and hopped in.

When Saafie turned out 12th St. from off of Pine St., the street was already starting to fill up with students going to lunch. He pulled directly across the street from the school and pumped the radio to its capacity, as the young girls shook their asses and did the latest dances.

"Damn these young bitches phat to def!" Saafie said discombobulated.

"Nigga you act like some ol'head nigga or some'em and you only like what? Twenty one?" Tyaire said.

"You too nigga."

"Oh I know nigga, but I ain't trying to act like some ol' nigga either. I'm trying to stay young forever nigga!"

"I heard that." Saafie said.

*   *   *   *   *   *   *

Tish and Trans left the school arm and arm and headed over to the corner store hugging. Just as they crossed the street, a black H-2 bent around the corner playing "Brush ya' shoulders off" by Jay-z and Tish nodded her head. When it came to a stop and Saafie hopped out, she spit on the ground, that's just how bitter it tasted in her mouth after she saw him.

"Ain't that Saafie, your baby's dad?" Trans asked.

"Yeah that's him, but so what?" She answered and cuddled up close to him, as if to insure his position as her man.

"No reason, I was just asking."

"Oh." Tish said.

*   *   *   *   *   *   *

"Man I know this bitch just seen me sittin' here," Saafie said to himself; as he watched Tish and that young nigga who stayed on the T.V., go in the corner store.

"Where you goin' cuz?" Tyaire asked, as Saafie stormed away.

"I'll be right back."

"I hope that nigga don't go do some'em stupid," Tyaire said to himself, and then noticed Rayon across the street standing next to Tasheena.

"Rayon!" He called three times before she acknowledged him, even though he knew she saw him in this pretty Hummer when they first came outside.

"What?" She yelled from across the street.

"So you goin' to act like dat?"

"Like what?"

"Like that. Now come here." He demanded.

"Who you talking to," She rolled her eyes, but came anyway.

Rayon bopped across the street with her Louis Vuitton bag draped across her forearm swinging her keys in her hand. Her hip hugging Baby Phat jeans brought every curve out, and the half cut, v-neck matching Baby Phat t-shirt damn near pushed her titties out of the small V.

"I see why I been trying to fuck dis girl," He said imagining how phat her ass was just by looking at her waist from the front.

"What? Whass up?" She asked.

"What'chu mean whass'up? You know I been trying to see you about some'em for I don't know how long now."

"Me and how many other bitches? See that's why I ain't fuckin' wit you" She said, but visualized it like it already happened. See truth be told, she'd been having these same feelings about Tyaire that he had for her, but wasn't trying to just be fucked like the rest of the bitches, so she stayed away.

"Why not?" Tyaire asked.

"Because."

"Girl, let dat shit go whatever you holding on to. I know you feelin' a nigga, damn!" Tyaire said and he was right.

"How you know what I am feeling?"

"Cause I know," He replied.

"Know what," She asked.

"Are you coming wit me or not?" Tyaire asked.

"Where we goin'?"

"To my crib." Tyaire said.

"For what? We ain't doing nuffin'."

"Girl just come on." Tyaire pushed.

"Well at least let me go get some kind of fake pass or some'em"

"Alright, hurry up." Tyaire said with a smile on his face.

21

*   *   *   *   *   *   *

Tish and Trans were paying for their little snacks and soda's when Saafie walked in, so they never saw him coming. He walked straight up on her and grabbed her arm, spinning her towards him.

"Yo, I know you saw me out there sitting on my truck."

"Boy get your hands off me!" She yanked away.

"Bitch! I'll slap da shit out of you," He snapped as a crowd began to draw.

"Yo, who you callin' a bitch, nigga? Don't get your lil' pretty ass knocked out in here," Trans said and meant it.

"What nigga? Do you know who I am? I'll have your lil' bitch ass come up missing, how about that?" He said then stressed the word "pussy!"

"Whatever nigga. I just know if you call her another bitch, I'mma knock ya bitch ass out!" He said scared to death. He knew he could knock Saafie out, but he also knew Saafie had enough money to probably do what he said, so he held back. It was a threat that Trans would remember for a long time.

"Why are you always making a scene?" Tish asked.

"That's his young ass! I only came to ask if I had to go get my son or not."

"Don't you bring him home from daycare every day? Well what you think?"

"Man you ain't gotta be smart." Saafie said.

"Be smart? Be smart? For what? You already slapped us in the face, your son and me. All that mu'fuckin money you got and my son don't have any new Timbs and sneaks, but I see you gotta new truck for your fans though, huh? Nigga you ain't shit."

22

"Saafie was about to go haywire, but saw Trans looming over Tish in back of her and decided to step off."

She was really hurt, as was he, to think that's how Tish thought he felt about his son.

"You know what, you got dat." He said and left the store.

"You alright baby?" Trans asked.

"Yeah, as long as you are," She said and tried to smile.

*   *   *   *   *   *   *

"Man let's get the fuck away from here," Saafie said when he got back to his truck.

"Hold up cuz, I'm waiting on Rayon."

"Where she goin'?" Saafie asked.

"She goin' wit me nigga! What's wrong with you?" Tyaire asked.

"Nuffin man, I'm just ready to go." Saafie said.

"Yeah nigga, that young boy wearin' Tish ass out, ain't he?"

"Not now nigga now is not the time." Saafie said pissed and hurt.

"I don't care nuffin' about you being mad nigga." Tyaire said then saw Rayon. "Hurry up baby, my boy trippin' again."

"Hey Saafie, whass' up?" Rayon said.

"Your mutha'fuckin girl keeps doing that bullshit, that's what's up."

"What'chu mean? I know you ain't talking about Trans are you? And you got a what? A wife at home!" Rayon said.

"That's what I told his ass," Tyaire added.

"Man, fuck both of you two mu'fucka's and get out my truck!" He said trying to hold back his smile as they reached the detail shop.

*   *   *   *   *   *   *

Tyaire disappeared into the detail shop leaving Rayon standing out front. When he came back, he was pulling his 500 SL from the back of the building as T.I. was screaming "24's are like 10's round here" on Memphis Bleek's new single "Round Here," as his Sprewell's spun oddly. He jumped out the car leaving the door open and told Rayon to get in as he walked back into the shop. Within minutes he returned with a man in a jumpsuit carrying a spray bottle. Rayon sat patiently and watched Tyaire in his Jim Brown throwback and butter Timbs give the man instructions. "I guess he would want it done right, paying all that money," Rayon thought as the man sprayed Armor All on his tires again. The man stood up after he hit the last tire and Tyaire peeled him off a couple dollars, and then got in the car.

"Was I too long baby?" Tyaire asked.

"No you wasn't too long, but can you play something else. Do you have Alicia Keys?" And with one press of a button the sweet sounds of "You don't know my name" poured through the system.

"That's what I'm talking bout," She said and reclined into the soft leather.

Tyaire pulled up to his three-story home in Hockeson and parked in the driveway. Rayon was shocked because he only lived right around the corner, well five minutes away, from her.

"Who lives here? I mean, how long have you lived here?" Rayon asked.

"For about six months now. See, my grandparents left me the house in their will when they died last year. I only lived here for six months because my peoples had fought the will saying my mom-mom and pop-pop were incompetent when they left me everything, but I won in court and got everything. I'm a millionaire."

"Well why do you still sell drugs?" She asked.

"I can't even answer that." He said and led her in the house.

Rayon walked into the house and was surprised at his set-up. She had figured that the house would be more glamorous than it was, but it wasn't. It looked as if older people still lived there. Don't get me wrong, the house was not like Sanford and Son's, but it wasn't Al Pacino's style either.

"You alright? I see you look a little puzzled." Tyaire asked.

"I was just thinking you would have done some things different to the house, that's all."

"Nah. I left it like my grandparents had it because it gives me that feel, you know?"

"I guess so." Rayon said.

"But if yo' ass was here a little more, then it probably would be decorated differently."

"What?" Rayon said hearing the unspoken words.

"You heard me," He said and headed upstairs. "Come on baby girl."

Rayon's heart pounded as she walked upstairs behind Tyaire. It had been over a year and a half since she'd had some and she's only did it with two people her whole 18 years. Her last boyfriend Joe and the person she'd never tell anyone about, Trans. They had made a promise to never tell anyone, besides they were best friends. When they entered Tyaire's

25

bedroom, she really began to tremble. Tyaire walked over to
her and asked, "Are you alright," but her mouth was too dry
to answer, so she just shook her head. "Come here," He
whispered and took her into his arms.

     The kiss was soft and their tongues twirled like they
wanted to become one. Tyaire gently laid her across the bed
and peeled her Baby Phat jeans off of her real easy. The way
he moved, so patiently, had calmed Rayon's nerves to the point
that she was starting to enjoy it. "You like that baby?" He
asked and kissed her navel. "Um-Hmm" She moaned and
arched her ass up off the bed, so he could get the pants the rest
of the way off. Rayon let out a soft cry and dug her manicured
nails deep into his back, as he eased himself into her. Her prize
was so wet and tight that Tyaire didn't want to move.
"Damn," He said to himself, but Rayon was too far aroused to
notice his reaction. She swiveled her hips like she was twirling
a hoola-hoop and then it was on. In less than five minutes they
both had came together and was starring into the ceiling, lost
in thoughts.

*   *   *   *   *   *   *

Chapter Three

If it hadn't been for Rayon's cell phone ringing, she could have slept all day. She reached over and grabbed it from her purse and sat straight up. "Damn! It's 3:00 P.M.," She said to herself knowing school had let out at 2:50 P.M., and when she saw her 18 missed calls, she knew why. "Tyaire get up, I have to go," She said nudging him on the side. "Alright, here I come." Tyaire said. When they arrived at Howard High School, the street and parking lot was near empty. Just a few after school activities students lingered, along with a very pissed off Tish and Tasheena.

"Damn where's this girl at?" She knows damn well I gotta go out here to grab this birth certificate, then go to work." Tish said anxiously.

"I don't know where the bitch at," Tasheena said, then remembered. "Girl I know where that bitch at, she's with Tyaire girl."

"No she ain't bitch." Tish said in disbelief.

"Word on everything, she is." Tasheena said.

"That's why she ain't been answering the phone." Tish said, then saw Tyaire's car turn the corner.

"Here da bitch come now." Tasheena said.

The moment Rayon pulled into the parking lot she saw her girls standing by the Honda, as they called it. She knew they'd be a little upset about her lateness, but they'd be alright once they got all the juicy info about her five-minute escapade. Tyaire pulled up right next to Rayon's Honda and parked. He rolled down his window and looked at Tish smiling from ear to ear.

"Hey sis! Thanks for putting the word in for me." He said knowing she didn't say anything.

"You're welcome," She said playing along while Rayon climbed out the passenger's side.

"Where you been at bitch?" Tasheena asked. "Oooh bitch, no you didn't!"

"No she didn't what?" Tyaire asked being nosy, and then called Rayon around the car to him.

"Give me a kiss baby and call me later," He said as they touched tongues one more time.

"Eeeewww bitch! Do you know where his mouth been?" Tish played.

"Fuck you," He responded with a chuckle and pulled off.

"Bitch what happened? And we want to know everything!" Tasheena asked as they piled into the car.

The whole ride from Howard High School to the Secretary of State office out on Limestone Rd., was filled with Tasheena and Tish laughing in stitches. Rayon had them laughing so hard their stomachs were hurting. It really got bad when Rayon was telling them about how much Tyaire was worried about his five minute performance.

"Baby look, I'mma make it up to you, o.k. Baby?" Rayon mocked in her deepest voice.

"That bitch is crazy, ain't she?" Tish said still laughing.

"As a bed bug," Tasheena responded as Tish went into the office building to get her birth certificate.

After planning their every move out for the night, they dropped Tish off at Che-Che's shop to meet her only client for the day, Ms. Barber. It was exactly 4:30 on the dot, four hours away from the big game at Chester High and Ms. Barber wasn't there yet.

"I got the right mind to schedule her for tomorrow," She thought the same time Ms. Barber walked through the door.

"Hey baby, I ain't late am I?"

"No you're not Ms. Barber."

"O.k. baby, let's get started then o.k?"

"How you want it Ms. Barber?"

"You know baby, like uh, what's that girl's name? You know, the one who sings that song, uh "Crazy in Love," oh I know now, the girl's name is Benonsay."

"You mean Beyonce."

"Yeah that's her name."

Tish couldn't do anything but grin as she walked Ms. Barber to her station.

"Now she now damn well she ain't goin' to look like Beyonce, when she already look like Florida Evans," She said to herself.

Ms. Barber was cool though and Tish liked her a lot. Her personality was animated and she always had something to say. Ms. Barber was the walking Channel Six news van and kept up with the latest gossip.

"Girl, you know I missed the damn Powerball by one number." Ms. Barber started as soon as Tish laid her back in the hair-washing sink.

"I know you were mad." Tish shot back.

"Not as mad my sister was when my niece, her daughter, left them kids on her and ain't been back in a week. I told my sister that damn girl got a problem; those drugs are killing her ass. See what we need to do is put her ass in rehab or jail, one or the other 'cause she need help! Anytime a mother can leave her children on someone, I don't care who it is and not check on them, some'em gotta be wrong!" Tish couldn't help but to think about Deon and how he looked earlier that morning.

"Dats a shame Ms. Barber," Tish replied.

"A shame it is baby, a shame it is." Ms. Barber finished and Tish sat her under the dryer.

By six-thirty Tish was finishing Ms. Barber up and Rayon and Tasheena were walking in.

"You almost done?" Rayon asked.

"Mmm-Hmm, all I got to do is clean my station," Tish answered.

"Damn Tasheena, that ass still phat," Che-Che said when he came downstairs.

"And is," She shot back, as they remembered the times.

"Tish, you don't have to come in tomorrow if you don't want to, unless you got some clients, alright?" Che-Che said and left out the door.

"Come on y'all, let's go." Tish said once she was done cleaning.

*   *   *   *   *   *   *

The Honda turned off of Todd's Lane onto Bower St. and headed down to 27th St. Veering through the front windshield, Tish saw Saafie's truck parked in front of her mom's house and became instantly agitated.

"What the fuck does he want?" She thought.

"Bitch don't get in here and start running your mouth." Tasheena said. "'Cause bitch we only got like an hour and some'em minutes until the game starts."

"I ain't, I ain't goin' to say a mutha-fuckin' thing to him," Tish said as the three walked up the busted sidewalk to the door.

When Tish saw the door knob, the first thing she saw was Saafie bouncin' his son on his knee saying; "Hey man!"

Then at his side, and in front of him sat bags and bags of clothes and sneaker boxes.

"I ain't impressed!" She snapped looking Saafie dead in the face.

"It's always some'em wit'chu, ain't it?" Saafie responded.

"And mom, you fake!" She said as Ms. Carla sat across from Saafie smoking a Kool cigarette.

"Y'all can sit down." Tish said and walked upstairs.

"They know they can sit down. They're just as much welcomed as you," Ms. Carla responded.

"Hey Mom Carla. Whass'up Saafie?" Rayon and Tasheena said in unison.

"Whass'up wit'chall? Where y'all goin' looking all jazzy?" Saafie asked.

"To the game up in Chester," Rayon said.

"Oh, that's right," Saafie said and pulled out his Nextel. "Hey baby boy, what'chu doing tonight? You know the big game between the boah Shakim Shabazz from Chester and da boah, whass his name." He paused then said, "Yeah dat nigga, is tonight. You tryin' to go? Yeah I'm goin' and I got a stack on da boah Shakim," He finished and hung up.

Tasheena, Rayon and Ms. Carla, all three were acting like they were in some deep conversation, but eavesdropping on Saafie's conversation the whole time. When he hung up the phone, he said, "Rayon, can you go get Tish for me?"

"Yeah, if you let me have a couple dollars 'cause a bitch is broke!" Rayon replied.

"Ahn-huh, I knew your mouth was just as filthy." Ms. Carla said, finally catching innocent Ms. Rayon swearing.

"I ain't say nuffin Mom Carla," She answered, busted.

"How much money you need?" Saafie said pulling out a sure enough hustlers' knot.

"However much you goin' give a bitch, I mean, sista." Rayon said.

"Well you might as well hit us all off now!" Ms. Carla said and he did giving each one of them a half a man, fifty dollars, to those who don't know.

"I'll be right back," Rayon said and darted up the steps.

Tish, fresh out of the tub, stood in her matching new blue panty and bra set in front of her favorite mirror. Rayon opened the door and damn near hit Tish in the face because she didn't knock.

"Damn bitch, smash my toes under the door." Tish said holding her arms out to stop the door.

"My fault girl," Rayon said and eased in through the lil crack in the door.

"Whass'up," Tish asked as she sprayed Berry Island by Victoria's Secret over her most intimate parts.

"Nothing, Saafie down there talking 'bout how he need to see you, that's all." Rayon said.

"Fuck Saafie." Tish said.

"Can I ask you a question?" Rayon said.

"Shoot." Tish said.

"Why are you so mad at Saafie and that's your baby's daddy?" Rayon said.

"Because dat nigga deceived me, and lied to me too many times. Plus I love Trans now, that's my baby," Tish said and Rayon squirmed again. It happened every time Trans was mentioned and they were together. For some odd reason Rayon thought Tish knew they had fucked or some'em.

"Oh I see." Rayon said.

32

"Ooo girl, grab dat shoe and kill dat roach right there,"
Tish said as she looked at Rayon through the mirror.

"Eeew girl," Rayon said smashing it into the
floorboards. "Go get me some tissue."

"Does this look right?"

"Bitch you know it look right," Rayon said picking the
roach up in the tissue with her thumb and index finger and
tossing it in the trashcan.

"You sure?"

"Yeah bitch! And the way those jeans, what are they
Parasucos, are fitting your hips and ass, girl got damn you
hurting 'um! I wish my hips were wide."

"Bitch they will be as soon as your ass drops a baby!"
Tish said.

"Not yet baby girl, not yet." Rayon said.

Rayon led the way downstairs and when she saw the
look on Saafie's face she said to herself, "Gosh, here she
comes." Tish stepped off the last step in her blue Bebe
sneakers, blue Parasuco jeans, white long sleeve t-shirt and
Trans' varsity jacket. "What" She asked making her way
towards the kitchen. Saafie just stared for a moment as he
took inventory on Tish. He knew he loved Pumpkin, but was it
wrong for him to still love Tish too? Those were his thoughts as
he sat his son down and rose from the couch.

"She swears she slick," He said, finding it humorous to
watch Tish trying to be smart.

Tish, who was at the refrigerator, bent down and looked
into the fruit drawers, making her ass spread out. She knew
he'd be looking so she wiggled it a little bit, and started singing
the chorus to Master P's new song "Shake what you got in
them jeans, them jeans." Saafie walked right up on her and

smacked her ass and said, "Now touch the wall and shake," but before he could finish, she stood up and pushed him away.

"Nigga! Keep ya dusty ass hands off me!"

"Why are you fronting?"

"Saafie I don't even like you no more," She shot back, the words cutting him deep.

"Why would you say that," He asked, eyebrows frowned up.

"Look, I don't want to get into it right now, o.k?"

"Come on Tish, we only got 15 minutes! You know we still gotta find a parking spot," Tasheena said.

"Here I come, I'm ready," She said and brushed right by Saafie. "Excuse me." Tish breezed by, as Saafie stood dumbfounded. There was nothing left for him to do, so he said bye to Mom Carla and followed them out.

"So you are going to carry me like that huh?" Saafie asked.

"No, you carried yourself like that," Tish said and got in the Honda.

*   *   *   *   *   *   *

Chester High School's parking lot was filled to capacity. Everything from school buses to news vans lined the lot, as well as the streets around it. Frustrated, Rayon popped the curb and parked next to a school bus with Delaware tags and Howard Wildcats painted on the windows.

"Bitch I told you we was going to find a spot, didn't I?" She said while they exited.

Tish, Rayon, and Tasheena, the most popular girls at Howard, stepped in the gym and watched as girls from their school and Chester give them evil eyes.

"Hey jealous bitches," Tasheena said waving at them with her tongue out.

"Dats why I don't fuck wit these bitches now and I don't like coming out 'cause I'll beat a bitch down!" Tish said seriously. She and Tasheena really were fighters, but Rayon wasn't. She knew they would fight at the drop of a dime, so she knew Tish was for real.

The three of them managed to find somewhere to sit in the stands although it was really standing room only. Tish had called her girl Renee from shop class and she held it down, by getting them some seats, so they were straight. As soon as they were seated, Tish looked down on the court at Howard's lay-up line and couldn't find Trans anywhere. She stood in bewilderment, looked harder, and then she saw him. There he was in the center of media frenzy. There were countless reporters around, cameras were flashing, questions were coming a hundred miles an hour, and microphones lined his face.

"Trans, what do you think about going up against Shakim Shabazz?" A reporter from Fox News asked.

"You know he's number 5 in the nation on the list of top high school basketball players." Another reporter added.

"Well it should be a good game then. I mean Shakim and me are good friends. We play one another all the time. I mean we even traveled together in the AAU league, so it'll be a good game." Trans answered.

"Trans, rumor has it that you'll forego college to play in the NBA. Is there any truth to that rumor?" One reporter from ESPN asked.

"As of now, I'm a UCLA Bruin," He replied.

"Do you have a prediction for tonight's game?" A local reporter asked.

"Yeah, Howard by 10!" He answered and jogged off.

35

"Trans wait!" The reporters called out, but he was gone.

The referee stood center court as the players from both Howard and Chester sought one another out to defend, but there was no Trans. Trans sat on the bench mad as he'd ever been, but he understood the disciplinary act. Coach Stormy saw the frustration on his face and walked down to comfort his star player; the nation's star player.

"The first three minutes Trans, that's all," and he turned his attention to the court when the crowd cheered.

Chester won the jump ball so their fans erupted in cheers. The center tipped it to Shakim Shabazz and he dazzled the gym with a no look pass on the break. The score was Chester with 2 points and Howard 0. Chester's full court press caused Howard to turn the ball over three times in a row, which led to 7 unanswered points all by Shakim.

"Hey Coach," Shakim yelled as he passed Howard's bench, "you better call a time out, 'cause I'mma kill your guard." He finished. Coach Stormy resisted, but had to do something because another turnover and another 3 pointer by Shakim gave Chester a 12-0 lead and only 2 and a half minutes had elapsed.

"Time out!" Coach Stormy yelled, and the chant of 'blow out' began in the gym.

"I told you nigga! Get dat money right!" Saafie yelled over the crowd to his boy Tyaire.

"Nigga, my man's ain't even hit the floor yet! You'll see when he gets in nigga!" Tyaire replied.

Howard huddled up around the bench and Coach Stormy stood in the center with a clipboard in his hand going crazy.

"What have we practiced all week long for? Yeah, that's right, the press! The press! I mean, y'all are panicking making careless mistakes and we look nothing like the number one team in the nation. This is the only game y'all all been waiting on. Scouts from every major division one college in the United States are in here, and y'all are performing like freshmen. What scout would want to recruit anyone of y'all?" Coach Stormy asked, and then continued, "Trans it's your stage baby lead your team!"

Trans stood up, snapped off his warm-ups and went to the center of the circle.   "Look y'all these muthafuckas can't beat us! We're the number one team in the country nigga's! Put ya hands in here," Trans said as everyone put their hands on top of one another.

"One, two, three fight!" They yelled raising their hands and then dropping them down.

When the Howard fans saw number 21 step on the court, they went cold-blooded bananas. They were so loud that chill's shot up Tish's back. The center for Howard got the ball and in-bounded it by passing it to Trans. He caught it, stood straight up and with the ball cradled under his arm waved three fingers to set up the offense before starting his dribble. Shakim stood before the number one player in the country and was determined to prove that he was better than his number 5 ranking. Soon as Trans passed the half court line, Shakim squatted down and smacked the palms of his hands on the floor as if to say "I'mma steal that ball." Trans smiled because he knew Shakim would play him to his left, so he went left confusing him totally. With a hard power dribble to the left and a quick stop, Shakim backed up like five steps. Trans then quickly crossed over to his right, looked down and stepped behind the three-point line for the jumper. The shot was nothing but net and it was on, Chester 12 points and Howard with 3.

By the middle of the second quarter, Howard had chipped Chester's lead down to two and Trans had 19 points. The halftime score read Chester 35, Howard 33. Shakim Shabazz led all scores with 20 points and 6 assists.

*   *   *   *   *   *   *   *   *
      *   *   *

"Girl we going to win this game." Rayon said as they headed to the concession stands.

"Yeah we are, ain't we Tish?" Tasheena asked.

"I don't know girl, I think I'm jinxing the team or some'em," Tish answered while they made their way into the crowded cafeteria.

Tish, Rayon, and Tasheena stood in line waiting on their hot dogs and shit for what seemed to be an eternity.

"They know damn well it don't take that long to put some mustard on a hot dog!" Tasheena complained loud enough for everyone to hear it.

"Girl chill out, 'cause if it was you you'd want to dress your shit up too, right?" Tish spoke up for the people.

"Oh shit! Ain't that Tyaire?" Tasheena asked spotting him through the crowd.

"It sure is bitch! Rayon you need to go cuss his ass out, I'll come with you."

"For what? He's not my man." She said, but was feeling some type of way about him being posted up like that.

"I'mma get y'all's shit, y'all go handle dat!" Tish told them while she stayed in line.

Tyaire didn't see them coming as he talked shit to the broad Tamia from up in Chester. She was his role dog, his home girl, who he just so happened to fuck on occasion.

38

"I'm trying to see about some'em tonight, you hear me?" Tyaire said.

"Nigga do you got my money? 'Cause that shit been in my house for too long now," Tamia reminded him.

"Oh shit, I forgot all about that. I was wondering where that shit was at." He said and lost his train of thought when he heard Tasheena's voice.

"And who da fuck is she?" Tasheena asked with her hands on her hips.

"Hold up, Hold up! How you going to just walk up on me and ask me some shit like that? I mean I don't have a problem explaining it, but you ain't got to act all ghetto about it, feel me?"

"Well who is she 'cause your girl does want to know, right Rayon?" Rayon didn't answer.

"Oh shit, why haven't you introduced me to your girl Tyaire? Hi, I am his cousin Tamia." She said and held her hand out to Rayon.

"I'm Rayon," She replied and shook the girls hand.

"See you came over here on some dumb shit" Tyaire said.

"Call me tonight at Aunt Cat's house," Tamia said and smiled as she walked away hoping he would catch the usage of the word cat.

"I will, I just hope she got the house fresh 'cause I don't like coming over there when it's not." He said playing along.

"Well you know she always has that part of the house clean." She said over her shoulder.

"Hey baby! Come here and give me a hug," Tyaire said and grabbed Rayon in his arms.

"That's what the bitch betta had been, 'cause I woulda beat her ass!" Tasheena told Tyaire as he hugged Rayon.

By the time Tish reached where Rayon, Tyaire, and Tasheena were Saafie had accompanied them. She started to turn around, but remembered that she had their food.

"Here y'all" She said passing them their food.

Saafie looked over at his baby's mom again and tried to think of what he did that made her feel the way that she felt about him. He stepped over to her and asked, "Can I please say some'em to you?"

"I told you now was not the time," Tish said. The rejection from Tish, along with the weed and Belvedere he'd been drinking was too much for Saafie to handle.

"Bitch I said come here!" He snapped and damn near ripped her jacket off 'causing her to drop her food.

"Boy you better get da fuck..." She tried to say, but Saafie grabbed her by the neck.

Everything was happening so fast that Tyaire and them couldn't respond fast enough.

"Bitch you goin' to stop playin' wit me," He said, with his hands wrapped around Tish's neck squeezing the life out of her. Tish couldn't breathe as tears soaked her eyes. It wasn't the actual pain, it was the anger built up inside of her that 'caused them to fall and then she blanked out. Tish let out a loud scream and clutched Saafie's face as the few onlookers present said "Dats right girl, don't let dat nigga do that shit to you."

"Muthafucka I told you to keep your hands off of me," She shouted and dug her nails in his face.

When Tyaire finally gained his composure, he broke them apart. Tish had managed to leave a trail of scratches on Saafie's light skinned face.

"Bitch I'mma fuck you up!" Saafie threatened Tish.

"Why you mad nigga! Why you mad? What, 'cause I
don't want you no more? Fuck you and you won't see ya son
no more! He gotta a new daddy anyway." She barked.

"What bitch?" He said frantically as he tried to break
Tyaire's grip.

"You heard me nigga loud and clear!" Tish said as the
police were coming to break up the new main event.

*   *   *   *   *   *   *

Howard in-bounded the ball to start the second half.
Trans, the 6'6" Phenom, dribbled the ball with grace, as if he
had a string on it and from the stands, you would have thought
it was an oversized yo-yo. When he took the first shot of the
third quarter, Chester knew they were in for a long night
because the three pointer left the nets stuck on the rim and
gave Howard their first lead.

"Wild Cats! Wild Cats! Wild Cats!" Tasheena started a
chant and Chester could feel the momentum changing.

The whole entire third quarter belonged to Howard
High School, as they began the fourth and final quarter with a
seven-point lead: Howard 60 and Chester 53. Shakim did
everything he could do, from passing, scoring and rebounding
to playing tenacious defense, but Trans and the Wild Cats were
just too good. The entire fourth quarter Trans went
unconscious and gave the entire world tuned into ESPN, a look
at why he should forego college and enter the year's upcoming
Draft. The final score was Howard 87 and Chester 70.

"Get my money nigga!" Tyaire yelled, as Saafie peeled
off a quick 10 big faces.

"Got damn I ain't know that boy was like that. It's a
shame he playing with his career like that." Saafie said
referring to Trans dealing with Tish.

"Man leave dat nigga alone. You should be glad she fuckin' wit a nigga like dat anyway. At least you know ain't no dumb shit around your son or nuffin'," Tyaire said defending Trans.

"Man who you wit? Me or dat nigga?" Saafie said.

"I'm wit da young boah on this one," Tyaire answered and meant it. He liked Trans. He loved the idea of a young boy doing his thing and going somewhere. It kind of reminded him of himself and his days at M.C.I. prep school playing football. Tyaire had a great chance at playing in the NFL as a premiere running back, but a torn ACL took all his heart and glory away. He was forever scarred by the injury and was too scared to play on it again. So seeing Trans was like reliving his own dream through someone else.

"Man fuck dat nigga!" Saafie said.

*   *   *   *   *   *   *

Trans exited the gymnasium and Tish was waiting right there for him. She ran straight over to him and tried to hug the life out of him. The incident that occurred earlier in the cafeteria with Saafie had almost ruined her night, but as she hugged Trans, her man, she felt like she was melting in his arms and felt like a brand new person.

"Damn baby! I need these kinds of hugs more often." Trans said.

"Me too," Tish responded and just like that their special moment was interrupted.

"Hey Trans! Hey Trans! Do you…? Are you…? You had a nice game!" Questions and comments were coming from all sorts of directions and they got caught up in another media frenzy.

"Here, here ask her," Trans said putting Tish on the forefront.

"Who is she?" A reporter asked.

"My good luck charm." Trans said with a smile.

"Oh, we see. She's the lucky lady." Another reporter said.

"Yeah, you got that right," He answered and Tish blushed.

Tish couldn't believe that Trans put her on the front line, but it was all-good though. She felt real important giving up little intimate things the reporters wanted to know about Trans, because it gave him a life outside of basketball. Trans was impressed at how well Tish handled herself the first time under the gun and when the slew of questions was done he let her know.

"Baby I'm proud of you. I don't even act that calm yet." Trans said.

"Its nothing, all you have to do is tell the truth and answer the questions." She said when she heard Trans' coach call him as the team boarded the bus.

"Baby look I have to ride with the team. What are you doing tomorrow?" Trans asked.

"Nothing." Tish said.

"O.k. well look, I'mma probably get my peoples car and come and get you so we can do some'em special alright?" Trans said.

"Sounds good to me," She said giving him a kiss as he walked away. "Fuck this, its time for us to handle ours!" She thought to herself as she walked to the Honda.

Tish had been with Trans since the end of the last school year, which was around nine months ago and still hadn't given him any. It had been plenty of times when they came real close, but she'd always chicken out. See, Tish had never been with anyone outside of Saafie, so there was a fear factor involved in the long wait. Plus with Saafie, it was always rough, so she never really saw the joy in making love. I mean, sometimes it felt good and sometimes it was just painful. But the time had come, she wanted some, and she was tired of making her baby suffer.

When Tish finally reached the Honda, she saw a CLK 500 parked next to it and two guys leaning in both the driver and passenger's side windows. They both raised their heads and spoke to her when they saw her approach, then went back to talking to Rayon and Tasheena.

"Girl you want to go with them to some bar?" Tasheena asked Tish as she closed the door.

"I don't know, you know my mom got Tymeere."

"Well call then, and tell Mom Carla its Friday night and you want to hang out for a little while."

"Who said I wanted to hang out?" Tish snapped.

"Bitch stop being a party pooper!" Tasheena snapped back.

Tish called her mom on the cell phone and told her she was hanging out tonight. Ms. Carla said she didn't mind and that Tymeere was already in bed, so it wasn't a problem.

"Just bring me some Kool's when you come in, that's all." Ms. Carla said and hung up the phone.

"Well bitch, is you coming or not?" Tasheena asked.

"Yeah I'm coming." Tish said unenthusiastically.

Chapter Four

Boots & Bonnett's, a popular bar & lounge located in Chester, was where the who's who frequented when they wanted to have a nice time. Rayon drove the Honda into the small lot and parked next to the boah Radee's CLK 500.

"Come on y'all" He said as he and his boy Fresh Mally walked to the door. Once inside the bar, Rayon cringed because the smoke burnt her eyes, but Tish and Tasheena paid it no mind.

"Girl your eyes don't hurt, do they." She asked.

"No. I'm cool," Tish said as they followed the two Chester boys over to a booth.

"Which one of y'all knows how to roll?" Radee asked pulling out a dutchie and some dro.

"Here I'll roll dat shit," Tasheena said, grabbing the weed and cigar from the table.

After blowing two dutchies and drinking about four Apple Martini's apiece, the music started sounding extra good.

"That's my shit," Tish said bobbing her head to the Young Guns 'No Better Love'."

"Chris and Neefie are my babies!" Tasheena said.

"They alright. I like O and Sparks myself," Tish replied.

> *Can't stop thinking bout her lovin'*
> *'Cause I'm crazy bout your lovin'*
> *Can't stop thinking bout your lovin'*
> *'Cause there's no betta love!*

Radee sat directly across from Tasheena and started going hard, while Fresh Mally stepped off and hollered at some

45

other broad. He figured he'd give up on Tish and Rayon because he wasn't getting anywhere and they seemed loyal to their men.

"So whass'up? You tryin' to dance for a minute?" Radee asked standing up.

"Yeah we can do that," She said and looked back at her girls with a smile and a wink.

"Girl watch this," She said sliding her purse over to Rayon.

Tasheena stood before the boy Radee and gave him a serious once over, starting at his crisp new Timbs, and then she worked her way up to his Miskeen jeans and matching shirt, then back down to his chain and iced out Jacob the Jeweler watch.

"This nigga got some dough," She thought. "And he ain't ugly. I can do some things with him."

"Why you staring at me?" Radee said and passed her another dutchie, this one was lit already.

"I'm just checking you out, dats all," She said as smoke escaped her mouth.

"I heard dat," He said and took the dutchie back.

Tish and Rayon sat in the booth knocking down the rest of their drinks really not feeling their surroundings, while Tasheena did her thing on the dance floor.

"Girl look at her, she makes me sick!" Tish said, watching as her girl Tasheena shook her ass.

"Mmm-Hmm they might as well be fucking," Rayon said as Tasheena threw her leg around Radee's waist.

"Come on, let's go get her and tell her we're ready to leave." Tish said to Rayon as they walked over towards Tasheena.

"For real girl, y'all ready to leave already?" She asked when Tish and Rayon approached.

"Yeah girl, I'm fucked up and I really don't feel like driving back to Delaware." Rayon said.

"Plus it's late, it's damn near two o'clock in the morning." Tish reminded them.

Tasheena turned to her new friend and broke the news of her early departure as easily as possible. She knew he'd be upset because he'd been talking slick all night, plus she felt he was hard while her leg was on his waist.

"Look, I'm about to bounce 'cause my girls are ready to leave," She said.

"Huh? So you are going to leave me just like that?" He asked.

"No, don't look at it like that. I'm saying my peoples are ready to leave, so I gotta go, feel me?"

"Let 'em go. I got you. I'll take you home."

"I don't even know you."

"Do it look like I'mma let some'em happen to you?" He asked, and then stepped back with his arms open.

"I don't know!" Tasheena said cautiously.

"Come on girl, what you going to do?" Tish said irritated.

Tasheena looked at Tish and Rayon then back at Radee and said "I'mma chill here, Radee is going to bring me home."

"You's a stupid bitch!" Tish said and spun on her heels in disgust. "Come on Rayon."

Tasheena felt the sting of Tish's words, but let them bounce off. "Shit she got a man, and so do Rayon, them bitches is straight. I gotta do me 'cause ain't nobody giving me shit!" She thought and grabbed the Dutchie from Radee.

"You alright?" He asked.

"Yeah, I'm straight."

*   *   *   *   *   *   *

During the entire ride from Chester back to Delaware, all Tish and Rayon could speak on was their friend Tasheena's actions. This wasn't the first time she pulled a stunt like this, but it was the last time it was going to happen without them speaking on it.

"She don't even know that boy." Rayon said.

"She don't give a fuck! I'm really starting to believe her when she says that shit. I mean, all a nigga got to do is look like he gotta couple of dollars and she wit it." Tish spoke more disgusted than anything else.

"It's a shame because Tasheena is the bomb!" Rayon said complimenting her girl because in reality she actually looked better than both her and Tish.

"I know, but she gotta realize that. It's crazy because she ain't starting acting like that until Deon got messed up. I hope he calls me because he's probably the only one who can talk some sense into her."

"You probably right too girl." Rayon said as they passed the sign that read: Welcome to Delaware, The Small Wonder.

"Look you might as well stay with me tonight girl. That way you ain't gotta drive all the way out Hockeson by yourself." Tish said as they pulled in the projects.

"Alright." Rayon said.

"Damn girl, you know what?" Tish asked as she put the key in the door.

"What?"

"I forgot my mom's Kool's!"

*   *   *   *   *   *   *

48

Radee held Tasheena's arm as she staggered away from Boots & Bonnets and led her over to his CLK. Tasheena was mad at herself for allowing herself to get so high, and couldn't shake the intoxicants. She was conscious and knew what was going on, but she felt as if she was moving in slow motion.

"Here take this shit," Tasheena said giving Radee the half of blunt she held in her hand.

"You got the lighter?"

"No, you got it." She said and flopped down in the passenger's seat.

"Yo, you staying with me tonight?" Radee asked.

"Where we staying at?" Tasheena asked avoiding the question she knew was coming sooner or later.

"I don't know, but it'll be somewhere nice you can bet on that."

"Well you're driving ain't you? I'm trying to figure out why we ain't left." She said and laid the seat all the way back.

The Guest Quarter Suites hotel was the final destination for the night, as the CLK pulled into the parking garage. Radee led Tasheena through the front doors and they stood at the desk waiting on someone to check them in. When the manager came to assist them he was more than friendly.

"Hello, welcome to the airport's Guest Quarter Suites where we take pride in assisting our guests. My name is Dave and how may I help you?"

"Damn dog. Do you gotta say that shit every time somebody come up in this mutha-fucka?" Radee asked.

"Well yes sir, I do." He replied, not catching Radee's hint for him to relax.

"Look man, Fuck it! Just give me a room, a presidential suite." Radee said pulling out a wad of hundreds.

"That'll be $275.00."

"No problem and keep the change," Radee said sliding him three hundred dollar bills.

When they reached the tenth floor, Radee slid the credit card type key into the door and waited for the green light before he turned the knob. He held the door open for Tasheena and she entered the plush room. The presidential suite was more like a condominium. Its large living room had a huge entertainment center and soft leather furniture, while solid oak frame doors lead to the bedroom. The bed was queen sized and placed against the wall in front of the huge bay window.

"I'm going to the bathroom," Radee said as Tasheena opened the drapes and looked out over the Philadelphia International Airport's runway.

Tasheena's eyes began to water as her thoughts drifted to Deon. She hated him for the way he abandoned her and chose drugs over her. "How could he do this to me?" She thought. Tasheena was crushed and as she watched an airplane take off down the runway and disappear into the sky, she silently wished it were her and Deon flying to some remote place and cuddling under a palm tree while eating some exotic fruit.

"Are you alright?" Radee asked when he came back from getting the Jacuzzi ready.

"Yeah, I'm alright, just thinking that's all."

"Well let me help you take your mind off of that because you are too damn sexy to be stressing." He said and Tasheena's sadness turned into vengeance.

"How you goin' to take my mind off of it?" She asked.

"Come on, I'll show you," He said.

Radee led Tasheena into the bathroom where the four men Jacuzzi was bubbling with steamy water. On its deck sat two glasses, a wine bottle, and a rolled Dutchie.

"You getting in?" He asked and started stripping down to his boxers.

"You know what?" She asked herself as she watched Radee stand before her cut up and in boxers, "Fuck Deon!"

Tasheena always did that. She would always have to channel her anger and resentment towards Deon to go forth with someone else. By doing that and wanting money, she managed to fuck her reputation up as being one of the baddest bitches around town into being a smut broad.

"Yeah I'm getting in."

Radee laid back in the Jacuzzi sipping the Moet while he watched Tasheena undress. She came out of her clothes piece by piece as provocatively as she could revealing her beautiful caramel skin. When she stood before him in her red thong and matching strapless bra, he could only shake his head.

"Whass wrong?" She asked as he starred at her oddly.

"Yo, anybody ever tell you how good you look?"

"I've heard it before," She said and stepped into the Jacuzzi.

Tasheena sat back against the other wall of the Jacuzzi and faced Radee while he poured her a drink. She let her arms spread out and rest over the base of the Jacuzzi and arched her back, pushing her titties up. Using her foot, she slid it under the water and placed it on his dick and wiggled her toes causing him to almost spill her drink.

"You alright?" She teased.

"Don't start nothing you can't finish," He said.

"I thought you'd never ask," She said and slid across the Jacuzzi and sat on his lap.

Tasheena wrapped her legs around his waist and her arms around his neck then kissed his forehead.

"Damn girl, you know how to make a nigga feel special with your phat ass," He said giving it a squeeze.

"Ummm," She moaned and ground her waist into his pelvis. "Squeeze that ass."

The two of them teased each other with foreplay for almost twenty minutes always touching and feeling spots trying figure one another out. Then just like that, Radee stood up with Tasheena still wrapped around his body and walked to the bedroom.

"You got a rubber?" Tasheena asked as he laid her down on the bed.

"Yeah, I got one," He said and went to retrieve it from the pants pocket.

"When he came back, Tasheena was laying on top of the bed buck naked.   Instantly seeing this dime on the bed got his man rock hard as he stepped from his boxers and slid the Trojan on.

"Take your time, I haven't did it in a while," She lied as Radee climbed on top of her. Tasheena reached down and grabbed him, then guided him into her. Radee began a smooth stroke and Tasheena held one of her own legs up and ground her hips in a circular motion.

"Ssss, damn baby," Radee squealed. "This pussy is blazin'"

"Is it? Tell me it's good again! Tell me my pussy is good again." She moaned.

"It's good baby! This pussy is good!" Radee said and Tasheena flipped him over.

"Let me ride it baby," She said and straddled him.

Just like that Tasheena snapped, she put her hands in his chest and rose, flopped, ground, and twisted until she felt him melt.

"Damn, you came already?" She asked and saw the look of shame on his face. He didn't answer, but Tasheena knew it was over, so she reached down and grabbed his man again to make sure the rubber stayed on when she got up.

"Don't feel bad, you said it was blazin'" She said and knew it, because Radee was whipped. They fell asleep.

*   *   *   *   *   *   *

The sound of the phone and the knock on the door woke Tasheena up.

"Room service, house keeping," a lady's voice spoke from beyond the door.

"Hello," Tasheena answered.

When she heard the voice on the other end say, "Check out time," She got up. She sat up with her back on the headboard and rubbed her eyes trying to shake the hangover.

"Radee" she called out, but there was no answer. Tasheena stood up, paced the floor, and tried to find her thong and bra.

"Housekeeping!" She heard the lady say again.

"I'm checking out!" Tasheena yelled as she gathered her clothes to get dressed.

"I know this nigga ain't play me!" She said aloud as she searched the room and for the first time she realized how she'd been playin' herself like some bum bitch as the tears flowed. For the first time it hurt, it really hurt and she needed Deon. She knew Deon could make it all better.

"Rayon where you at?" Tasheena asked, calling her Nextel.

"I'm over Tish's. Where you at?"

"I need y'all to come get me." She said through sniffles.

"Girl are you alright? Where are you at?" Rayon asked concerned.

"At the Guest Quarter Suites by the airport like you're going to Philly." She said as her voice broke up.

"What? The boah left you or some'em?" Rayon asked, but before Tasheena could answer she said "Never mind. Look we on our way," and hung up the phone.

"Bitch guess what?" Rayon asked Tish.

"What?" Tish asked as she washed the last few dishes from breakfast that morning.

"The nigga done left Tasheena up in the hotel in Philly."

"Bitch stop playin!'"

"Girl I'm dead serious. We gotta go up there and pick her ass up." Rayon said.

"We should leave her stupid ass up there," Tish said thinking Tasheena got what she deserved for being so stupid.

"We can't do that girl," Rayon said.

"Oh, I know that. We'll never do no shit like that, I'm just saying that's how I feel that's all."

After Tish strapped the car seat in the Honda and put Tymeere in it, Rayon pulled away from the curb. Tasheena sat patiently in the lobby until she couldn't take it anymore. "Damn where they at?" She asked herself as she paced the floor. She felt as though the staff and every guest that came through the door knew what had happened to her because they all were looking at her. Or at least that is what she thought. Tasheena stood at the door for what seemed to be an hour and was about to return to her seat when she spotted the Honda.

"Look at her, looking all stupid in the face." Tish said when she spotted Tasheena at the entrance door.

"I don't know what for? She did the shit to herself." Rayon said.

Tasheena hesitated for a moment as the thought of what her girls were going to say to her entered her mind. It was

54

already bad enough that she actually went through the ordeal herself, but to hear it again from them would almost be too much to bare.

"Fuck it! I'mma hear it anyway," She said herself and walked out the door with her head down.

"Bitch pick ya head up! You made the decision." Tish started as she approached the car.

"Look, I'm not trying to hear that shit right now," Tasheena stated aggressively.

"Who you talking to like that bitch! Don't get it twisted 'cause I'll fuck you up!" Tish said.

"You'll fuck who up? Tish, I'll beat ya ass!" Tasheena said and meant it.

"Well what then bitch?" Tish said stepping out of the car.

"What?" Tasheena said as they stood face to face.

None of them threw a blow; they just stared at each other. Tish and Tasheena were like sisters, they grew up together and even though Tish knew she couldn't beat Tasheena, her sisterly love made her snap like that.

"Y'all come on and get in the car." Rayon yelled as she stood beside the car.

Tish didn't say a word the whole ride back, but Rayon had a mouthful to say. She went from how Tasheena was with Deon, to how she had transformed, and Tasheena didn't like it.

"I'm sayin', who are you to judge me?" Tasheena asked.

"I'm not judging you, I'm just telling you how I see it that's all. You fuckin' up, and then wondering why nobody won't take you serious," and the words couldn't have come out simpler. Rayon was right and Tasheena knew it. The only thing she could do was sit in the back seat and play with

Meere-Meere and he even sensed something was wrong as he wiped the tears from her cheeks.
*   *   *   *   *   *   *

Chapter Five

Tish answered the phone on the first ring.

"Hello," She said into the phone, and then smiled when she heard his voice.

"Hey baby, what'chu doing?" Trans asked.

"Nothing, waiting on your call."

"Look, I want to take you out somewhere special, but a nigga only got like $30.00 dollars, so we limited, you know?

"I got money. I did Ms. Barber's head yesterday, plus I've had clients all week."

"Man, what I look like taking money from you and my lil man's, that's y'alls money."

"I'm saying if I got money, then so do you." Tish said.

"Look, I'mma think of some'em so you get ready alright?"

"I ain't got no babysitter."

"So what? He coming wit' us anyway."

"Excuse me," She said and they said their goodbyes.

That's why Tish loved Trans so much because he always included Tymeere in everything. She knew someday he was going to make a good father.

"Damn what I'mma do?" Trans said rotating in circles around his bedroom as he held the twenty dollar bill and two fives.

"Man some'em gotta give! I'm tired of being broke and all my boys are hustling and shit! Man fuck dat, I'm turning Pro!" He said to himself and for the first time felt sure about the leap.

"I got it!" Trans said and stuffed the money down in his pocket.

"I know just what I'mma do."

Trans left his bedroom and went downstairs to the kitchen where his mom was preparing dinner.

"Mom we got some potatoes?" He asked as she prepared the roast for the oven.

"Why?" She asked.

"'Cause I want you to make me some potato salad right quick."

"What for? And what's right quick?"

"'Cause me and Tish getting ready to go on a picnic."

"Where at?"

"Probably down to Battery Park."

"Alright, I'll make it, but it ain't going to be ready for an hour."

"Alright then. Hey mom, let me use the car so I can go to the supermarket right quick," Trans said grabbing her keys from the counter.

"Come straight back 'cause I have something I need to do for myself today, that's why I'm getting dinner started so early."

"O.K.," He said and left out the back door.

Trans drove his mom's station wagon Volvo to the Ginardi's right around the corner. Since he wasn't going to be long, he parked in a handicap spot and ran in. The first thing he saw was some fresh roses, one for two dollars. "I'll grab that on my way out," He thought and walked to the back of the store to the deli. Trans ordered a pound and a half of Turkey, a pound and a half of Turkey Ham, and a pound of American cheese and threw it in the carry around basket. He then made his way down the snack isle and grabbed some chips & dip.

"Oh I almost forgot," He said and stopped on two more isles grabbing sub rolls, sodas, and some Tasti Cake pastries.

58

After grabbing a rose, Trans stood in line awaiting the total amount on his little shopping spree.

"Twenty three dollars is your total." The cashier said to Trans.

"Damn. I barely made it." Trans said as he handed the cashier twenty five dollars.

When Trans got home, his mom was in the kitchen peeling eggs in the sink.

"Did you get everything you needed boy?" She asked when he came through the back door.

"I think so. Don't we got lettuce and tomatoes?" He asked.

"Yeah we got plenty of that."

By one o'clock, Ms. Carmen, Trans' mom, had everything prepared and laid out on the table. The subs had been made, the chips and dip had been placed in Tupperware bowls and the sodas and fruit were in an Igloo. Ms. Carmen told Trans to go downstairs in the basement because she had a brand new picnic basket she never used before and to grab one of those comforters from on top of the dryer.

"Look boy." She said when he came upstairs. "I done made the subs, potato salad, packed the snacks and I'll be damned if I pack the picnic basket too!"

"Alright mom, I got it, but can I use the car because dad ain't here yet?"

"Go ahead."

*   *   *   *   *   *   *

Battery Park, located in Historic New Castle, was crowded on the first day of spring. Children were running around playing everything from Frisbee to flying kites, while their parents enjoyed some quiet time to themselves stretched out on blankets. Trans put Tymeere up on his neck and grabbed the picnic basket and started walking onto the parks ground.

"Baby, grab the radio and Igloo," Trans said to Tish.

Tish followed behind her man proudly as he carried her son on his neck without any complaints. It was as if Trans was really Tymeere's daddy because Trans was all Tymeere knew. Whenever he came around he would drop everything or stop anything he was doing to run to Trans for him to pick him up. Just thinking about those kinds of things and the way Saafie acted towards her son made her angry. "Mutha-fucka can't even watch his son when I need to work or some'em," She said and sat everything on the ground next to Trans.

Tish lay on the comforter next to Trans while Tymeere ran around. They never let him get out of their sight, yet they could still concentrate enough on each other to enjoy themselves. Tish was so impressed at how Trans went out of his way, on the spur of the moment, to come up with something so beautiful. The sky was blue, the sun was shining brightly, and for March, the first day of spring, and it was relatively warm. He had planned it perfectly.

"Baby," she asked, "What made you think of a picnic?"

"I don't know? I guess 'cause I only had $30.00 dollars," He answered and she smiled.

"You want some more?" She asked dipping a potato chip in some dip, and placing it to his mouth.

"Nah, I'm straight. I do want to listen to the radio though." He said and Tish laid it flat on its back in between the both of them.

I think I might wife her
You know,
Powder blue Roca-wear suite white Nike her!

Young Guns, Chris & Neef

The Young Guns new single was burning up the charts and as the tunes came through the portable radio, Trans became lost in the lyrics, and so did Tish. It was talking about them, the whole song was about them, and as if they read each other's minds they turned to face one another.

"You hear that?" They asked at the same time, and broke out laughing.

Trans and Tish stayed in the park until the once crowded place had become almost empty. Only about four other couple and a few kids skipping rocks into the river remained.

"Let's go," Trans said and he and Tish began to pack up.

"Get Meere-Meere baby and try not to wake him up," Tish said and watched as Trans' stealthily lifted him into his arms.

"I got'em" Trans said.

After dropping Tymeere off at home, Trans invited Tish to dinner and she accepted. She liked going over to Trans' house because it was family structured and motivated Tish to attain that part of life. Every time she left, she envisioned her and Trans one day living like a family with plenty of kids.

Trans pulled into the driveway of his parents three story home and parked next to his dad's F150 pick-up truck. He looked over to Tish, smiled and said, "What'chu thinking about baby?"

"Nothing," She replied as they got out of the car to enter the house.

Tish followed Trans into the house and that family feeling struck her instantly, as Trans' dad, Mr. Carl, lay back

in his lazy boy. On the floor, his brother Carron and sister
Kiesha lay in front of the TV watching a basketball game.
    "Hey Tish," Kiesha said and jumped up when she came
through the door.
    "Hey girl, whass'up?" Tish said bending down to hug
her.
    "Yo Trans UCLA is gettin' blown out by USC and yo
they mentioned your name like five times." Carron said.
    "For real?"
    "Yeah I'm for real. Hey Tish, whass'up?"
    "Hey Carron."
    "How was y'all's picnic?" Mr. Carl asked.
    "It was nice," Tish answered giddily. "Where's Ms.
Carmen at?"
    "Over there in the kitchen, should be almost ready to
feed us our dinner."
    "Well let me go help out," Tish said and turned to
Trans before disappearing through the den with Kiesha.
    Ms. Carmen was Tish's girl. They shared a bond
together that the two of them made stronger every time they
saw one another. See, Ms. Carmen was just like Tish and they
shared a similar story. They were both from the projects, both
mothers at an early age and both in, what they seemed to be at
the time, love with their baby's daddy's. Ms. Carmen shared
her story with Tish and how Trans' real father, a drug dealer,
had received a life sentence for shooting someone at a drug
buy, leaving her pregnant and alone. But she made it. Ms.
Carmen's story got better when she met Carl, a regular dude.
They strived together, made goals together, but best of all they
stayed together through everything, and now they were
reaping the benefits.

"Hey Mom Carmen!" Tish yelled as if she hadn't seen the woman in years.

"Hey baby! Did you bring my grandson?" She asked with just as much enthusiasm.

"No, he's home asleep."

"Well can I come get him tomorrow?"

"Yes."

"Good, I gotta check on Carla anyway. How's she doing?"

"She's alright. Just about ready to move though."

"Oh yeah. Where to?"

"I think somewhere on the east side."

"Oh, well I'mma find out tomorrow anyway, so are you still over to Che-Che's shop?"

"Yeah," Tish answered then went to get a better look at her hair. "It's about time to come see me, huh?"

"I know girl, I just ain't had the time. It's been so busy around here lately with me playing hostess to different college recruits and coaches that I just ain't had the time. I should be free now because they stopped coming every since Trans committed to UCLA" She finished as Tish washed her hands and joined her in making dinner plates.

*   *   *   *   *   *   *

At the dinner table, Tish sat directly across from Trans, while Ms. Carmen and Mr. Carl sat at each head of the table. The roast beef was tender and the greens were perfect with the macaroni and cheese, as they ate together like a family. Tish loved it. This was her vision and she just couldn't shake the feelings. Trans kicked his shoe off under the table and ran his foot up Tish's leg causing her to jump.

"You alright baby?" Ms. Carmen asked seeing Tish jump in her periphery view.

"Yeah I was daydreaming," She said then looked at Trans and frowned her face.   "Stop" she said under her breath looking at Trans.

"No!" Trans said and nodded his head to the side and got up.

Tish waited for a couple of seconds before she got up and left, not to seem obvious, but Ms. Carmen caught it all. She smiled to herself as she thought how obvious they looked trying to be sneaky.

"Boy! Why you do that?" Tish said and smacked Trans' shoulder playfully.

"Do what?"

"Rub your feet on my leg."

"Because," He said and took her in his arms. "I want some baby!"

"Me too," Tish said feeling as shocked as Trans looked. It was the first time she actually told Trans how she felt.

"Come on then," He said.

"No boy! Your mom is right there."

"She ain't gone say nuffin."

"Yes she is."

"Come on, watch," He said and led her past the dining room.

"Where y'all going?" Ms. Carmen asked as they headed to the living room.

"Upstairs to my room mom and watch a couple of movies."

"Mmm-Hmm. I hope they rated PG," She said letting them know she wasn't stupid, but still keeping their slick stuff from Carron and Kiesha's young 16 and 14 year old minds.

"They are," Tish and Trans said in unison.

Trans opened up his room door and hit the switch on the wall. Instantly his TV came on along with the lamp on his dresser and he stepped in. Trans' room looked more like a showcase display of trophies than a bedroom, but it still had a bedroom feel. His more than thirty pairs of sneakers lined one wall and his stereo system occupied the other with more trophies.

"How many trophies are in here Trans?" Tish asked standing next to a six foot MVP trophy.

"Almost seventy," He answered and flopped down on the bed. "Come here," He said.

Tish's heart pounded so hard she could hear it in her ears.

"Oh my God." She said to herself as she moved over to Trans.

Tish wasn't nervous, instead she was borderline terrified as she sat next to Trans on the bed.

"Whass wrong baby?" He asked taking her hands into his.

"You remember what I told you, don't you?" She asked.

"What? About only being with one person?"

"Yeah."

"I told you baby I'mma make it special, real special," He said and kissed her lips.

"Your mom might come up here," She said pulling away.

"Look I got this" He said and slid the dresser behind the door that couldn't lock.

Trans laid Tish down on her back and slowly peeled off her clothes as she melted beneath his touch. They hadn't even got into the actual act of making love, but Tish felt better now than anytime she had been with Saafie. Just the way he was moving so smoothly had Tish soaked between the legs and squirming.

Trans felt her moving beneath him, as she lay topless on his bed. He kissed her neck and then moved to her titties where he licked and nibbled softly at her nipples. Tish let out a soft moan that only 'caused Trans to intensify his foreplay. He licked down between her cleavage making his way down to her navel, where he unbuttoned Tish's jeans with his teeth.

"What are you doing?" She asked with a jolt and lifted his face up to hers.

He didn't answer, he just continued licking all around Tish's stomach and navel, while pulling her pants the rest of the way off.

Tish couldn't believe the way his tongue felt stabbing in and out of her intimacy. She panted and sucked air between her teeth rapidly to a feeling she never felt before.

"Oh my God! Oh my God!" She cried, unable to control anything that was happening to her, as Trans' hands never stopped exploring her body.

She was about to burst with pleasure and tried reaching out to grab something or anything to hold and squeeze on and that's where she found Trans' ears.

"Oh my God! What are you doing to me?" She cried louder, as she tried to pull his face inside her and when she stiffened her legs she shook uncontrollably.

Tish was in awe. She never knew it could feel like this and as he climbed on top of her and guided himself into her the feeling was even more intensified.

"Oh my God baby! Stop! What are you doing to me?" She continued to cry with pleasure, as Trans stroked uncontrollably.

The more she moaned and cried, the more Trans was aroused. In and out, up and down, side-to-side, he stabbed at her love box, as she lay beneath him in a daze. She was lost in total bliss and didn't even know how hard she was throwing it back, but when they came together it was like they were the only two people in the world.

"Trans! Open this damn door!" Ms. Carmen yelled.

Chapter Six

The closer he got home, the harder the rain started to fall. He crossed Gov. Printz Blvd. and passed the K.F.C. hungry as a slave. Twenty Seventh Street and Van Buren was a long walk from where he stood.

"Damn man, I gotta do something." He told himself, as he passed the once known notorious Bucket Projects that had been renovated into town homes soon to be open.

Talking to himself had become a regular thing now since dope had become his life and sometimes he actually had to catch himself doing it because he didn't know he was doing it. Deon pulled the half cut straw from his pocket and bag of 7-up dope from his coin pocket and opened it up, as he stood under one of the unfinished house porches. Digging the straw into the bag, he pulled out the fine substance and held it to his nose and sniffed hard, causing him to choke.

"Don't make no sense!" He talked to himself again as he realized he was actually outside at an abandoned house in the pouring rain sniffing dope.

When Deon finished his bag, he checked himself to make sure he knew where everything was.

"Yeah that's about right," He assured himself as he checked the dummy rocks he had bagged up and the couple of dollars he had.

"Three mu'fuckin' dollars!" He said disgusted.

"I can't even get a pack of cigarettes, let alone some'em to eat!" He said and stepped off the porch headed to Market Street.

Deon's whole world had caved in. He lost everything. He lost his cars, his house, his money, his girl, and the love of his life, his mom. The crazy part about it was he lost her to the

same shit that he just sniffed up his noise; it was sickening. At
that thought, he flicked what could have been a tear or
raindrop from his eyes and understood he had a disease. His
tears fell.

When Deon hit 27th and West in-between Market
Street, he was rejuvenated. The dope had kicked in and he felt
normal again, like he hadn't a problem in the world.

"Whass'up my man? I got dimes of straight drop and
pop!" Deon said holding out his bag of dummy rocks, and they
even looked real.

Deon had managed one day, high as hell, to clone some
cooked up by mixing candles, Bisquick, and Ambesol. The
results were what seemed to be a weight or whatever you
needed.

"Is it real my man?" The crack head asked.

"Do it look like I'mma sell you some fake shit nigga?"
Deon snapped, as he dug a couple of rocks from his bag.

"How much you spendin' 'cause I could break you off
some'em if you spendin' enough."

"I'mma spend $50!"

"Alright cousin look I got you. Here take these 7 for
$50," He said and dropped the rocks in his palm.

"Come on cousin, where da money at 'cause it's hot as a
mu'fucka out here!" He said and grabbed the money, as the
crack head left.

As soon as he turned the corner, Deon took off. He
knew the dude would be back for his money, but it was a done
deal. With his new found $50 dollars, Deon went to the
Chinese store and ordered 5 wings, an ice-tea, and some
shrimp fried rice.

"Oh and let me get a pack of Newport's." Deon said to
the lady.

When Deon gathered his food and came out the store, the rain had become a drizzle.

"I need a ride down River." He said to himself.

Jenson Drive, the horseshoe, was the new drug market. Everybody from over in the Bucket Projects had just made their way across the street and brought the heroin to Riverside. The crazy thing about Riverside now was that they made all the streets one-way. For as long as the projects stood, they never even thought about changing the streets into one-ways. The state was cool with drug dealing amongst the blacks, but as soon as the whites got caught up on the dope and heroin, the state made every street a one-way. Just goes to show you who's a priority in this country!

Deon made the dude he caught a ride from park in front of Pop's house and he got out and disappeared through the cut.

"Hot Sauce!" He called out. "Who got it?"

"I don't know baby, but it's some out here somewhere. Did you check up there where Spotty be at?" She asked.

"Ain't nobody around there."

"Come on then baby, let's go around T-dog's house 'cause I know she knows who got it." And Hot Sauce was right; T-dog had 7-up herself and gave him a play, 4 bags for $30 dollars.

"Thanks Hot Sauce. Baby you alright?"

"Yeah I'm cool; I'll catch you next time."

Deon got back in the car with the dude, paid him a fake rock, and got out on 27th street again. Nobody was outside this time though, so Deon looked at his watch.

"Damn, I ain't know it was this late!" He said to himself as he checked his Movado, the only thing he had left from his hustling days, which he refused to sell.

Deon sat down on the step, pulled a bag from his pocket and began to sniff again.

"Man I can't even quit!" He said to himself and put the straw to his nose.

Deon sat in that same spot and sniffed three of his four bags before nodding out. When he came out of his nod almost an hour later, the same brother he hated seeing so much, Brother Aziz, greeted him. Brother Aziz, a tall, thick, dark skinned Akee with a salt and pepper Sunni stood before the nodding young brother.

"Oo thoo be la hi min a shaitan a rahzeem," He said kicking the brother's foot.

"Brother Deon, brother Deon! Get up!" The shame on Deon's face spoke a million words when Brother Aziz greeted him.

"As Salaam Alaikum!"

"Wa-laikum As Salaam," Deon replied remembering when Bro Aziz taught him the proper greetings a while ago.

"What are you doing out here asleep on a step, Akee?"

"I don't know Bro Aziz."

"Listen Ak, are you tired of living like this? Do you want to change Akee? I mean, because it's only going to work if you want it Akee. See this dunna that your living in will kill you Akee, literally drown you to the hell fire in this life and the next life." Bro Aziz said and began taking off his jacket.

"Brother Deon," he started again, "You see this! You see this Akee!" He shouted into Deon's face, as he pushed his arms into Deon's view.

"These are my scars from the dunna Akee! They are never going anywhere. Every time I look at my arms, or go to the doctor's office to get blood work done and them mu'fuckas can't find a good vein to draw from, I remember and say alhum-du-liallah, praise be to God that I made it up out of there. Listen Akee, my arms look like Popeye's arms and not from muscles either, and that's from shooting dope! If you don't get ya shit right, one day these will be yours too. I know its hard brother Deon." Bro Aziz said and took a crying Deon into his arms.

"I done tried everything from weed, dope, coke, pills, women, and so on, but I have never tried anything as sweet as Allah." Deon said.

"Brother Deon, try Allah!"

Deon couldn't answer. He just stayed in the big brothers arms and sobbed away his pain. The loss of his mother was an unresolved issue, the loss of Tasheena was a fresh wound, and the loss of his own dignity and pride was a hard blow to Deon. Brother Aziz kept an arm around the brother he had talked to almost every morning before work, just like now, for a whole summer and his words finally penetrated Deon's armor clad facade.

"Allahu Akbar!" He popped open his trunk and gave Deon a pamphlet on Islam's five pillars and the six articles of faith.

"Brother Deon, take these and read them. If you have any questions contact me Insha Allah. I'll help you with anything, but right now Akee I gotta get down this highway to Chrysler and make this money." He smiled and departed, "As Salaam Alaikum."

Deon couldn't believe what Brother Aziz had just revealed to him, as he watched him pull off. He was just like him. He looked down at the two pamphlets he held in his hands about Islam and the tears started again.

"Please Allah, help me!" He cried out in his head as he watched the nighttime sky turn into an early morning pink and purple.

*   *   *   *   *   *   *

Tyaire was at Deon's door at eleven o'clock in the morning Sunday. His aunt Sheila let him in and said that Deon was still sleeping, so Tyaire ran up the steps and walked in Deon's room to wake him up.

"Get up nigga!" He shouted and pulled the covers off of him.

"Yo man, what da fuck is you doin'?" Deon snapped and snatched the covers back.

"Yo man, get up and go to the game with me."

"Man fuck da game! I just went to bed, plus I'm on some new shit."

"What type of new shit?"

"Some stop getting high and get some money again new shit," He said clearly.

"About time nigga! That's what I'm talking about. When you going to start?"

"Man I started this morning. Some deep shit happened to me cuz. A nigga just broke down and cried; I been needing to cry since my mom dukes died."

"I heard that," Tyaire said with understanding, but he couldn't relate. He still had his mother, so he could only imagine.

"So whass'up? You coming to the game with me or not?"

"Man I ain't got nuffin' to wear and I ain't goin' nowhere until I'm right."

"I got'chu cousin. You know I ain't going to let you go nowhere fucked up."

73

"Alright. Let me go take a shower right quick and get my shit together."

"Go ahead nigga," Tyaire said grabbing the remote control. "I'mma watch Sports Center." And right off the bat a segment on the next high school phenom, Trans Owens, appeared on the screen.

*   *   *   *   *   *   *

The park on 6th and Madison was the sight of one of the longest rivalry games of this generation. It started way back at the P.A.L. league over at George Gray Elementary School and extended into high school. Riverside versus Eastside; just mentioning these two sides playing one another could draw a crowd. Whether it was a softball game, flag football game, or basketball game these two sides of town were archenemies, but they shared a bond that extended and would last a lifetime. Trans, Lenny, Tail, Bo-Bo and MC made up the team from Riverside, while Mr. C, Showtime, Duff, Steph, and Shahid represented the Eastside. The stage was set and the park was flooded, as people once again came to see the rivalry.

Rayon drove up Madison Street towards the park and didn't see a parking spot in sight.

"Damn, all these people out here, I hope they don't start acting like they ain't got any sense." She said as she tried to squeeze into a spot in front of the daycare center across the street.

"I know girl, 'cause you know when a lot of nigga's get together it's always some'em." Tish added.

"Who you telling. It's either over who's fuckin' who, or just plain jealousy." Tasheena spoke then added, "Damn bitch, you is a parking ass" as they got out.

Tish, Rayon, and Tasheena walked across the street into the crowded park and felt the eyes on them. As usual they

74

were sharp as a tack, so they were used to the odd feeling, but something felt different today. The sky was gray and the air almost smelled like rain, but it was warm. Cliff's hot dog truck was parked on the corner and as always there was a line that never ended in front of it; people were waiting to kill their munchies urge.

"Girl, does it feel crazy out here, like somebody is really staring at us?" Tish asked.

"Yeah girl," Tasheena added.

*   *   *   *   *   *   *

"There go that bitch right there," Pumpkin said as she stood with her girls Cherell and Lisa.

"Whass'up then bitch? Do you want to handle this now or later," Lisa asked aggressively.

"It can wait 'cause the game ain't even started yet. Wait till they start playing, then it won't be no scene." Pumpkin responded.

"O.K.! I heard that." Lisa said.

Pumpkin kept her eyes on Tish the whole time the game was going on; never letting her out of her sight for one minute. She despised Tish for having a baby by her man and still denied it was his because he cheated with Tish, while they were together. Saafie used to snap on her at first when he bought the lil boy over to the house because she didn't except it, but as time went on he understood. So to please Pumpkin he at times denied or deprived things from Tymeere in order to keep her happy. "I'mma beat dis bitch's ass!" She thought as she watched Tish jump up and down when Trans dunked the ball.

*   *   *   *   *   *   *

Tyaire and Deon stepped up out of the 500 laid like a mutha'fucka. Deon, who hadn't been out to a major outing

75

since his glory days was almost frozen stiff. He had missed all
this and felt like he didn't belong, as he stood amongst all the
people. He actually forgot how to interact with people who
didn't get high and it felt crazy. He looked down at himself in
his throwback U.S.C. (O.J. Simpson) Jersey, blue Roca-wear
jeans, and butter Timbs Tyaire had just brought him and
noticed that he was sharp, but still felt odd. He had lost touch
with the hood and the who's who by staying stuck in the hood
and couldn't relax. The first thing that crossed his mind was
"I need a bag."

Tyaire crossed the street on 6th and looked back only to
see Deon still standing by the car. "Come on nigga!" He
shouted and waved his hand, as Deon finally stepped across the
street.

"You alright nigga? You ain't dope sick are you?"

"Nah I'm cool," Deon answered, as they made their way
through the crowd.

"Oh shit! I know dat ain't dat nigga Deon!" The boah
B-Mizzle asked as he approached.

"Hey cousin whass'up?" Deon asked and felt good
knowing that at least someone knew who he was.

"Damn baby, where you been?" Asked B-Mizzle.

"Stuck baby boy, stuck, but I'mma be back like the old,
ain't nuffin' changed nigga, just a small set back." Deon spoke
confidently and the thought of the bag was gone.

When he and Tyaire stepped off, they saw a couple
more people they knew and received props of all kinds and
right then Deon found his cure.

"All I gotta do is get over the moment, that first urge
because I don't feel I need a bag now," He talked to himself as
always.

"Look cousin! There go Tasheena." Tyaire said and pointed across the basketball court at Tish, Tasheena, and Rayon sitting down.

Deon was stuck like chuck as he felt his heart drop down in his stomach. He had to remember that Tyaire had taken him to the mall and barbershop to get a total make over, but he still felt dirty like "I know I ain't living right," as he watched Tasheena.

"Damn, my baby still sharp!" He said to himself, but refused to speak to her.

"Hey cousins, whass'up? Where y'all two niggas coming from?" Asked Saafie as he gave Deon a double take.

"O.K. baby boy, I see you! You lookin' real good too, you hear me?" He said and asked Tyaire to bet something.

"Nigga you always trying to gamble," Tyaire said.

"But I'mma break you out of that shit, you hear me? Bet everything in your pocket!"

"Nigga that's like twenty five hundred!"

"Bet it!"

"Bet it then nigga!"

"My young boah goin' to make you a believer yet, watch nigga!"

"Man fuck dat nigga!"

*   *   *   *   *   *   *

They switched baskets at 22 and Riverside was leading but with these two teams you could never tell. Out of all the years they'd been playing one another, I think the record is damn near dead even. Mr. C dribbled the ball over the half court line talking shit as usual as Tail guarded him.

"You know what it is nigga!" He boasted.

"I don't know shit!" Tail shot back.

Mr. C crossed over and stood straight up to see the court. If you knew anything about the game you'd love Mr. C's style because it was strictly fundamental, but if you came for the flash you wouldn't like it. Put it like this, on any given night he could give you 30 or better and you'd never see it. Mr. C threw a swift bounce pass to a slashing Showtime in the paint who laid it barely over the fingers of Lenny.

Tail in-bounded the ball and got it right back. Rumor had it that his jump shot range was anywhere in the gym, but he dribbled even nicer. Always low to the ground, Mr. C rode his jump down the court until he spotted Lenny going baseline. They played with each other on the same team all their lives, so when they made eye contact it just happened. Tail lobbed the ball and Lenny caught it out the air for a two handed alley-oop dunk that left the court rocking, as people grabbed the pole to steady it out. The crowd went berserk.

After about four to five lead changes, ten rim shattering dunks, long-range jump shots, and hard fouls it was a one-point game. The whole park knew who it was going to and so did Eastside, but there was nothing they or anyone else could do. Trans was a man in a young man's body and playing amongst boys or so it seemed. See because Delaware just didn't breed tall people, it was like no one could grow beyond 6 ft 3 in. and that stopped everyone on both of the teams from going to the league, except Trans. He had it, and it was all packed in his 6 ft 6 in. frame. Bo-Bo, a football star, but designated point guard for Riverside, passed it to Trans at the top of the key. A pump fake, a hard dribble down the land, and a leap from the dots had the crowd ooo-ing and aaah-ing, but the finish made them go absolutely crazy! Trans, in mid air, twisted his body in the air and placed the ball in between his legs with his back to the backboard and threw it backwards.

"Get my mutha'fuckin money nigga! Did you see dat nigga?" Tyaire said to Saafie before asking Deon did he see the dunk.

"Here nigga!" Saafie said pushing the money into Tyaire's hand, then watched as a big crowd formed by the fence.

*   *   *   *   *   *   *

As soon as the crowd swarmed the court, Pumpkin, Cherell and Lisa made their move.

"I'mma beat dis no good ass bitch's ass!" Pumpkin said hyping herself up as she walked.

"Bitch, I said stop calling my mutha'fuckin' house!" Pumpkin said poking Tish in the face.

Tish couldn't even react for herself because Tasheena was already on Pumpkin's ass.

"Bitch you gotta be crazy!" was all Tasheena said before smashing her from the side.

Tish regained composure and went right on Pumpkin's ass, as Pumpkin's girl Lisa went at Tasheena. Rayon stood on the side and watched as her girls fought their asses off. She jumped in when she saw Cherell trying to pull Tasheena off her girl Lisa. Tish and Pumpkin were getting at each other like two niggas, ducking and slipping blows, but Tish was getting the best of her. Cherell turned around as she caught a glimpse of Rayon coming from the side and pulled out her straight razor. In one swift motion she swung the blade. Rayon saw the blade in her hand, but couldn't move quickly enough. She tried to put her arm to block the swing, but Cherell was too quick. Rayon clutched her breast and let out a scream that pierced the ears of everyone in attendance, once

the blade cut her. The razor had sliced through her Baby Phat t-shirt and gashed her tittie as blood oozed through her fingers.
*   *   *   *   *   *   *

When Tyaire saw that it was Tish fighting, he instantly scanned the surroundings for his baby Rayon and made his way over to the commotion. He tried to get through the crowd before things got too serious, but he was too late.

"Rayon!" he yelled for her to stop, but she charged Cherell.

He knew from always being with Saafie that Cherell was crazy and known for keeping a blade or knife and when she turned he saw it. The next thing he heard was a deafening scream.

"Pop! Pop! Pop," the 45 Cal. Ruger Tyaire held in his hand sounded, causing everyone to scatter as he bust in the air. He did that so everybody would clear out and they would stop fighting.

"Man grab your girl nigga," Tyaire yelled at Saafie getting mad at him. "You can't even control your girl nigga!"

Saafie grabbed Pumpkin up and pulled her off to the side and other people separated the rest of them. Deon grabbed Tasheena from behind and when she turned around, she could have melted.

"Deon!" she thought, and then heard Rayon still weeping.

Tasheena snatched away from Deon and like Tish ran to her girl's aid.

"Yo! Get my baby to the hospital," Tyaire said and Tish ran to the car.

"Help her over here Tasheena," Tish said as she got behind the driver's seat.

80

"Alright, here we come."

Tish sped off down Madison St. and turned on 8ᵗʰ Street, headed to St. Francis Hospital. Through stop signs and red lights she drove rapidly under control.

"You alright girl?" Tish asked Rayon who was still clutching her breast.

"Yeah I'm cool. I can't believe that bitch cut me," Rayon replied.

"Yeah, well the bitch done fucked up, 'cause I'mma beat her ass." Tasheena said. "Don't nobody fuck with my lil' sisters!" she continued and meant every word.

"Bitch did you see Deon!" Tish asked. "Oh my God, he looked good."

"Yeah, I saw him." Rayon said, but Tasheena didn't answer, she was still shocked to have seen him.

"Bitch, why you ain't saying nuffin?" Tish asked Tasheena as she pulled into the emergency.

"I ain't thinking about Deon." Tasheena lied.

"Yeah bitch, imagine that!" Tish shot back.

*   *   *   *   *   *   *

Tyaire's car came to a screeching halt in front of the hospital's emergency room and he jumped out his whip.

"Cousin, park this," he said leaving the car running in the middle of the street.

Deon slid across driver's seat and closed the door, then circled the block for a place to park.

"Damn I miss my baby!" Deon said reminiscing about his 7 series BMW, as he rode the big Benz.

Then he had another mood swing. He went from feeling good to feeling like shit in seconds. This happened all the time; it was as if he couldn't control his emotions anymore. The drugs had altered his emotions for so long that he couldn't function without them. Then, Deon remembered as the urge approached to try and get over the moment as he parallel parked the Benz and suppressed the urge at the same time.

When Deon walked through the emergency room doors, he spotted Tish and Tasheena sitting in the back near the double doors that lead to the actual rooms.

"Whass'up y'all?" Deon asked, as he got comfortable in the chairs across from them. "Where's Tyaire at?"

"Back there with Rayon," Tish answered and nodded her head towards the double doors.

"Oh," he replied and looked down at the floor.

Deon sat across from them in total silence as they talked amongst each other never lifting his head from the floor. He didn't want to have to make eye contact because he thought they'd see right through him. See his secrets and all the crazy shit he'd been doing for the last year and a half.

"Whass'up though Deon? How you been?" Tish asked turning her attention to him.

"I'm alright, trying to stay focused on some shit that's all, you feel me?"

"I heard that."

"So you just ain't going to say shit to me, huh?" Tasheena asked looking for more of an explanation than anything else.

"What can I say? You knew my situation. I was fuckin' up, so I just bounced," he answered.

"I mean, but you ain't say nuffin. You could have at least said some'em."

"What was I going to say Tasheena? Huh? That I'm on dope and can't stop! That I can't take care of myself let alone YOU! I wasn't going to expose you to that, so I bounced" he said loudly, causing people to stare.

"Shhh, be quiet. Why are you so loud?"

"Man, I don' give a fuck about them people!" Deon snapped, his emotions getting the best of him.

"Calm down Deon," Tish said in a rational tone, sensing Deon was about to go off.

"Nah sis, I'm saying. I love this girl and always have and she coming at me crazy like she don't know that I got a mutha'fuckin problem that I need to address. Do you think she ever once said Deon are you alright? Hell no! All she said was nigga you weak! Nigga you a follower! Nigga you a junky! Now she got the gall to ask for an explanation 'cause she sees a nigga half ass looking good! Man fuck Tasheena!" He vented, his words plunged deep in the heart of Tasheena.

"What'chu mean fuck me nigga? I stood by your sorry ass even when your own people's didn't, I tried!" She defended herself. "I tried!"

*   *   *   *   *   *   *

Rayon was happy to see Tyaire when he came through the door.

"Hi baby," he said and made his way over to the bed and sat next to her.

"Hi," Rayon replied, and then scooted up close to him. "I'm cold," she said as she sat naked, down to her panties underneath a paper blue gown.

"What the doctor say?" he asked.

"He said the cut was so deep that I'mma need staples," she answered the same time the doctor came through the door. "Baby stay with me while he does this, O.K.?" She asked scared.

It took everything Tyaire had inside him to stay with her because the smell of the hospital was unpleasant to him. It brought back too many memories. The smell alone reminded him of his two favorite people in the whole world and the answer he got from the doctor when he came out of the operating room. "I'm so sorry, but they didn't make it." His grandparents were gone. Just thinking about those memories made his eyes water, but the squeeze Rayon gave his hand brought him back to reality. He watched the doctor stick a needle of Novocain into her wound and staple it up and then he appreciated the job that doctors do.

*   *   *   *   *   *   *

Chapter Seven

Pumpkin stomped through the duplex with her lips poked out and an attitude for about two hours after they got home. She couldn't believe Saafie would actually take up for the bitch Tish, especially in front of people. "You gone have the nerve to tell me I'm wrong!" She said as she continued to rant. Saafie got up from the couch and walked into his bedroom and shut the door, leaving Pumpkin downstairs with her dogs. Pumpkin was dead wrong for starting that shit with Tish and he let her know that. The way he said it might have been a little harsh, but it was the truth. Tish would always be a part of his life because they shared a son.

"It ain't my fault she can't have no kids!" He thought then felt bad for allowing that thought to cross his mind because it wasn't her fault either.

Some crack head raped pumpkin one night while she slept. She woke up and tried to defend herself, but her little 10-year-old frame couldn't fend off the skinny intruder. It took Pumpkin years to get over the incident. When she met Saafie years later, she showed him the man and never saw him again. She found out later that the man was gunned down and once she found out about the incident she was filled with relief. She didn't know who gunned him down, but she had a clue; she was just glad to know she'd never see him again because the sight of him brought back painful memories.

Saafie flopped down on his bed and called Tyaire's cell phone to see how Rayon was doing. He smiled because he never seen his boy Tyaire act that way over a broad before. Tyaire was some'em like a pimp, but for the past few days all that came out of his mouth was Rayon's name.

"Hello," Tyaire answered.

"Whass'up cousin? Your girl alright?"

"Yeah, she's cool. Just had to get some staples that's all."

"Damn!"

"Yeah, but none of this shit would've happened if you could control your bitch, nigga!" Tyaire said getting madder as he talked.

"Yo nigga watch your mouth!" Saafie said aggressively.

"My bad cuz, I'm just a little salty, that's all."

"So you dead serious about the broad Rayon, huh?"

"Damn right! This is my baby nigga." He said looking at her while she got dressed.

"I heard that cousin, so what'chu about to do now?"

"Talk to Deon and see what's up with him. You know dat nigga went cold turkey on the dope."

"Say word!"

"Word nigga! I think dat nigga about to bounce back like the old Deon on some real shit you heard!"

"I hope so cousin, 'cause a nigga ain't have shit on that nigga!" Saafie said remembering the times.

"Word, well look I'mma get wit'chu later alright?"

"Alright cousin." Saafie said.

Tyaire hung up the phone as Rayon put the last of her clothes on. "Who was that," she asked eavesdropping on the whole conversation. "It was Saafie," he answered.

"Oh, so I'm your baby now, huh? Which one am I, number one, two or three?"

"The only one baby! Ever sine we been together for these past few days, I can't see myself without you." Tyaire said sweetly.

"Well if you wanna be with me there are some things that are going to have to change," She said.

"Anything for you baby, anything!" Tyaire said.

*   *   *   *   *   *   *

When Tyaire and Rayon came through the double
doors leading to the lobby, they were surprised to see Deon
sitting by himself. From where they were, it looked like he had
an attitude about something, but they were unsure. They
continued out into the lobby until they could see the whole
lounge area in its entirety and saw Tish and Tasheena talking
across the room. Tasheena's mouth was moving a hundred
miles a minute and her hands were motioning back and forth
at Deon, so they knew something happened between the two of
them. Tyaire walked over towards Deon, and Rayon went to
Tish and Tasheena to see what was going on, but before Tyaire
could ask, Deon said, "Come on man. Get me the fuck up outta
here!"

"Hold on cousin, whass' wrong?" Tyaire asked puzzled.

"Man dat bitch got to be crazy! Gone come at me out
the side of her neck like I'm some lame or some'em. Man I
cussed dat bitch out!"

"For what?" Tyaire asked.

"Fuck for what! Just get me da fuck up outta here
before I snap," He said and walked towards the exit.

"You got the keys?" Tyaire asked.

"Yeah I got'em. I'll be out in the car."

Tyaire walked over to where Tish, Rayon, and
Tasheena were shaking his head.   "Whass' up y'all?" He
asked setting his eyes on Tasheena.

"Your punk ass boy, dats whass' up." She answered his
indirect question, then continued "Gone have some nerve to
cuss me out like I'm the one getting high or some'em!"

"Well why did y'all start arguing in the first place?"

87

"All I did was ask why would he just up and abandon me like that and he went off. All I ever tried to do was help his ass, but you know what? Fuck Deon, Tyaire. And tell him the next time he do some dope I hope his muthafuckin' heart explodes!" She said out of anger.

"Girl chill out wit dat shit! You know damn well you don't mean it. Look, I'mma go holla at dat nigga. You know he stop getting high and he's trying to get his shit right, don't you? Right now that nigga is on pins and needles. He feels like everybody is against him and shit. Just give him some time to get his shit right. You know he loves you girl! That nigga is just ashamed right now, you know that!"

"I hear you," Tasheena said and then remembered what her aunt said, "Baby he's going to be alright. He just has to hit rock bottom," and maybe this was Deon's rock bottom she thought to herself.

*   *   *   *   *   *   *

After walking Rayon to her car and saying bye to Tish and Tasheena, Tyaire leaned in the car window and kissed Rayon on the cheek.

"I love you," He said, the words slipping out of his mouth.

"I love you too," She replied, surprised at her own words.

"Damn! Is it like dat?" Tasheena teased from the backseat.

"Yeah it's like dat!" Tyaire said surely.

"Well excuse me!" Tish said, adding to the fun.

"Whatever," Tyaire said and walked away.

Tyaire walked over to his 500 and got in on the passenger's side. "You alright cousin? Relax baby boy, you can't change the past, but you can change the future. That

88

dope shit is in your past now. You on some new shit now, just get dat money, stack dat money and spend dat money nigga!" Tyaire said as Deon pulled away from the curb.

Deon drove the Benz in the direction that Tyaire gave him, while *The Black Album* by Jay-Z played smoothly. When they finally stopped, they were in front of an old ran down looking house on the west side, not too far away from the park on 8th and Franklin. "Come on nigga," Tyaire said as he got out of the car.

"You said you were ready right?"

"Yeah I'm ready," Deon answered, half sure of himself.

"Look," Tyaire said as he turned the lock on the door. "I don't give a fuck what you do with what I'mma 'bout to give you, but I'm tellin' you like this, if you fuck up, I'm done wit'chu! I mean dat shit cousin, 'cause I love you too much to see you killing yourself," he said as he continued into the house. "What can you stand?"

"What'chu mean?" Deon asked.

"I mean, if I give you this, can you handle it or are you scared to take it 'cause you ain't ready yet. See 'cause I can just give you this," he said and held out an ounce of crack cocaine. "Or I can give you this," he said and held out a rubber inner tube containing a kilo of the same thing. See it all depends on you. Do you want money again or are you bullshittin'?" Tyaire asked seriously.

Seeing everything lay out in front of him like that scared him half to death. Not because he couldn't move it, but because he was unsure of himself.

"Just get over the feeling, the moment" the answer to a sober life popped in his head.

"Yeah I'm ready nigga, give me a brick." Deon said and Tyaire tossed him the thirty-six.

*   *   *   *   *   *   *

For the next two months, Deon isolated himself from society. He pulled around the clock shifts in the base house on 23rd and Market St. everyday until he reached his goal and that goal was to be back on top. Like clockwork, Deon pulled his rental up in front of the base house ran by Wanda at six o'clock in the morning. The sun hadn't even broken through the clouds yet and the base heads flooded the street awaiting his arrival.

"Deon whass'up? You workin'," One of the base heads asked as he got out the car?

"Yeah give me about twenty minutes," He said, as he walked up the busted sidewalk to the base house door.

Deon knocked twice, hesitated, and then knocked three times simultaneously before someone came to the door. He heard someone unlocking the locks, he heard the floorboard being lifted, and then he said, "Hurry up," because he was standing on the porch dirty! Deon clutched the book bag full of powder cocaine close at his side as he stepped into house. Wanda's man stepped to the side as he brushed through the corridor and made his way to the lab, the kitchen.

"Whass'up baby? How'd you make out last night after I left? Deon asked Wanda, who looked like she hadn't moved from that spot all night.

"I did alright, but you know me and that nigga out there fucked up my share." Wanda replied referring to her man.

Wanda was Deon's girl. She was bonafied good peoples and the first one he looked up when he first got that kilo from Tyaire two months ago. He knew that Wanda's house was where everybody went to get high, so why not have the shit to get high with there also. He remembered the days like they

90

happened last night when he used to sit at that very table and
sniff dope and roll crack weed joints all night long while people
came to buy drugs, but there weren't any drugs there. Wanda
would usually take the peoples money and go cop the drugs for
them. On many occasions, he would take the money and just
not come back, but Wanda didn't mind. She remembered
Deon from way back; when he was the largest thing moving
next to those boys Rasul, Dog, Pretty E, and Hit Man, bless his
soul. She knew what Deon was going through was only
temporary and that one-day he'd be back. Now, as he stood in
the kitchen with his book bag over his shoulder she knew her
intuitions were right.

"Wanda, where's the Pyrex pot at baby?" He asked.

"Ain't it under the sink?" She replied as he bent down
to get it.

"Yeah, here it goes."

Deon tore open one of the kilos he had brought with
him and poured half of it in the large glass pot. He grabbed a
box of baking soda and shook some on to the cocaine and then
added a little water before placing it onto the slightly lit stove
to cook. Thanks to his childhood friends down in the projects,
he knew how to make the 18 ounces he just poured in the pot
look more like 36 when it came out. The water began to
bubble up and the smell of raw cocaine filled the kitchen. Deon
smiled to himself because he remembered when this smell
would give him an urge, now it didn't have an effect on him.
He always just 'got over the moment' now and felt good about
doing it. As the baking soda boiled off and the water became
clear, he held the pot up to the stove light, rotated it in a circle,
and watched as oil filled the once rocky substance pot. Then
he worked his magic thanks to good old let's just call him P.R.
"Puerto Rico."

Deon made the kilo of cocaine look like one and a half then went and sat on the porch. The twenty minutes he told everybody it would take turned into more like an hour and a half, but like zombies they were patiently waiting for their fix. One by one they came onto the porch to get served and in less than twenty-five minutes he had a stack, one thousand dollars. Twenty third street was at least a twenty thousand dollar a day drug trap, but since Deon was back it jumped up increasingly over the past two months to somewhere around $150,000 dollars a week and Deon seen every bit of about $70,000 dollars of it. The fiends and junkies loved Deon to death because he treated them fairly. That was Deon's advantage over all of the other hustlers because he was once there. He knew how it felt to be addicted, so he understood them. Deon wouldn't turn down a dollar and on more times than none he contributed if they didn't have nothing, so whenever he was outside they'd bypass every dealer to see him.

By two o'clock, Deon had managed to knock off the whole kilo and half of the half by selling everything from dimes to ounces. He took a break to eat when the base head Smokie came back from the Jamaican store with his platter. "Did you get yours Smokie?" He asked, as he reached into his bag of drugs. Deon pinched a little crumb from the big rock and paid Smokie with it, then stepped in the house and said "about time" when the first person he saw was Wanda knocked out on the couch then her man George on the floor. "Them muthafuckas never get any sleep." Deon said to himself.

Deon wiped off the table and pushed Wanda's crack pipe, Brillo pad, broken hangers, and empty crystal palace bottle to the side. He opened up his platter of curry shrimp said, "Bis-Mil-Allah," in the name of God and dug into his cabbage first. When he bit down on his mouth full of cabbage, he noticed how much he'd been using the name of Allah and speaking in Arabic manners and thought, "I need to take my Shahaada," as he felt Islam and Allah more present than ever before in his life.

*   *   *   *   *   *   *

Chapter Eight

The months of April and May flew by without the slightest inclination that time was moving so rapidly. Graduation day, June 4th, came faster to Tish, Rayon, and Tasheena then they'd ever expected and walking across the stage didn't seem so fulfilling now. Yes it would be great to finally get a chance to relax for a while, but then what? College, marriage, and growing up that was enough to put a butterfly in any 17 or 18 year olds stomach that wasn't ready to give up being a mommy's or daddy's little boy or girl.

"Girl, are you nervous?" Tish asked Tasheena as Rayon went to the bathroom for the third time in less than ten minutes.

"A little bit, because I really don't have any plans to do anything yet," Tasheena replied.

"Girl you ain't going to college?"

"I might. I'm thinking about Clark Atlanta or Spelman."

"That's good. I heard it's the shit in Atlanta."

"Me too." Tasheena said as Rayon came back into the room.

"Damn bitch, what'chu got the shits or some'em?" Tasheena asked Rayon while Rayon spit into a napkin.

"I don't know what's wrong with me girl?"

"I do bitch, I just need a little more time to make sure that's all." Tish said, as they killed time in her room waiting for graduation.

Tish, Rayon and Tasheena sat around Tish's room going through yearbooks dating back to when they were in grammar school. With each page they turned, they remembered a day or time from back then and understood the phrase 'time flies' because it seemed like yesterday.

"Girl do you remember him?" Tish asked pointing to someone from her second grade class picture.

"Girl yeah I remember him! How any of us going to forget pissy ass Dave!" Tasheena said as Tish and Rayon joined in on the pissy ass Dave part.

"Eeeew girl! Look at you!" Rayon said to Tasheena when they came across a picture of her smiling ear to ear with no fronts.

"Bitch I was still da shit!" She shot back.

"And look at her!" Rayon continued, this time pointing to Tish, as Tasheena fell out laughing.

"Bitch I remember that turtleneck!" Tasheena said still laughing as she looked at the picture. "And bitch look at the lights!" she continued and laughed harder, as she pointed to the reflection on Tish's forehead.

"Ms. Carla knew she was wrong for using that whole jar of grease."

"Fuck you bitch," Tish said through a laugh as Rayon darted for the door.

This time they didn't wait on Rayon to come back though they went right behind her. Tish put her ear to the door and when she heard what she heard, she busted in the door. Rayon was on her hands and knee's face in the toilet throwing her brains up.

"Bitch I knew it! Yo' ass is pregnant!" Tish said.

*   *   *   *   *   *   *

Trans could barely sleep all night long or for the past couple of months far as that's concerned. He was under an enormous amount of pressure coming from all angles. The decision he had to make between going to college or entering

95

the NBA Draft was stressful, not to mention that he would still be broke in the process. Then there was Tish, his baby, the love of his life, and his inability to do shit for her or her child. That kept him in the dumps, but last night took the cake. She actually had to pay for everything from gas, the movies and dinner and he was definitely not feeling that. "I gotta talk to my Pops."

Trans walked down the hall and knocked on his parent's door.

"What?" his mom hollered.

"Mommy, I need to talk with dad for a second."

"Alright he'll be right out," She said.

"Alright then, tell him I'm downstairs in the living room," he said and walked down the steps.

Trans flopped down in his Pops Lazy Boy recliner and cut on the television. ESPN Sports Center was just coming on, so he ran to the kitchen and poured himself some orange juice. When Trans came back the host of the show was showing highlights of the Yankee's game and their all-star team.

"Man's that's crazy! How they going to get A-Rod too?" He said to himself talking about the signing of Alex Rodriquez, the best in-fielder in the game.

Mr. Carl, Trans' step dad, came down to the living room to see what was so urgent that Trans would need to talk to him this early in the morning for. He sat down on the love seat still dressed in pajamas and slippers, faced Trans and asked "What's going on son?" Trans found out by a letter written to him when he was in the six grade that Mr. Carl wasn't his Pop. The letter was from his real dad, Terrance Carter. He explained how he got to where he was at and how much time he had to do. He also explained how much he loved him and wanted to be a part of his life, but Trans didn't know

this stranger. His mom told him more about his father
whenever he asked, never holding back one thing and even
took him down to Smyrna to visit him once. When they
walked through the big steel gate into the actual prison visiting
room all his questions were answered.

Trans felt all his life as though he was different. He
didn't look like his brother or sister and he definitely didn't
look like his dad, so he felt out of place. He did however favor
his mom, but when he stepped in that visiting room it was if he
looked into a mirror. The visit was a good one because his dad
explained everything he wanted to know. Trans knew it was
sincere because of the eye contact he received when he talked.
He would occasionally look over to his mother and watched the
pain and hurt on her face and he knew that sometime and
somewhere long ago that she loved his father. It almost hurt to
the point of tears when it was time to leave, but it really
shocked him to watch how much it hurt his mother, as Terence
kissed her softly and said "Carmen, I'll always love you and
my son, always!" She cried.

Trans cleared his head of those thoughts and said to
himself, "Yeah I love my dad, but that's my father right
there," referring to Mr. Carl. Mr. Carl had been in Trans' life
from day one and he respected the fact that he raised him like
one of his own, but he still kept in contact with Terrance
through letters and their bond had grown tremendously.

"Dad, I need to ask you your opinion?"

"About what?"

"I-I-I," he stuttered. "I'm skipping college and going to
the league" and as soon as Trans finished saying that the
basketball segment kicked in.

*   *   *   *   *   *   *

Hello, I'm Cris Dishman and I'm joined here in the studio with Kenny Anderson and Kenny Smith.

"Men, what do you think of this year's Draft?"

K.A.: "I think there's a talented group of young men coming out, but none matches the talent and skill level that Trans Owens possesses.

K.S.: "I agree Kenny. But the only problem is that he said he's going to UCLA."

K.A.: "I don't think so, after that performance he put on a few months back against Shakim Shabazz, and here recently against Oak Hill Academy and the number two player Leroy Willcotts, there's nothing else for him to prove."

K.S.: "You might be right, there's still a lot of talent though, and where do you think he'll fall in the Draft?"

K.A.: "Well after the way LeBron James came into the league and Carmelo Anthony, I think he'll be in the top two."

K.S.: "I'll agree on that because no one wants to pull a bone head Draft like Detroit did last year picking that what's his name, over Carmelo?"

*   *   *   *   *   *   *

The commentators went on and on about the Draft and even ran a few highlights as they talked about the lottery picks. Trans looked back over to his dad and said, "So what do you think?"

"What'chu going to do about school?"

"What'chu mean school?"

"I mean your mom wants you to go to school. If you can promise me that somehow you can play ball and do school during the off season, I'm all for it."

"Thanks dad." Trans said.

98

"Well are you ready to announce your decision at graduation tonight?"

"Yeah."

"A lot of people are going to be surprised."

"Tell me about it."

*   *   *   *   *   *   *

Howard High School's gymnasium was filled beyond capacity, as students, parents, and alumni filled the chairs and bleachers for the 80th class to graduate from its classrooms. Tish, Rayon, and Tasheena stepped in the gym and were escorted to a row of seats up front by Mr. Scott, the plumbing teacher at vo-tech. They made their way through the makeshift rows of chairs that occupied the basketball court and sat down.

"Damn girl! It's a lot of people in here." Tasheena said, then continued, "Heeey girl!" she spoke to Munch from across the room.

"Why are all these cameras and news reporters here?" Rayon asked without thinking, and then remembered, "Oh, that's right, they're here for Trans."

"Mmm-Hmm girl," Tish said. "He's supposed to be speaking tonight."

Trans walked through the gymnasium doors and instantly bulbs began flashing and cameras began snapping. It almost looked like a sea of lightning bugs, as he waved his hands for them to stop.

"Hey Trans," A reporter yelled.

"Listen, I'm here to graduate from school and spend some time with my friends. I'll answer all your questions later!" He said, as Mr. Scott escorted him to the same area where Tish was seated.

After about an hour speech from the principal, followed by a half hour from the Superintendent, the crowd was getting restless. They all sighed of relief when the principal came back to the podium and started calling names. Tish, Rayon, and Tasheena all held hands in support of one another and were proud to be walking with their class. Since Rayon's last name was Anderson, she was one of the first five to be called. "Ms. Rayon Anderson," the principal called as Tish and Tasheena lost their minds. They led all cheers in the gym as she took her diploma from the principal and walked across the stage.

Ms. Rachael, Rayon's mom, Ms. Judy, Tasheena's mom, and Ms. Carla, Tish's mom, went just as bananas as their daughters did when Rayon walked across the stage. It was a feeling of accomplishment for each one of them because it was a many of phone conversations during their children's scholastic years that they'd thought they'd never see this day.

"Ms. Latisha Wallace." Tish stood up and Trans gave her a peck on the lips as she headed to the stage. She received the same attention as people cheered and went crazy, especially when they kissed.

"Ms. Tasheena Younger," the principal said and Tasheena went buck wild crazy. She stepped on the stage yanked her diploma from him and bowed to the crowd. They erupted with laughter and camera's flashed everywhere when she grabbed the mic.   "Class of 2004 whass'up! We did it y'all," She said into the microphone keeping it away from the outstretched arm of the principal. Ms. Judy couldn't do nothing but shake her head saying, "That damn girl ain't got no sense."

The last person to be called to graduate from the class of 2004 was Trans Owens. The entire gymnasium stood to their feet and gave the high school standout an ovation as he made his way up front to stand on stage with the rest of his graduating class. Humbly, he approached the mic and asked everyone to be seated. "Thank you. Thank you." He said motioning for the few standing to sit down.

"Today is a very special day for me because I'm standing amongst my peers. Some of who go back as far as first and second grade," He began "It's also a special day for me because I'm about to make the biggest decision of my life. I thought long and hard about it and my father helped me decide. Mom, don't have a heart attack." He joked, then continued, "I'm going to forego my college years and enter this year's NBA Draft!" the crowd erupted. Every reporter in the gym hurried to the front of the stage in a frenzy. They all had questions to ask. Trans' decision caught everyone off guard and it would cause teams in the NBA lottery to make some swift changes about their Draft picks.

Trans turned his back to the media and faced his class. He grabbed his cap, along with the entire graduation class, and on three they heaved them into the air. They were high school graduates.

*   *   *   *   *   *   *

It was the first time in more than two months that Deon had come out, but he wasn't going to miss Tasheena's graduation for the world. He looked at his newly renovated Movado with an iced out face that he added and saw that he had three hours until graduation. "Plenty of time," he thought as his return debut unfolded as planned. It was time. It was time for Deon to show all the haters, backbiters, and half ass hustlers how to really stunt. Deon was back like he left something and they were about to once again feel his presence. Deon managed to get over the many moments he had when he thought about doing drugs in the last couple of months. He flipped, tumbled, and tucked off the kilo Tyaire had given him back then, and turned it into five. Just like that he was feeling like a pimp and brushing his shoulders off. Deon opened his closet door and looked at his new wardrobe and footwear. If the closet was a suitcase, it'll be busting at the seams. "Damn what I'mma wear?" He asked himself as he came across some real fly shit. "Yeah, this'll definitely set it off."

Deon stood in front of his mirror on the dresser and took off his wave cap, then combed his Sunni. It wasn't as long as the rapper Freeway's beard, but it was getting close. "Damn Al J is a beast!" he said as the shape-up Al gave him two days ago was still crisp like he did it today. Deon grabbed his soft bristled brush and brushed his hair in circles as his waves spun endlessly. "Man I'm back like I never left," Deon said to himself as he backed away from the mirror to get a look at his whole body. His chain hung oddly to his stomach overtop of his cloudy white button up shirt, while his Roca Wear jeans sagged just enough off his ass to lie smoothly on his white and blue S. Carter sneakers. Deon walked over to the closet and pulled out the stash that was hidden in Timberland boxes and smiled, "twenty-five thousand a box" He said to himself as he stacked the six boxes on top of one another. Deon reached in the one that he stacked back up in the closet last and took out $5,000 wrapped in rubber bands and left the room.

Deon came down the stairs an hour away from graduation and said, "Hi Mom Auntie," a nickname he gave his aunt who was more like a mother to him.

"Hey boy, where you going at all sharp?" She asked seeing Deon dressed and groomed for the first time in a long while.

"To Tasheena's graduation," he answered, to see the lady he loved so much. Ms. Erica was Deon's Aunt and his mother's older sister. She took him in when he was about ten years old after his mother became strung out on heroin and kept him every since.

"How's my baby doing?" She asked.

"She was doing well the last time I saw her, but that was over two months ago."

"Oh, so she hasn't seen you since you got yourself together?"

"Nah, but I'm quite sure people told her that they haven't seen me out running the streets."

"Oh, so she's going to be surprised, did she see that car of yours yet?"

"No Mom Auntie ain't nobody seen that yet because I only drove it that one time. That's when it got done getting the seats piped and rims changed, but after that I came straight home."

"Oh, so you finally are going to drive it today, huh? Good, now I can use it when I want to." Ms. Erica teased about driving his car. That was part of the deal they made when she put it in her name, but she already had a Jag of her own copying off of her older sister Ruthie.

"Yeah you can use it," he said and walked towards the door. "Mom Auntie, can you come back your car up for me please?"

Deon walked outside, stood up on the porch, and inhaled as much of the fresh air as he could. For it to be the tail end of spring, it sure felt like a mid-summer's day. Deon stepped off the porch and walked to the car that was hidden under a cover. He unsnapped the cover by the front fender and peeled it back revealing a white on white 745.I sitting

handsomely on 24 inch Giovanni's. He rolled the cover up and
put it in the backyard, anxious to pull the car out. He popped
the locks on the car as he approached it and stopped at the
front tire 'cause it looked funny. After seeing it was nothing
wrong with it, he hopped in and started the engine. Deon
pressed the power button on the steering wheel, and then the
disc changer button until he found the CD he was looking for,
and played song number 5…

> *I'll teach you how to stunt*
> *My wrist stay rocked up*
> *My TV's pop-up in the May Bach Benz*
>
> *I'll teach you how to stunt*
> *Man you can't see me*
> *My Bentley G.T. got smoked gray tent*
> *Stunt 101*
> **G Unit**

*   *   *   *   *   *   *

After Trans was called, and the entire graduating class
tossed their caps in the air, Deon made his way to the floor. He
patted his pocket and made sure the money was still there,
knowing it was, as he bobbed and weaved through people to
get there. He couldn't wait to get up on them, because he knew
they'd be glad to see him, and know that he was doing well.

Tish, Rayon, and Tasheena were joined by their
mothers receiving congratulations when Trans and his mother
walked up. "Hey ya'll whass'up?" Trans said to Tish and
them, while his mom spoke to Ms. Carla first.

"Hey girlfriend, what's been going on?" Ms. Carmen
said.

"Nothing girl just glad to see they finally made, it makes me feel like I one some'em right, you know?"

"Yeah, I know what'cha mean."

"Here let me introduce you to Judy, 'cause you already know Rachael right?"   "Yeah I know Rachael, that's Rayon's mom. Her and my son have been best friends for years. You know they live four doors down from us, right?"

"I didn't know that. Hey Judy girl; I want you to meet my girl Carmen, this is Trans' mom."

"Oh, hi. How are you, my name is Judy, I'm Tasheena's mom."

"Hi, I'm Carmen." They embraced with a hug. Trans stood off to the side exhausted from the media barrage he experienced, and then looked around at all the people he knew. "Damn I'm getting ready to be in the pros." He thought, still unable to believe it. It seemed like yesterday he was out on the court by himself counting down from five. "Five, four, three, two, one," he would say before heaving the ball from half court wishing it would go in, so he could celebrate the game winning shot. Now it was a reality.

"Whass'up cousin?" Tyaire said snapping him out of his daydream. "Hey whass'up cousin," Trans answered giving Tyaire the right hand, followed by a half hug. Trans and Tyaire had become close over the past couple months, by him being involved with Rayon. They talked on the regular, and on more than one occasion he had offered Trans a helping hand. "Yo man." Tyaire would say." If you need me, I'm here for you. I know shit is tight cousin. I was once where you were at, in school, broke, frustrated, look man I know. If you need some'em, holler at me." Trans never accepted his offers though.

"Congratulations cousin, I see you making that leap!" Tyaire said confident about the move. "You're definitely ready!" He finished.

"Thanks." Trans said.

"How long have you been here?" Rayon asked as she interrupted Tyaire and Trans.

"The whole time." Tyaire said.

"Well come meet my mom, 'cause she wants to meet you, excuse me Trans." She said and they walked off.

When Deon finally made it to the floor, Tasheena was standing in a circle with her mom, Tish, and Tish's mom. His heart was pounding harder and harder the closer he got, but he had to get to his baby. Deon, for the last couple of months, since that day at the hospital, couldn't keep Tasheena off his mind. She was his baby, his other half, and even though he was back, without her, he was empty.

Tasheena just so happened to look past her mother into the crowd, and saw him coming.

"Oh my god!" She screamed in her head, yet held her composure as he approached. She had heard through the grapevine that Deon had stopped using, but she hadn't seen him to verify the rumors. The only thing she knew was that he was on 23rd street all the time, and she heard he was getting money again. When Deon got smack dead up on her, she and Tish were speechless.

"Hey baby girl, congratulations!" He said real smoothly. Tasheena placed her hands over her nose and mouth and couldn't say a word, but her tears that fell told the story she'd been holding for over a year. "Don't do dat baby, you goin' to make me cry," he said and took her in his arms.

"Dats right brother, get your woman," Tish said, then continued, "Rayon and Tyaire! Look who's here?"

"Is that Deon?" Ms. Judy asked, then playfully popped him in the back of the head, "Boy where you been at?"

"It's a long story," He replied as they all reunited like old times.

*   *   *   *   *   *   *

Chapter Nine

Rayon was up bright and early Tuesday morning pacing the floor. She had slept with a pad on last night praying on a visit from Eve's wrong doings, but still no cigar. Mother Nature hadn't come. "Well I'mma know everything today anyway," She said to herself, as she thought about her ten o'clock appointment at Planned Parenthood. She could have gone to the family doctor, but decided not too, because he'd definitely spill the beans to her mother about a positive test result. Rayon, tired of pacing the floor, sat down on her bed and stared into space. "What if I am pregnant? What am I going to do? What about college? Then again, I might have a little girl. Tish is doing fine with Tymeere. They can be like cousins." Rayon fought the emotional roller coaster as best as she could. She got up again, this time to get dressed, and left her room. "Let me go get Tish," she said and grabbed her keys from the kitchen counter.

*   *   *   *   *   *   *

Planned Parenthood, the free clinic and consultation center for young women was located in the heart of the city. Rayon pulled the Honda into the parking lot and sat in the car with Tish for a minute before they got out. Tish was explaining to her that this is what she needed to do, because if in fact she was pregnant, at least she'd know how far along, and what type of pre-natal care to use.

"Girl I'm tellin' you, I went through this exact same shit." Tish said and they exited the car.

Inside, the lobby was more occupied then Rayon expected it to be this early in the morning. Young ladies like her filled the chairs accompanied by their mothers, and some by friends, like she was with Tish, but there wasn't a happy

face in the room. Everyone looked or seemed to be so scared
and it put a knot in Rayon's stomach. Tish grabbed an Essence
magazine and flipped through its pages, occasionally looking
up at her surroundings and empathized with every one of the
girls in the room. She was in their shoes once upon a time, and
knew exactly what they were felling. Some were weighing the
decisions to have an abortion or keep the child, and some were
weighing the rights of an adoption; but she definitely could
relate. She herself had thoughts of terminating her pregnancy
at one time, but every time she looked at Tymeere in the face,
she couldn't see herself without the little guy. "Keep your
kids." Tish said to herself, hoping each and every one of them
felt the vibe.

"Ms. Rayon Anderson." The R.N. called into the lobby.

"Go 'head girl. Get this over with." Tish said, and she
stood up.

"Ms. Anderson?" the nurse asked when Rayon
approached.

"Yes." Rayon said with hesitation.

The nurse led Rayon down the hallway past rooms and
rooms of young girls all in her same predicament. "At least I'm
not alone," she said to herself, trying to make herself feel better
as she followed the nurse in the room.

"Hello Ms. Anderson, I'm Lynnette and I will be taking
your vital signs, and urine analysis, then a doctor will be right
with you." She said and took her blood pressure. When the
nurse completed her vital signs and logged them down on the
chart, she handed Rayon a paper gown and left the room.

"Here, put this on," she said. The doctor, Mr. Williams,
a middle aged black man, reminded Rayon of Bill Cosby when
he played the role of Mr. Huxtable on the Cosby Show. He

walked through the door about ten minutes after the nurse left, carrying a chart and went straight to work.

"Hello," he said and laid Rayon back on the examination table. "How are you feeling today?" He asked.

"Fine." She replied.

Dr. Williams poked and pressed his hand into and around her stomach feeling for lumps, or anything odd. The urine analysis test had come back positive for pregnancy, so yes she was pregnant. The question now was how far along.

"Ms. Anderson, the test results prove that you are indeed pregnant, but what I'm about to do now is try to see how far along you are, so we can see what's best for the baby." He said as tears welled up in her eyes. "Are you alright?" He asked, and Rayon nodded her head "yes."

Dr. Williams walked over to the cabinet and put on some latex gloves and grabbed a tube of something, but Rayon couldn't tell what it was. He lifted her paper gown and squirted the cold gel that looked like K.Y. Jelly onto her stomach and rubbed it all over. He grabbed a device that looked almost like a microphone and turned on the machine. Dr. Williams placed the device on her stomach and Rayon saw the image pop up on the screen.

"There's your baby Ms. Anderson," the doctor said and Rayon felt an emotion she'd never felt before. It was the motor response only a first time mother would get, but when she heard the heart beat on the monitor, she was overwhelmed. Tears of wonder stained her face as she asked, "How far along am I?"

"About three months" he answered.

"Do you know what I'm having?" She asked again.

"No Ms. Anderson" he smiled then continued, "It's too early to tell."

"Oh" she said. The doctor explained to her the importance of eating healthy for the child and what type of vitamins to take.

Rayon threw her Fendi bag over her shoulder, grabbed the image of her child off the counter, and walked out the examination room. Tish stood up the moment she saw her coming and walked towards her. She knew by the way Rayon held her arms across her belly like she was carrying a child that she was pregnant. So she eased the question in.

"So how did it go?" Tish asked

"I'm pregnant" She responded.

"How far along are you?" Tish asked.

"The doctor said about three months." Rayon said.

"So, what are you going to do? Have you thought about that?" Tish said.

"What do you mean?" Rayon asked.

"I'm talking about college, and your future. Are you going to keep the baby?"

"Yes I'm keeping my baby!" Rayon answered astounded at the question. She couldn't believe Tish would ask her a question like that, and when she glanced at the image on the picture she said, "How could I kill this?" and handed it to Tish.

"Rayon I didn't mean anything by that, but I had to ask. You're my sista and I needed for you to think it over because it's not easy. I struggle with Meere-Meere every day. The last thing in this world I would want you to do is terminate your pregnancy, but I needed for you to look at all aspects."

"You are right. I'm sorry I snapped." Rayon apologized.

"Don't be. Does Tyaire know you came here today? Does he even know you thought you were pregnant?"

"No, but I think he's kind of thinking that I am because for the past couple of days, all he did was sleep, and get sick in the morning."

"They said that the baby's daddy sometimes gets am symptoms like the mother," Tish said.

"For real?" Rayon said surprised.

"Yeah" Tish replied.

"I ain't know that," Rayon said as they headed out the door.

Rayon gave Tish the keys as they stepped outside the doors of Planned Parenthood still baffled about the pregnancy.

"What is my baby going to look like? Is he going to be dark chocolate like his daddy, or light skinned like me? I hope like his daddy. What is my mom going to say? She ranted in her mind, getting stuck at her mother. Ms. Rachael was Rayon's best friend, slash worst enemy. She could, at times be the sweetest person in the world, but her Jekyll & Hyde personality could change at the drop of a dime. All she preached was education and financial stability to Rayon, because she was a single mother When Rayon's father died, he didn't have any insurance, so it left her stuck with no money and a child to raise on her own.

She had to start selling things like the cars and jewelry she owned just to stay on top of the bills, until eventually she lost everything. That ate Ms. Rachael up because she was always on a pedestal, above her brothers and sisters and really arrogant about it. It literally almost killed her to have to move back in with her mother until she got back on her feet, but she made the move anyway. Ms. Rachael was young, a single mother, and had no work skills. The only thing she did was please her husband and take care of the house, but after he died she was lost. After about a week in her mother's home, and a ton of ridicule, she put her plan in effect. For the next six years straight, she kept her face in the books. The odd jobs, and part time gigs she did on the side managed to take care of Rayon, and helped out her mother, then it all changed. A degree from U.D. in Science, and a Chemist position at Dupont put her right where she needed to be. A year later she was in a better home than the one she lost, and back on her self-imposed pedestal.

"I can hear her now!" Rayon thought.

"Girl why you so quiet?" Tish asked breaking the silence.

"Huh?" Rayon asked when she heard Tish, but not the question.

"I was just thinking that's all. You know how Rachael can get."

"Who?" Tish asked confused.

"My mom girl. You know she simple."

"Mmm-Hmm." Tish responded and then asked, "Is your mom coming tonight?"

"Where?" Rayon said.

"Over to Trans' house. You know his mom is having a Draft party over there."

"That's right that is tonight. Yeah, you know she'll be there" Rayon answered.

"O.K., well I'll see you tonight then," Tish said as she pulled up to her house. "Call Tyaire and give him the good news!"

"I am!" Rayon replied as she slid across the seat and into the driver's seat and dialed Tyaire on her cell phone. "Hi baby, guess what?" Rayon asked.

*   *   *   *   *   *   *

Chapter Ten

The Owens residence was elbow to elbow with news cameras from every local station in the Tri-State area. Channels three, six, ten, and Fox 29 crammed in whatever spot they could fit in because ESPN controlled the living room. Trans sat on the couch with Tish, Carron, and Kiesha, while his friends, teammates, and agent sat where they could. The television was tuned to ESPN on the Draft in Auburn Hills, MI.; live via satellite from the Owens living room.

Trans had been invited time and time again to attend the Draft live, but refused the invitations. He wanted to experience the feeling of being drafted around his loved ones.

"Hey everyone! It's coming on!" Kiesha yelled.

Everyone turned to face the television. David Stern was giving a Pre-Draft speech on the rules of the Draft as always. It was the same every year. He explained how much time each team had to select, and about the trade before pick rules and then the Draft began.

Trans' agent, Monty Rammano, already explained to Trans that the Clippers would take him with the number one pick, and then they would trade him to Atlanta for the second pick, two future Draft picks, and some money. At first, Trans didn't like the idea of being traded to Atlanta because they were dead last in the Eastern Conference, but after weighing his options, he realized it would be the best move.

The Los Angeles Clippers had three minutes remaining to select their first pick, as time ticked off the clock that was visible in the left hand corner of the television. The executive staff of the Clippers scrambled through paperwork, picked up and hung up phones, and negotiated amongst themselves until coming to a decision. Monty Rammanos' phone rung at a minute and forty seconds remaining on the clock, then after he said a few words, he told Trans to be ready to answer the house phone.

"Hello," Trans answered on the first ring.

"Hello Trans?" The voice on the other end asked.

"Yes," replied Trans.

"Hello, my name is Michael Homestead, and I am the president of the Los Angeles Clippers.

"Hey man, whass'up," said Trans.

"Well I'm calling you to let you know we're selecting you with the number one pick overall!" He said, and highlights of Trans started playing across the screen. "Welcome to the N.B.A!" He tried to finish, but Trans couldn't hear him because the entire house was in an uproar. The news cameras were trying to focus in on him but his teammates were going crazy, and his friends were crowding around him.

"What did you say?" Trans asked, putting one hand over his open ear.

"I said, Welcome to the N.B.A! Now stay on the phone until our selection is official, and then the commissioner, David Stern, would like to speak to you."

"O.K." replied Trans.

"Do you have a Clippers hat?" Homestead asked at the same time Monty Rammano passed one to him.

"Yeah, I got one," said Trans.

"Alrighty then, hold on" and Trans held the phone.

The highlights were still playing across the screen, the house was still ecstatic and Trans sat still. He was in a daze. He couldn't believe that he was going to the league. His heart was pounding and his mouth was bone dry, as he watched clips of himself shooting jumpers, fade aways, dishing off passes, and dunking the ball on all of his competition. He knew he was ready and apparently the league did too, but he still had a feeling of uncertainty inside him.

David Stern walked up to the microphone and said, "With the first pick of the 2004 N.B.A. Draft, the Los Angeles Clippers selects from Howard High School, Mr. Trans Owens."

Instantly, his face popped up on the screen T.V. in the living room and the globe-a-tron set up in Auburn Hills, MI., live via satellite.

"Good evening Trans. I see everyone is excited about the Draft" the Commissioner said, looking into the globe-a-tron and seeing him on the couch surrounded by his people.

"Yeah, we're all excited here." Trans replied.

"Who are the people with you?" the Commissioner asked.

"These are my teammates. This is my lil brother and sister. This is my mom and dad behind me, and this is my girlfriend slash best friend Tish. Oh! And these are my two other sisters Rayon and Tasheena."

"Oh I see. Well how does it feel to be the number one pick overall?"

"I don't know yet. It still hasn't hit me. I'm just glad to be in the league." And just like that he was traded to the Atlanta Hawks for Jamir Kelson of the St. Joe's Haks.

*   *   *   *   *   *   *

Tyaire and Deon were sitting in the living room that Rayon remodeled watching the N.B.A. Draft on ESPN. The new furniture and bright paintings did give the house new life, and Tyaire liked it. It wasn't gloomy anymore, and sad thoughts of his grandparents didn't pop up in his head regularly like they used to. Tyaire was just feeling all around good today. He even felt better when Rayon called him and said, "Hi Daddy!" Now as he and Deon sat patiently waiting on the Draft to start, he was about to enjoy seeing one of his new closest friends be drafted into the N.B.A. At first, he felt like he was betraying Saafie by befriending Trans, but he later realized there was nothing wrong with being his friend. He admired the young boy's strength to stay focused and headstrong because the mean streets of Wilmington, Delaware would suck you in if you let them. The hating and people wanting to see you stay down in a rut was enough to will bad shit to happen to you. I mean, so many people could actually hate on you, or backbite you so bad, you'll never prosper. It was crazy but that's how Delaware was. It was like crabs in a barrel 'round here. That's why if you wanted to come up, you must move from round here.

"Don't get me wrong" Tyaire thought, "It's still the shit 'round here you just gotta watch out and know who your friends are round here."

"Yo nigga, here go the young boah right here." Deon said snapping Tyaire from his trance. Tyaire and Deon knew Trans was nice, but they never expected for him to go so early in the Draft. The Clippers had the number one overall pick, so when they selected him, it caught them off guard.

"Oh shit! Dat nigga went number one overall!" Tyaire snapped, and grabbed the bottle of Cristal he had chilling in the wine bucket.

"Got Damn!" Deon added, and drunk from the wine bottle Tyaire just passed him.

"Look at my baby!" Don't she look good nigga?" Tyaire asked when he saw Rayon sitting in the living room at Trans' house live via satellite.

117

"Yeah, she sharp! But look at my baby." Deon said and was right. Tasheena was the shit!

"Yeah cousin, Tasheena is a bad mu'fucka!" Tyaire said feeling a little guilty about a situation. Although nothing happened, he remembered the day ever so clearly when he tried to go at her when Deon was getting high. He figured Deon wouldn't care anyway especially since she was fucking everybody, but when she turned him down, he respected her more.

"I'm saying, ain't Deon your boy?" She paused, and then continued. "Well that's my baby and I don't do boys feel-me?" Tyaire remembered Tasheena telling him.

"Yo, I need my baby back cousin" Deon said.

"Yeah cousin, y'all made for each other" Tyaire said, and then answered his cell phone.

*   *   *   *   *   *   *

Once again it's on nigga, Segal hard like corn liquor
I'll take you out this world, like you was born nigga
Butt naked, covered in blood, gasping for air
Clinging for dear life.

Once Again It's On
Jay-Z and Beanie Segal

Saafie nodded his head to the State Property Chain Gang CD, as he waited on the broad Monique to come outside. He would occasionally check his mirrors, a habit he picked up from being around Pretty E., so much to see if anyone was following him or trying to creep up on him. He dialed her cell phone number again. "Yo, is you coming or not?"

"I said I'm coming!!" Monique answered irritated, and hung up. "Damn whass' taking them so long? They should've been here." She thought as she pressed the speed dial button to

Boog's phone. "What are y'all going to do? I got this nigga outside right now."

"We're on our way. We only right around the corner." Boog said and hung up the phone.

Boog, also known as Young Grams, was Tish's little cousin from the projects. He promised her the day that Saafie did that dumb shit up in Chester at the game, that he was going to handle that, which was over three months ago. Now was the perfect time to retaliate on Saafie because no one was expecting it now. They knew Tish would run and get her lil cousin Boog so if some'em would a happened to him, they would of known who done it.

Boog and O.D.B. turned the corner on Monique's block and saw the Jag double-parked with the hazard lights on. Boog pulled the white Grand Marquis up on the side of the Jag and slammed on the brakes. He and O.D.B. jumped out of the car so fast, Saafie couldn't turn the ignition fast enough. The A.R. 15 and Desert Eagle sounded off simultaneously ripping through the metal and fiberglass Jaguar like it was paper mache.

Saafie had lunched, and it almost cost him his life. He was fiddling around with the equalizer on his face-off Alpine, when the car pulled up. His instinct said smash the gas pedals, but the car was turned off. He turned the ignition and the car came to life, but the bullets started flying. There was nothing he could do but duck down from the ambush. He balled up as tight as he could in the fetal position up under the steering wheel as glass and pieces of the upholstery shattered all over him. Saafie stayed crouched under the steering wheel for what seemed to be an eternity then he heard the tires of his assailants squeal off.

Saafie eased up from the floor and peaked out the
window to see if the coast was clear. When he did, the only
thing he saw was a crowd of people standing around watching.
He stepped out of his battered Jag and shook glass from his
clothes as his mind raced "Who the fuck was that? What the
fuck did I do? Who even had the balls to disrespect me?" he
thought, getting madder at the fact that someone tried him and
then at the fact that he almost died. He looked down at his
white t-shirt and saw blood, but didn't panic. He checked
himself smoothly and realized he had only been grazed on the
shoulder and then he pulled out his cell phone.

"Yo, where you at nigga?" Saafie asked pissed off and
breathing heavily.

"I'm at the crib watching the Draft. You know the boah
Trans went number one!" Tyaire answered so excited that he
didn't hear the urgency in Saafie's voice.

"Man fuck dat nigga! I almost got shot da fuck up!
Nigga's just came through and sprayed up my Jag!"

"Did you get hit?" Tyaire asked surprised.

"Nah nigga, but I got grazed. I was up under the
steering wheel."

"Who was it?"

"I don't know, but we going to find out. Somebody
goin' to say some'em."

"You got dat right. These mu'fuckas around here can't
hold water."

"Well look, I'm on my way over there alright?" Saafie
said then called Triple A to come get his car hoping they'd get
there before the police.

*   *   *   *   *   *   *

Boog and O.D.B. sped away from the scene on 30th and Washington St. and headed all the way out past Lea Blvd. and jumped on I-95 by way of Marsh Rd.

"Man you think you hit him?" O.D.B. asked as he spit tobacco out his mouth from the blunt he was rolling.

"I don't know cousin, do you?" Boog asked as he bent into traffic. "I hope so." Boog replied.

"I hope I did too, 'cause that's like the third or fourth time dat nigga put his hands on my cousin. I don't know who da fuck he think I am, but it ain't goin' down like dat" Boog said picturing Tish as she explained to him what happened.

Boog and O.D.B. were live wires that could spark off at any moment. They had the projects and everywhere for that matter on pins and needles as they shook up the town.

"Where we goin' nigga?" O.D.B. asked as they entered Pennsylvania.

"Up Philly on 18th and Masters nigga. I need a shot of yellow, and about four of them zanies."

"I heard dat. I need one too." O.D.B. replied, and held the bic on the end of the Vanilla Dutchie.

"Yo, you know dat nigga goin to pay mu'fucka's to tell'em who shot at him right?"

"Man I don't give a fuck. I want da nigga to know who did it." O.D.B. said and patted the Desert Eagle that was still warm in his lap.

*   *   *   *   *   *   *

Saafie pulled up to Tyaire's house in a cab fifteen minutes after he called. His heart was still pounding and his knees were still trembling as he walked up the driveway to the house. He couldn't believe that someone actually tried to murk him in broad daylight. The whole ride over there he called everyone he knew who might know some'em, but no one did.

121

The only person or people he knew who had the balls to do some shit like that was the young boahs Boog and O.D.B., but why? Then he remembered. Boog was Tish's cousin.

Tyaire was pacing the floor back and forth with the door wide open. The call he received minutes ago had made him forget all about the Draft and what he was doing minutes ago. Saafie's call had put him on edge. He was now trying to wonder what he did or they did, for someone to be shooting at them.

"Was it meant for me too?" he asked himself, and then he saw the cab pulling up.

"Whass'up cousin?" Saafie said when he stepped through the door. "You know what? I think I know who did that bullshit!"

"Who?" Tyaire asked.

"The boah Boog. Tish's lil cousin."

"Who? The crazy lil young boahs?"

"Yeah them two young nigga's."

"Yeah, it probably was them two nigga's you know they ain't got no sense."

"Yeah, well neither do I. I'mma kill one of them young nigga's!"

"Yeah, well we better be careful 'cause them young nigga's is reckless. That's why they're so dangerous. Them nigga's don't care if they get knocked, shot, or what!"

Deon was relaxing. He didn't say one word about nothing that was going on. On some real shit, the shit didn't make any sense to him. He was stuck on why two nigga's with so much cash would even put themselves in a position to be shot or locked up.   "These two nigga's sound stupid as hell." Deon thought as everything he came across in life started to unfold so clearly to him. The pamphlets that Bro Aziz gave him and the Holy Koran he brought from the Islamic store Mecca changed his outlook on things.

"What'chu think cousin?" Tyaire asked Deon for his advice.

"I'm saying you're your own man. I can't decide for you. If y'all want to kill them nigga's, kill 'em! But for what? So y'all can get life bids or get killed y'all selves? Man y'all got to use y'alls heads." Deon replied and saw that his words were taking affect on Tyaire.

"Man fuck dat soft shit Deon! Them mother fuckers tried to kill me!" Saafie said.

"Soft shit! Nigga, I ain't ever been soft! I'm just on some different type time. Why you think I isolated myself from you two nigga's? Because y'all too hot! You mufucka's stay in some shit because y'all too flamboyant. Man grow the fuck up!" Deon shot back.

"What type of dumb shit you on nigga?" Saafie asked.

" I'm on some getting to know me type time, trying to get my life right. I have been down too long. Nigga tired of all types of wrong. Whether it's beef, drugs, money, bitches, whatever, I'm trying to stay sucker free and happy. That's why I be by my mu'fuckin self."

"Well dats on you nigga! I'mma handle my B.I.!" Saafie said.

"I ain't stopping you." Deon said, while Tyaire weighed his options.

*   *   *   *   *   *   *

Chapter Eleven

The planes wheels came to a screeching stop two and a half hours after it left the Philadelphia International Airport. Atlanta's Hartsfield-Jackson International Airport in Riverdale, GA was right next to College Park and just as big, if not bigger then Philadelphia's airport. Trans and Tish stepped off the plane and into Atlanta, GA at 11:30A.M., Tuesday morning, just two weeks after the Draft. They walked into the airport and went to baggage claim to claim their belongings and were stopped by an older black couple in their fifties.

"Hey!" the older black man in his fifties said. "Aren't you Trans Owens?"

"Huh?" Trans asked, not sure of what the man said, because of his southern accent.

"I said, aren't you Trans Owens, our number one pick?"

"Yeah, that's me." Trans said, his head swelling up a little bit.

"Well I sure hope you can get us back to the Playoffs like when we had Dominique Wilkins."

"I'mma sure try my best."

"Well I know you are son, I know you are. Look here, can my wife and I have your autograph if it's not a problem?"

"Sure you can." Trans said and signed a piece of paper he pulled from his wallet.

After Trans signed his autograph he turned and looked at Tish. Tish's eyed were as wide as his when he turned to her, and they both said. "Can you believe that?"

"Baby, people know you already down here." Tish said surprised.

"He was just a sports fan." Trans said as he grabbed the luggage.

Trans and Tish headed towards a door where Monty Rammano, Trans agent, was supposed to be waiting, and realized that wasn't the case. Instead awaiting he and Tish were a mob of news reporters and Atlanta Hawks fans everywhere.

"Do you see my agent?" Trans asked Tish as they tried to spot him through the crowd.

"Hey Trans! Welcome to Atlanta!" A fan yelled.

"Hey Trans, how was the fight? Who's the lady?" A reporter asked.

"My Fiancée and my flight were good." He answered holding Tish's arm with one hand and dragging the luggage on its wheels by the other.

"There goes Monty right there baby." Tish said, when she saw the agent standing by a stretched limousine.

Trans and Tish weaved their way through the media barrage and fan-welcoming stand, answering as little questions as they could while they made their way to the limousine. They were amazed at the amount of people who came to greet him because this was the N.B.A and it was full of stars, so he thought he would be another pea in the pod. However, this wasn't high school anymore, and Trans wasn't just another player either. He was the high school phenomenon. He was slated to be the answer to LeBron 'King' James and Carmelo 'Michael's Student' Anthony's showcase of talents, but most of all, the ATL's savior. Trans lay back in his seat and got comfortable as the limo driver drove off on I-20 West towards downtown Atlanta.

For the first time since being drafted into the N.B.A., Trans felt pressure. He didn't feel it when he signed his three

year, nine million dollar contract. He didn't feel it with the
three million dollar signing bonus and didn't feel it when he
signed a seven-year, eighty million-dollar contract with
Reebok, but he felt it now. It felt like the weight of the world
was on his shoulders.

"Whass' wrong baby?" Tish asked feeling his
discomfort.

"Nothing baby, just thinking that's all." He replied.

"Well Trans, this is it babe." Monty said, then
continued, "Welcome to the N.B.A.! Now just relax because
everything is the same. Play your game, stay focused and
breathe easy. Today is your official meeting and team shoot-
around with your teammates. Right now we're going to the
motel, get you checked in, and then get you down to Phillips
Arena for your shoot-around."

"Alright." Trans answered and tried to relax.

"Relax man," Trans said to himself. "You been doing
this shit since you was five years old, ain't nuffin changed!" He
finished, trying to hype himself up.

Tish listened to Monty talk just as attentively as if he
were talking to her. She really didn't know what they were
referring to most of the time, but she used her intuition to
come up with clever explanations. When the conversation went
over her head, she turned her attention out the window to look
at her surroundings. The first thing that stood out to Tish was
the cars on the interstate. It was like nothing she ever saw
before, nearly every one of them; let's say eight out of ten, was
occupied by a black man or woman. Then as they approached
downtown Atlanta she saw the city line from a distance.
Atlanta was huge. The buildings were beautiful and there was
this one particular building that stood out to her. It was huge,
almost looked round and it had a huge gold dome as a roof.

126

Tish promised herself to come back one day and see it in the near future. The limousine exited off of I-285 after coming off of I-20 at the Windsor and Spring Street intersection and made a right at the stop sign. The first thing that caught Trans' eye was the big blue sign that read "Magic City." "That's that strip club the rappers be talking about in their lyrics." Trans said to himself, then thought, "I'm coming back to that joint," as the limo headed towards the city.

The limousine driver made a left on Mitchell Street and took it down to Peachtree Street. He rode the main street of downtown Atlanta, Peachtree Street, all the way down to Piedmont, passing everything from the Underground Mall, Gladys Knight's Chicken & Waffles, to the Fox Theatre.

"Ooo Baby, let's get some'em to eat from Gladys' later on!" Tish said excitedly.   "Alright," Trans answered, as they pulled up to the Piedmont Suites, a five star hotel.

*   *   *   *   *   *   *

The guest suite at Piedmont Suites was located on the 15th floor overlooking downtown Atlanta. Monty explained to Trans that he had to be ready for the shoot-around in two hours, and then called him out into the hallway.

"Here do you want this now?" Monty asked Trans, holding out a box from Gordon's Jewelers.

"Yeah, let me get that," He said, placing the 10 carat ring in his pocket.

"Alright, now remember. You got two hours to be ready."

"Alright, I got you." Trans said.

Trans walked back into the room and found Tish standing on the balcony overlooking the city. He tried to creep up on her from behind, but she heard him coming in.

"I heard you the whole time." She said, not flinching when Trans suddenly grabbed her from behind.

He stood at her side and they both took in the sights in pure astonishment. From where they were, they could see the Georgia Dome, Phillips Arena, and Peachtree Street in both directions and the rooftop of Lenox Square Mall.

"Atlanta is big as shit," Trans said, comparing it to the other cities he visited.

"I know, especially compared to our city. If it wasn't for Philly, Jersey, and New York, we wouldn't have anywhere to go. Down here is where it's at. I read in Essence magazine last month that one of the ten most popular places for black people is in the South. It said that our people our migrating back to the South and Atlanta, Georgia and Charlotte, North Carolina are two of the most popular places for black people."

"For real?" Trans asked.

"Mmm-Hmm." She answered.

Trans put his hand in his pocket and fiddled around with the ring box. His heart was beating to the point where he could feel it in his neck and ears, but he had to do it. He placed his hand on Tish's shoulder and spun her around to face him, then pulled out the ring. Getting down on one knee, he looked Tish in her eyes and said, "Baby I love you," as he opened the box. Tish stood there speechless. She threw her hands over her mouth and watched the love of her life get on one knee and propose.

"Baby you are my everything, you and Tymeere. I don't know what I'd do without you. I can't see you anywhere else except with me for the rest of our lives. Baby my money is right, my career is about to take off, and we're young and in love. Baby let's grow old together. Will you marry me?"

Tears stained Tish's cheeks as he spoke. What Trans pulled off had her stupefied with emotion and at a loss of words.

"B-B-Baby," she stuttered, "How much was that r-r-ring?"

"It doesn't matter. What matters to me is if you will place it on your finger and be my wife."

"Of course I will! Yes, I'll marry you!" She said and sprang into his arms.

Trans stood with Tish in his arms and spun in circles on the balcony.

"Baby, I'm going to make you the happiest woman in the world," He said and placed her down.

"Baby, I'm already the happiest woman in the world." She said and kissed him deeply.

Trans grabbed her hand and led her from the balcony into the luxuriant room, straight through the living room into the bedroom area. He stood in front of her at the foot of the huge king sized bed and kissed her softly, as his hands explored her body. Tish moaned and purred softly as his hands made her cream in her panties. It was a feeling that she was becoming accustomed to with Trans and one to which she looked forward. Trans slid his hand down into the front of Tish's jean shorts and slid his finger in her box, as secretion nearly poured out over his fingers.

"Mmm baby, is it like dat?" Trans asked, as she moaned and ground her hips.

"Ssss," She sucked air through her teeth and said, "Mmm-Hmm, it's always like dat when you touch me baby."

Trans peeled her clothes off piece by piece and she did the same to him until they stood stark naked in front of one another. Tish ran her hands down his chest and grabbed his tool and stroked it gently until it became rock. She had been watching movies that Tasheena had brought by for her to learn what she was about to do and hoped she was about to do it right.

"Girl you better suck his dick!" Tasheena's words echoed through her head as she dropped to her knees.

"Here goes nothing," she said, and licked the head before sliding down to his balls.

Tish mimicked everything she could remember from the tapes and realized all was well, as Trans fell under her spell. Trans couldn't believe it when Tish fell to her knees and grabbed his man. She barely liked kissing, so this was way out of character for her. He thought that maybe in the near future she'd try, but right now was blowing his mind. Tish was going hard. She worked her hand and mouth like a pro. The more he squirmed, the more confident she became. She laid him back on the bed and licked between his thighs as he squirmed up the bed and begged for her to stop.

"Please baby stop! I want to feel you. I want to cum in you!" he begged, as Tish climbed his six foot six frame and eased him into her.

Tish rose up and down slowly while she raked her freshly manicured nails over his torso to the point where he felt he would bust at any moment. He arched his back to meet her every stroke until he began to shake.

Tish knew what Trans' shaking was all about. He was about to explode, so she sat all the way down on it until it hurt her stomach and ground her hips roughly. Back and forth, side to side, and up and down she went until they exploded together, then she lay flat on his chest.

"Baby was it good?" She asked.

"Out of this world," He replied.

*   *   *   *   *   *   *

Trans and Tish were showered, dressed and ready to leave when Monty returned to pick them up. The two hours flew by more like one, and the jitters that Trans once felt, reappeared the moment he heard Monty at the door.

"Trans come on man it's time for the shoot-around." He said from the other side of the door, still standing in the hallway.

Trans held Tish's hand as the three of them exited the hotel. The second they stepped out the door cameras started flashing again. This time Trans didn't even acknowledge them; his mind was too pre-occupied with the shoot-around he was about to attend then to speak with some reporters.

Inside the limousine, Trans was mute once again. Tish placed her hand on his leg and rubbed the back of his knuckles trying to relax him, but it didn't work. It was almost as if he were meditating. The limousine drove down Peachtree St. and made a right on Martin Luther King Jr. Drive, then took it straight around to the player's entrance at Phillips Arena. European cars of almost every make and model filled the little parking lot beneath the arena, and Trans visualized his whip being parked there real soon.

"Trans!" Monty said, snatching him out of his fantasy. "Listen the shoot-around will probably last two hours. Then after we get you changed into something more casual, you'll meet with the front office."

"I didn't bring anything casual." He said.

"Baby, I'll get you some'em while I'm out." Tish said.

"Yeah do that. Now let me get in here to this shoot-around." He said

"I know I can get a kiss, right?" Tish asked as he leaned in to give her a peck on the lips.

Trans stepped into the locker room carrying his gym bag over his shoulder, nodding his head to the Best of Oschino glaring through his headphones. The first person he saw was Sharif-Abdul-Rahim, the 6'10" quiet storm of a forward, with his back turned.

"Sharif!" Trans yelled louder than he thought because of the headphones.

"Hey man, whass'up?" Sharif asked. "I was looking forward to meeting you. I saw some film on you and you look bigger in person that's good though, now the trainers won't be on you so much about dieting."

"Oh," Trans responded.

"Hey folk! What's da deal?" J. Terry asked when he stepped in the locker room.

"Ain't shit my nigga. Bout to go out here and shoot dis pill, dats all folk," Sharif answered, then continued "J.T., here goes our phenom."

"Oh shit folk, I ain't even notice you standing there. Just don't be a busta like dat boy in Detroit." He teased.

After picking up teams, J.T., Trans, Jackson, and Crawford were on one team against Theo, Sharif, Thomas, and Vaughn. The team reporters lined the baseline with their cameras and the coaching staff stood courtside, all to get a look at the number one pick. J.T. in-bounded the ball at the top of the key and the pick-up game began. Trans got his first touch and patted the ball like he was in the park, before dishing it to Jackson who cut across the lane. His lazy lay-up was swatted away by Theo and hustled down by Vaughn before being bounce passed to Sharif. Trans tried to get over to cut off the lane, but then he heard whistles. The pick Theo set sent him sailing to the floor, holding his head as he lay there.

"You alright?" J.T. asked extending his hand to help Trans up.

"Yeah, I'm cool." He said using the help.

"Welcome to the league. It's a big jump from high school."

"Yeah, but I'm ready!" Trans said. "Check da ball."

Trans in-bounded the ball to J.T. and got it right back. Everyone in the gym was eager to see how he'd respond after being leveled like that. Trans faced the boy Vaughn up and knew by his stance he was done. His feet were spread too far apart to be standing in front of him. Trans, with one quick bounce, threw the ball between Vaughn's legs and ran around him. He caught it on the other side of him as Theo slid over, which was exactly what Trans was anticipating. Theo was too slow and Trans had a step on him. The stage was set and just like that, from the blocks, Trans took flight. The only thing Theo could do was cover his head as the phenom showed everybody in the gym that the Hawks were back.

*   *   *   *   *   *   *

Tish walked through the doors of Lenox Square Mall with Monty in tow, armed with a Platinum Visa card. Lenox Square was a shopper's paradise and Tish was a true shopper. There were so many stores to choose from she just stood still for a moment and took it all in. Tish reached in her Chanel bag and grabbed her Nextel and called Rayon.

"Damn bitch! Why are you just calling me?" Rayon asked knowing it was Tish from her caller ID.

"Girl I was with my fiancée."

"Your who?"

"My fiancée bitch! Trans asked me to marry him! Girl, wait till you see my ring!" She said excited.

"Congratulations bitch! I'm so happy for you!" Rayon said just as excited. "Where are you at now?"

"Girl I'm at the mall."

"What mall?"

"Lenox Square, girl it is big as shit! And got a nerve to have all the stores in it, Bloomingdale's, Louis Vuitton, Cartier, and the list goes on and on!"

"Get da fuck outta here, you serious?"

"As a heart attack." Tish said.

"I know you going to bring me a gift right?"

"Bitch you know I got'chu. Where's Tasheena at?"

"I don't know, but you know her and Deon been hanging out."

"Yeah."

"Mmm-Hmm. I think they trying to put it back together again, you know? Oh shit, girl I almost forgot. You know they said Boog and O.D.B. were the ones who shot at Saafie a couple of weeks ago. They supposed to have a hit out on them."

"Who?"

"Saafie and some boy. I told Tyaire to stay his ass out of it, so did Deon."

"Girl you know mu'fucka's a whole lot of talk. Ain't nobody goin' to do nuffin." Tish said, hoping her words were true. She knew Saafie would probably try some'em like that, but since Boog was her cousin she didn't think he'd follow through.

"Girl I don't know. They seem pretty serious to me."

"Oh, well that's his stupidity." She said referring to Saafie. "Well look girl let me go, I'm trying to shop not talk about dumb shit, you know?" She said as she held a Chanel sandal in her hand.

"Alright bitch. Don't forget me!"

"Alright."

Tish put the cell phone back in her Chanel bag, then as fast as she put it in there she grabbed it back out. Her conscience was starting to eat at her to the point where she couldn't shop, so she called Boog. The stuff that went on up in Chester happened so long ago, she thought he had been confronted Saafie or just let it ride.

"Hey cousin," Boog answered, as her name popped up on his phone.

"Whass'up boy?" Whass' goin' on wit'chu?"

"What'chu mean?"

"I don't know? You tell me. Whass'up with you and Saafie?"

"Oh that shit? Dat ain't nuffin. I just finally got around to dat nigga dats all. One of my bitches let me know dat nigga was tryin' to fuck her, so we handled dat. She called da nigga up and I laid on him."

"Well somebody said he gotta hit out on you and O.D." She said calling O.D.B, another nickname: O.D.

"Man fuck dat nigga! I was goin' to call it off on dat nigga, but you like the third person dat told me dat shit, so it's on! I'mma get dat nigga before he get me!" Boog snapped. "Watch!"

"But don't do all this on the count of me." She said and took a blouse to the dressing room to get away from Monty.

"Oh this ain't for you. This is for me."

"Alright then cousin, just be careful and don't forget? He is Meere-Meere's dad." She said trying to feel better about what she started. "If it wasn't for me running to his crazy ass, none of this would be happening." She thought as the cashier rung up the sandals and blouse.

*   *   *   *   *   *   *

135

Chapter Twelve

Deon drove his 745i towards 27th and Tatnall St.; his old hang out spot when he used to get high and parked in front of Fat Cat's corner store. It was early Friday morning and as usual Bugs was out front on the step sweeping and talking shit.

"Hey Deon. Why I gotta speak first? When your punk ass was getting high, you broke ya neck to speak to Bugs, now you won't speak at all." He joked.

"Fuck you Bugs, always talking shit!" Deon said and stepped out the car. "Who's in the store?"

"Nurk and Sha'booda."

"Nurk got the grill on yet?"

"You know it."

Deon walked up the steps and through the door and saw Sha'booda sitting behind the register reading *Bloody Money*, a book by her peoples Leondrei Prince.

"Get your head out that book girl." Deon said as he entered.

"Hey cousin! They said you back! Throw me some'em, I can catch." Sha'booda said and stood up to give him a hug.

"Damn! Now you know your jeans ain't have to be that tight."

"Why not? Shit, I'm, tryin to keep up with da young girls. I ain't 18 no more, plus my young boy said he likes it like dis!" She said with her hands on her hips, and then turned so Deon could see why.

"I bet he do." He said and tried to smack it, but she moved out the way.

"Ahn-ahn only he can do that."

"I heard dat." Deon said and walked to the back of the store. "Hey baby!" Deon spoke energetically as Fat Cat (Nurk)

136

stood over the grill scrambling eggs and getting prepared for
them orders.

"Hey whass' happening nigga?"

"Ain't shit. I know I need one of them turkey bacon and
eggs."

"I got'chu, you want jelly on it?"

"Yeah cousin and give me some grits too."

Deon walked out the store with his food and saw
Brother Aziz coming out of his house with his two sons.

"Brother Aziz," Deon called. "Hold up for a minute," he
said and jumped behind the wheel of his car. Deon drove the
half of block instead of walking and parked in front of Brother
Aziz's squatter.

"As Salaam Alaikum!" he said as he got out.

"Wa laikum As Salaam Akee! I see your doing well. I
was worried about you brother. I thought maybe them boys
snatched you up and took you to jail or some'em, but I see my
prayers for you have been answered. Allah has been blessing
you Akee. So I ask again how many of Allah's blessings will
you deny."

"I don't know? I mean, I know he has been blessing me
because I stopped getting high, I got my new car, I got a couple
of dollars again, and I just don't think the same way anymore.
It's like those pamphlets you gave me have got me seeing stuff
in a different light. I know the Fatihah and two Surah's, I even
try to make prayer. So denying blessings, I don't think I do
that anymore," he said to Brother Aziz, who seemed to be
impressed.

"Al Humdu Allah," he replied then said, "What are you
doing today Akee?"

"Around what time?"

"About 12:30 P.M."

137

"Nuffin."

"Good, meet me here at 12:15 then we'll go to Jumah together, how about that?"

"That's whass'up."

"Alright, see you then Akee. As Salaam Alaikum!"

"Wa laikum As Salaam!"

Deon pulled away from Brother Aziz's house and made a right onto Market St. He drove two blocks up to 25th St. and parked in front of Renee's Beauty Salon, where he dropped Tasheena off at before he went to Fat Cat's. Using his two way, he twirked Tasheena and told her to come outside. Tasheena walked down the steps of the salon with her hair blowing all over the place, like it just been relaxed or some'em and came to the passenger's side window.

"Whass'up?" She asked then said "Ooo, whass' dat you eating? Give me a bite." As she saw the aluminum foil spread in his lap.

"Damn can I eat?" he said, holding the sandwich for her to bite.

"Boy shut up! Just give me some!" Tasheena said.

"Damn, why you goin' to bite it like dat? Here take it!" He said shoving it at her.

"Oh I know you ain't mad are you?"

"Man just take the sandwich."

"You should a brought me one anyway!"

"Well look, what time are you going to be done here?"

"I don't know, probably about 1 or 2."

"Well look, I'mma drop the car off around 12 o'clock and walk around Brother Aziz's," he said and was cut off.

"Brother who?"

"Brother Aziz. I'mma walk down his house 'cause I'm going to Jumah service, but I don't know where the Masjid is?"

"Yeah."

"Well come get me from there at two o'clock."

"Alright, but where you going now? It's not even ten o'clock yet."

"Damn, can I handle my business?"

"I ain't say nuffin about you handling your business, I'm sayin stay out of bitches faces!"

"Girl I ain't thinking about no bitches."

"You better not be!"

"Alright back up. Let me get outta here."

*   *   *   *   *   *   *

Allahu Akbar! Allahu Akbar!
A-Shadu-In-Allah Elahah Elallah
A-Shadu-Inna-Muhammada Ra-Sul Allah

Hey Allah Salat Ha Allah Salat
Ka Kamma Tu Falat Ka Kamma Tu Falat
Allahu Akbar, Allahu Akbar
La-Ilahah Illallah!

The Adhan was being called as Brother Aziz and Deon entered the Masjid.

"Come one Akee, let's go make Wudhu." Brother Aziz said before continuing, "Did you know that one of the companions of the prophet (P.B.U.H.) said that the prophet (P.B.U.H.) said one who performs Wudhu well, his sins come out of his body, even under his nails."

"Nah, you never gave me anything on that brother."

139

"Insha-Allah (God Willing) I'll give you something later Akee."

"O.K." Deon said, as he followed every step Brother Aziz made performing Wudhu.

After Deon had washed himself clean from head to toe with water from the Wudhu station, he followed Brother Aziz inside to hear the Kutbah. Deon fell into the ranks of the brothers sitting down listening to the I-man and focused in. It seemed as though everything the I-man said was focused directly at him.

"Yeah brothers." The I-man said. "See we get a little blessing from our lord and think that we made it happen all by ourselves, but surely Allah is the best of planners. Do you think you came here today or tried to grasp this Dean of Al-Islam by yourself, or because a brother may have enlightened you on something that made sense to you? La! No! Man doesn't make Muslims, Allah does. So again, how many of Allah's blessings will you deny?"

Deon heard it again, "how many of Allah's blessings will you deny?" and the question lingered in his head for the rest of the day. He listened to the rest of the Kutbah and learned even more about Islam, but the one thing that stood out the most was the question "how many of Allah's blessings will you deny?" The I-man and a brother called the 'Akammah' finished the Kutbah as they stood in ranks to perform congregational Salat. Deon, not quite sure he had his Salat perfected, slid to the back of the ranks. He didn't want to take a chance on making a mistake and having whoever was at his side blow their Salat on the account of him.

"Allahu-Akbar!" the I-man led, placing his palms up and thumbs to the lobe of his ears before letting his arms fold across his navel. Everyone in the ranks did the same thing on

140

one accord. "Allahu-Akbar!" he said again, this time everyone bowing with their hands on their knees. "Allahu-Akbar!" he repeated and everyone stood before posturing themselves in total submission to Allah. They went through these same steps one more time before prayer was complete, then they stood up and greeted one another again,

Deon was heading to the doors of the Masjid when he heard Brother Aziz calling him. He was feeling so good and rejuvenated after hearing the Kutbah and making Salat that he forgot he even came with the brother.

"As-Salaam-Alaikum Akee! What? You trying to leave me or something?" He asked with a smile.

"No brother. It's just that my mind is on another stratosphere that's all."

"Is that a good thing?"

"Oh, for sure." Deon said.

"Al-Humdu Allah," he replied. "So what'chu goin' to do?"

"About what?" Deon asked.

"About taking your Shahada."

"I want to take my Shahada." Deon said.

"Al-Humdu Allah, maybe next week we can get that done for you." Brother Aziz said, then handed him a Hadith.

"What's this?"

"It's sort of like questions being asked and answered by the prophet (P.B.U.H.) and recorded by his companions. It's a guide for a Muslim to try and be as much like the prophet (P.B.U.H.) as he can, feel me?"

"Oh, o.k. I see." Then Tasheena pulled up.

"Is that your peoples?"

"Yeah, that's her."

"Well you know Muslims don't have girlfriends or boyfriends right? You need to convert her or marry one of these Muslims."

"I heard dat, but its one step at a time right, Brother Aziz?"

"Ma-sha Allah brother, Ma-sha Allah" he said, as Deon jumped in his car.

*   *   *   *   *   *   *

"Hey baby! How was service?" Tasheena asked when Deon got in the car.

"Baby I can't even explain. You would have had to been there yourself." He replied.

"I would a came if you would a asked me." She shot back trying to be as supportive to Deon as she could. Her aunt had told her a while back about a person in recovery. "Baby," she said, "you're going to have to be there for Deon every step of the way, like I was there for your uncle. He's delicate right now in his recovery because he hasn't been clean that long, so be careful how you say things. Encourage him don't bash him. Love him, don't criticize him, he needs you girl and you need him." Was what her aunt said all the time and Tasheena took heed.

"You wouldn't have come."

"I would have come." Tasheena said seriously.

"You serious?" Deon asked.

"Yeah I'm serious, I been wanted to learn more about Muslims anyway." Tasheena answered.

When he realized what she said as they pulled away from the Masjid, the question popped in his head again; "how many of Allah's blessings will you deny?"

*   *   *   *   *   *   *

Saturday morning came and went, as the sun melted away like cotton candy on a moist tongue. She'd been lying in bed all day long, groggy and watching Lifetime on T.V., in yet another hotel. The only good thing about this one was that it was home in Delaware. From the moment they landed in Atlanta last Tuesday, she and Trans had traveled to three other states, and they just landed back in Delaware last night. It was becoming tiresome. Tish heard the special ring on her Nextel and rolled over in bed to retrieve it from the night desk.

"Hey baby!" she said answering the phone like she was wide-awake.

"Hey what'chu doing?" Trans asked.

"Nuffin, just laying here."

"Do you know what time it is?" he asked.

"No, why?"

"Cause you need to start getting ready. You know how long it takes you to get dressed."

"I'mma be ready and so will my girls. Baby, can you actually believe we're leaving?"

"Yeah, its what we gotta do, you know?"

"Yeah I know, but you know what? I'm having a hard time keeping our secret."

"Why?" he asked.

"Because I want the world to know that you're my husband," she replied.

"They'll all know next year when I give you a Cinderella wedding!" Trans assured her. "Now relax o.k."

"O.k.," Tish said and went to the shower.

Tish stood under the showerhead and let the water beat the suds from her body. She still couldn't believe that she and Trans had enough nerve to get married while they were on their three state tour. They left Atlanta, flew to Florida, and then to California to meet some friends he played basketball with on the travel league team A.A.U. The third and final state they stopped in was Nevada, where they journeyed to the infamous "Sin City," Las Vegas.

The planes wheels touched down at approximately 1:45 in the morning and the city that never sleeps was living up to its name. The cab ride down the main strip was like riding through an amusement park, as the lights lit up the night sky. Tish and Trans could've both used neck-braces when they finally reached the marriage chapel, because they twisted and turned their necks trying to see everything in sight.

"Baby are you scared?" Trans asked, as they came upon the chapel's entrance.

"No are you?" she replied.

"No because this is what I want to do. I'm not rushing you am I?"

"No because I want to do this as much as you do. I just always thought we'd have a real big wedding." Tish said with a hint of disappointment.

"Baby we will, I promise! We'll have it at the house next year, o.k. That's my promise to you." Trans said referring to the nine room mini-mansion he purchased off of Old National Hwy in College Park, not too far from Evander Holyfield's estate.

"O.k.," Tish answered as they walked in.

Tish and Trans were both glad that the wee-hours of the night attracted everyone into the casinos and restaurants, instead of the chapels. They filled out all their information on the marriage certificates and handed them back to the receptionist before taking their seats in the lobby of the chapel. Within minutes a young white chaplain in his late 20's to mid 30's called their number and they stood up.

"Do you have any witnesses?" he asked when he only saw the two of them.

"Yeah we got witnesses. Hold on." Trans said and walked over to the drunken couple that came in behind them.

"Sure we'll be your witnesses." They said and it was over as fast as she stepped out the shower.

Tish was dressed in her Atlanta Hawks Jersey dress with the number 21 on the back, right under the name "Owens." Her sneakers, the "Trans 1 Reeboks" hadn't even come out yet, but she made sure Rayon and Tasheena had their own pair too. She also brought them the same jersey dresses, along with a slew of other gifts, but tonight they were dressing alike. Tonight was going to be the party of the year, it was the going away party for Trans "the phenom" Owens, her husband.

*   *   *   *   *   *   *

Chapter Thirteen

Club 2000, on South Claymont Street, in the northeast section of the city was the location for Trans' farewell party. The sign outside of the club read: "Congratulations Phenom" and the line stretched all the way around the corner to Vander Ave. Trans, Tish, Rayon, and Tasheena pulled up in front of the club in a white stretched Hummer limousine and stepped out in front of the club. "What More Can I Say," track number two off of Jay-Z's *Black Album* blasted out the doors of the Hummer, as they felt the knives being thrown from people's eyes at their backs. It was sad that in this little city people felt that way. I mean, you would think that you would be all for someone in or from your town that made it, but not in Delaware. No one in Delaware wanted to see the next man shine not even if it was in a positive way, especially if it was at the expense of their own little shine. Trans shook his head at that thought and smiled knowing he was outta there after tonight.

"They can keep that petty shit to themselves," he thought, as him, Tish, Rayon, and Tasheena were escorted through the doors of V.I.P.

*   *   *   *   *   *   *

For some reason Tyaire wanted to chill for the night, but it was Trans' going away party and he couldn't miss it. He wanted to see his boy off and put a few words in his ear before he left. He called Deon on the phone earlier that day to see if he would ride with him, but he said he wasn't going. He was so far into this Islamic thing now that he hardly did anything anymore, he or Tasheena but that was beside the point. Tyaire had already told Saafie that he would go with him, so he wasn't going to back out now. He stood in front of his mirror, checked his cufflinks on his buttoned downed shirt and tucked the 40 cal. in the small of his back. After adjusting his belt to keep the pistol secure, Tyaire grabbed his keys from the dresser and left the house.

*   *   *   *   *   *   *

Saafie was going to Club 2000 for one reason and one reason only, to catch the young boys Boog and O.D.B. He knew they'd be there tonight because Boog was Tish's cousin and since she was moving Saafie knew that Boog would be there to send her off. He did everything he could to keep her from going to Atlanta; even threatening to battle her for custody of the baby, but her mind was made up. For years Saafie had been going off of the bullshit street tale the old heads told him when he was younger. "Young nigga, listen here." they would say, "If you take a young girls virginity, she'll love you forever nigga! I don't care what you say or do nigga!" the one talking would say before slapping five with the brothers who were lost, with no clue just like him. Saafie thought back on those days and realized he couldn't have been more misled even if a fool would've taught him. When Tish said, "you can save that bullshit! I don't care nuffin' bout you crying, begging, lying, ranting, apologizing, none of that! Nigga you don't care nuffin' bout nobody but yourself Saafie! Oh, and you can take me to court, but you won't win, not with the 'job' you got! Fuck you! I hate you bastard!" She finished.

Saafie loaded the last bullet in his clip and hoped he wouldn't have to use it tonight. He would much rather handle the beef by knocking the young boy out, but he wasn't going to be left armless either. Saafie checked the straps on his vest, put the gun in its holster, and threw his blazer over his button up.

He gave himself one last look over then left the house to meet
Tyaire.

*   *   *   *   *   *   *

She skeet so much they call her Billy Ocean
          Roll, like an eighteen-wheeler
     This hoe bad, but that hoe will kill her

              She drippin' she soaking wet
              She drippin' she soaking wet
              Shake it like a saltshaker!
                     Salt Shaker,
Ying Yang Twins & Lil' Jon

     The Ying Yang Twins and Lil' Jon's 'Salt Shaker'
pounded off of the walls in the club and the women went crazy.
They poured out onto the dance floor like it was going to be
snatched away and did the latest dances. The Dirty South was
making a whole lot of noise on the East Coast and throughout
the West Coast with their heavy bass lined music. Their style
was even making an impact, as Pimp cups started popping up
on the regular. Chingy, T.I., Ludacris, Lil' Jon, Pastor Troy,
and all the rest of them were making some real street bangers
that were ruling the airways and it was a good thing because it
was time for a change.
     "Bitch I forgot to ask you!" Tish said over the loud
music. "Why you ain't put on your jersey dress and what's
that on your head?"
     "I'm trying to tune it down some for my baby, plus I
feel better about me, that's why I don't wear tight shit no
more. Oh and this thing on my head is a 'Kemar' Muslim's
wear them!" She shouted back.
     "So what? You a Muslim now?"

"No, but I'm leaning more to it than away from it. Deon is one though."

"Yeah, that's why he ain't coming tonight. He don't really do nothing anymore, but learn the Dean of Islam. Do you remember 'Wiz' from the Westside?"

"Mike, uhm?"

"Yeah dats him. Well anyway his name is Abu Malik now and they all be on 30th Street at the 'Dawa' center. Girl that's who Deon is with most of time."

"That's whass'up."

"Oh and he doesn't go by Deon anymore, it's Yasir."

"Yasir?"

"Yeah," Tasheena said and then walked to the bar with Tish.

"Bitch what you drinking?" Tish asked.

"Orange juice."

"Bitch I'mma fuck you up!" Tish smiled proudly at her girl to see that she was really changing.

Tish and Tasheena left the bar and directed themselves back to their table where Trans and Rayon sat. On the tray that Tasheena was carrying sat two orange juices, one for her and the other for Rayon, a Remy Martin for Trans and an apple Martini for Tish. Trans grabbed his drink, kissed his wife on the cheek and excused himself to leave.

Trans stepped through the V.I.P. lightly on his toes as if he was walking on air. He gave handshakes to those he knew and signed autographs to those who wanted them, and then made his way over to the window to look out over the dance floor. For it to be only eleven o'clock, the small club was packed. Trans called the waiter and told her to keep her carry around tray full with glasses of Cristal and walk around passing them out, and also to spread the message to the rest of the waiters. "Yeah tell everybody in here it's an open bar tonight on me" He said giving his hometown something to remember.

*   *   *   *   *   *   *

"It's a secret society, all we ask is trust! No G-money shit, all we got is us!" Boog recited along with Beanie Segal as the song 'Once Again It's On,' blasted through the speakers of the Grand Marquise. "My guns shoot like fast forwards on! We dress cute when the war is on! What'chu doing dog you playin' wit it!" he shouted as he ran his hands down his clothes as if to say: "Yeah, I'm cute and I'm warring wit bitch ass Saafie."

O.D.B. just listened with his face frowned up as he gripped the steering wheel while he drove. It was as if every word was meant for him. The yellow syrup he drunk earlier on top of the 'Zannies' he popped had him numb. He reached down in his lap, grabbed his Desert and said, "B-Seg, Fred Krueger nigga's nightmare to your medulla nigga!" as he pulled up to Club 2000.

O.D.B. drove around the club like three times taking inventory of the cars that was outside. Once he was sure he didn't see Saafie's car or his boy Tyaire's car, he parked on the short street across from the club. "Yeah, right here cousin." Boog agreed because where they parked, they had a clear view of the exit door. Boog got out the car and smashed his two shot Dilenger down in his Timbs and told O.D.B., "Cousin, leave dat big shit. You know they at the door searching. I got us through; I got the Dilenger in my boot."

"Alright," O.D.B. said and put the Desert on top of the car tire for quick retrieval.

Boog and O.D.B. walked up to the front of the V.I.P. line and told security to get Trans. Trans came back to the door with security and nodded his head and Boog and O.D.B. were led through the door.

"Damn I would a brought my gun in if I would've known that." O.D.B. said to himself as they passed security without even a pat down.

"Cousin, where Tish at?" Boog asked Trans as they followed him to the back of the V.I.P.

"She back here," Trans said as they approached the table.

"Hey cousin!" Tish said and jumped up when she saw Boog.

"Hey baby, whass'up? I heard you outta here tomorrow, dats whass'up! I'm just glad you ain't chasin' behind tat sorry ass nigga no more." He said for her to hear and no one else.

"I was never chasin' behind him!"

"Whatever!" he shot back.

Rayon was feeling a vibe that wasn't good at all, as she watched Tish talk to Boog, and observed O.D.B. stalking the club. She knew they had heard about the hit that was on them, but she wasn't sure if they knew Tyaire wasn't responsible for it. It was all Saafie's doing and she wanted to tell them that, but maybe her assumptions were wrong. She turned to Tasheena and asked, "Do you think that they know Tyaire ain't got nothing to do with what's going on?"

"I don't know? I don't even know why they're beefing."

"I heard it was over money."

"Well I heard it was about him putting his hands on Tish."

"But Tyaire ain't got nuffin to do wit dat!"

"I know, but you know he ain't gone let nothing happen to Saafie either, don't you?" Tasheena said and Rayon didn't say anything.

"Whass'up Tasheena? Where you been at? Why you ain't call a nigga?" O.D.B. asked remembering the times.

"I been chilling, you know? Trying to study this Dean and leave the Dunna alone, that's all."

"Oh that's why your head is wrapped?"

"Mmm-Hmm."

"Then why your whole body ain't covered up?

"Because when your learning Islam brother, it's one step at a time."

"I heard that." He said, but didn't have a comeback for her.   Her presence and the way she carried herself in conversation had O.D.B. messed up. Her words were sharp and clear and having her head wrapped exemplified her change.

"Alright then sista, I'll see you around," He said and stepped off.

"As Salaam Alaikum, Brother." She said and enjoyed the newfound respect she commanded. Every since Tasheena started wrapping her head and dressing in loose fitting clothes, she received much more attention. Good attention, not the negative stuff like "hey baby that ass is phat" or "Damn what I could, would, or will do to that!" Now, she heard things like "Hey sista! How are you doing?" or "Al-Humdu-Allah, all praise be to God." And she loved it. For the first time in a long time she felt respected instead of degraded and the feeling was exhilarating.

*   *   *   *   *   *   *

Saafie and Tyaire stepped in the club strapped and ready for whatever lied ahead of them. They paid their boy

152

Larry, the security guard at the door, and they slid right
through without being checked. Tyaire stayed close on the
heels of Saafie as they made their way through the packed
club. It was so crowded that they could hardly move, let alone
find someone by just looking from where they stood. You
would actually have to walk around the club to find who you
were looking for unless you were in V.I.P. because it
overlooked the entire club.

"Yo, you see them nigga's!" Saafie asked as they pushed
through the crowd.

"Nah, it's too many mu'fuckas in here to see anything
from right here cousin." Tyaire responded as they went to the
belly of the club.

"Well look let's go over there and post up by the bar
until we see them nigga's. Then we'll handle our business."
Saafie said leaning towards Tyaire, so he could hear him over
the music.

Saafie and Tyaire pulled up two stools at the end of the
bar and scanned the club. Saafie's whole focus was on finding
the two young boys who tried to kill him and Tyaire's was on
Rayon. Rayon was his baby girl, plus she was about to have
his baby girl or boy and he couldn't wait to play daddy. He
thought about being a dad every second of the day and right
now was no different.

*   *   *   *   *   *   *

O.D.B. spun away from Tasheena feeling more
embarrassed that anything else. He was looking forward to
another one of their late night fuck sessions, but instead was
brushed off so respectfully he didn't know how to respond.
Usually Tasheena would cuss him out when she refused him
and that gave him a reason to cuss her back, but the way she
did it tonight, he couldn't respond. Her words were so sharp

and clear and her conversation was so positive that he couldn't hold it with her. That's why he felt embarrassed because he knew now that she was on a whole different level.

O.D.B. ordered a bottle of Moet from the bar to clear his head and then went back to his post at the V.I.P. window. He watched over the whole club for about ten minutes before he spotted them, and then he called for Boog.

"Yo Boog!" He yelled over the music and motioned his head. "Come here." Boog, full of energy as always, bounced over to O.D.B. and put his arm over his shoulder. "Whass'up cousin?" he asked breath smelling like a liquor store.

"Look, there go them nigga's right there!" O.D.B. said excitedly.

"Well come on then let's go handle our business!" Boog said and headed for the steps of the V.I.P.

Rayon kept her eyes on Boog and O.D.B. all night long and when they headed down the steps into the party she did too. "Come on Tasheena walk down here with me." She said and grabbed Tasheena's arm.

"Bitch where we goin'?"

"Down here for a minute bitch, just come on!" Rayon answered as they hit the first step.

*   *   *   *   *   *   *

"Whass' happenin' nigga! You supposed to be looking for me!" Boog asked as he approached Saafie.

"Yeah I'm looking for you nigga!" Saafie said as the right hand clenched into a fist caught Boog on the temple.

Boog stumbled underneath the blow, but the bar kept him from falling. Saafie threw another right, this one an uppercut and nearly stood Boog up. O.D.B. couldn't stand seeing his man's getting his ass kicked, so he threw a right that caught Saafie on the ear. The blow was enough for Boog to

gain composure, but the blow O.D.B received from Tyaire
nearly knocked him out. O.D.B. tried to get up, but he was still
dazed. He reached up to grab a stool and used it for leverage as
he pulled himself to his feet. The crowd in the club moved out
of the way of the fight and the four men kept fighting. They
fought for a good five minutes straight before the music
stopped and the lights came on.

By the time security reached the fight to stop it, Boog and
O.D.B. were battered. Saafie and Tyaire were too much for
the young boys three years their junior, as they slung and
tossed them all around the club.

"I'mma kill your bitch ass nigga!" Boog shouted
through a busted mouth as blood leaked down his chin.

The security guard who was holding him back held him
as good as he could, but the skinny frame managed to wiggle
away. Boog reached down in his boot and "Pow!" the shot
rang out from his .38 Cal. special Dilenger and the crowd
stampeded to the exit doors.

"Come one bitch!" Tasheena said snatching Rayon out
of the way of the stampede.

"No, I gotta go get Tyaire," She said trying to pull away.

"Girl you better worry about that baby and come on!"
Tasheena said this time dragging Rayon towards the V.I.P.

"Tyaire!" She screamed at the top of her lungs.

Tyaire heard Rayon calling his name, but he couldn't
see her through the crowd of frantic partygoers.

"Tyaire!" She screamed again causing him to stop this
time and look her straight in the eyes. Tyaire saw her standing
on the steps leading to V.I.P. and ran straight over to her.

"Where you going cousin?" Saafie asked, when Tyaire
ran in the opposite direction.

"To check on my girl right quick!" He said as he weaved and dodged through the excitement.

"Tyaire, come on. Let's go home don't go out there yet. I got a real bad feeling. They're probably outside waiting for y'all." She said almost crying.

"Baby, I'mma be alright, o.k?" He said pulling his gun from the small of his back.

"Look just go home and wait till I get there. You got your keys don't you?"

"No baby I want you to come home now," She pleaded.

"I'm coming, just be there when I get there," He said and kissed her on the lips. "Here Tasheena come and get her for me and take her home." He said and ran back with Saafie.

*   *   *   *   *   *   *

Outside of Club 2000 the rain was pouring down like cats and dogs and the stampeding people ran right into it. Huge lightening bolts lit up the night sky like the Almighty One was taking pictures with a huge flashbulb and thunder echoed repeatedly. The booms were so great it put even more speed into the people running to their cars from yet another turned out party. Boog and O.D.B. splashed through puddles of water as they raced to the car to grab their guns. O.D.B. was grateful that he had left his out on the tire because as soon as they got to the car the gunshots rang out.

"Pop! Pop! Pop! Pow! Pow! Pow! Boom! Crackle! Crackle," the gun shots and thunder mixed making a horrific sound in the ears of Boog and O.D.B. Boog grabbed his set of keys from his pocket and fumbled with the locks, while O.D.B. tried to keep them at bay with the Desert Eagle.

"Hurry up nigga! Get dat shit open!" O.D.B. said as he ducked on the side of the car.

"I'm trying nigga!" Boog shot back still fumbling with the lock and then dropping his keys on the ground.

Saafie and Tyaire burst out of the club in the stampede and kept their eyes glued to the backs of Boog and O.D.B. With their guns drawn and held out in front of them, they searched for a clear shot but it was impossible. People were screaming, pushing, crying and even trampling over people as they ran crotched over with their hands over the back of their heads in fear of gunshots. There were just too many innocent bystanders that could have been banged up, so they held their fire until they had a clear shot.

"Pop! Pop! Pop!" Saafie fired.

"Pow! Pow! Pow!" Tyaire followed with rounds and then there was a big boom of thunder. The frantic people really went out of control as they made their way to their cars.

"You going to do what pussy!" Saafie yelled across the street to Boog, who was fumbling with some key. "Pop! Pop! Pop!" He fired again, sending one bullet through the passenger's side door, and the other one's through the front and back windows. Saafie let out a whole clip of 40 cal. rounds and so did Tyaire. However, the war had yet to begin.

*   *   *   *   *   *   *

Trans, Tish, Rayon and Tasheena, along with some of the security guards, piled into the stretched Hummer for Trans' protection. Armed with their own weapon's they were going to make sure the 'Phenom' and his peoples made it out of there safe. "Come on driver let's move!" One of the security guards said, but the traffic was bumper to bumper, and at a stand still on the small street.

"I can't get out" The driver responded and then the shots started again.

157

Tish, Rayon, and Tasheena dropped to their knees on the floor of the Hummer and gazed through the front windshield as the wipes slung water from its surface. Trans and the security guards lay across the seats, guns drawn until the gunfire stopped. They asked Tish, Rayon, and Tasheena to do the same, but they didn't respect the call. They sat on their knees and watched everything unfold, as bullets pierced car doors and bust through windows, as Saafie and Tyaire chased behind Boog and O.D.B.

Boog picked up the keys from the ground as fast as they fell, and this time had no problem with the door. He slid in the car and reached underneath the beach towel that was stretched across the back seat, and grabbed his toy. Boog slapped in the 80 round clips and emerged with the A.R. 15 and an "S" on his chest as the A.R. 15 stuttered out bullets.

"Tat-Tat-Tat-Tat-Tat-Tat-Tat-Tat-!" the shots rang out as bits and pieces of brick chipped away from the club's walls, and holes the size of plums appeared in car doors. "Yeah nigga! Aaaahhh!" he screamed through gritted teeth, as he squeezed the trigger of the A.R. 15.

"Oh my God! Oh my God! Oh my God!" Rayon screamed as fire jumped out of the gun Boog was holding. "Please God, Please! Please don't let anything happen to my baby!" She prayed, as she watched bricks and glass shatter like fine china under the guns bullets.

"Run y'all! Run!" Tish said to herself, silently wishing Saafie and Tyaire could hear her, but she knew they couldn't.

Tish watched horrified as her cousin shot the gun at her child's father. She disliked Saafie to the point of hatred, but she never wanted to see him dead. He was, for God's sake, Tymeere's daddy. "Damn I hope don't nobody get shot." Tish said to herself again thinking back on why this whole thing got started anyway. "If I never got his crazy ass, this shit wouldn't even be happening right now." She thought, and then tried to make herself feel better. "Shit, Boog said this ain't about me anyway. It's about the hit they put on them." Then her wish came true, they ran.

When Saafie and Tyaire heard the gunshots instinct said run. The gunshots they had just heard spat off about 30 rounds in 3 seconds, so the little 40 Caliber pistols they held were useless. They ducked down behind a parked car for coverage, but when a bullet came clear through the other side, they were off to the races. The moment they stood up to run, Boog squeezed the trigger again, causing them to duck back down. "Man we gotta make it to the truck so we can get da fuck out of here!" Saafie said to Tyaire in almost a whisper.

Boog waited patiently for them to move again, while O.D.B. changed clips in his Desert Eagle. "Look cousin" O.D.B. said. "Imma sneak up on them nigga's from this side of the street, awight?" and pointed along the row of parked cars.

"Alright." Boog said eyes glued on the Cherokee they were hiding behind.

O.D.B. crept along side of the parked cars until he got directly across the street from Saafie's H-2, and looked back at Boog. The minute he nodded his head, Boog unloaded the rest of the rounds into the Cherokee.

"Go man! Go!" Tyaire said, but Saafie was frozen. His heart was pounding with fear, and the thought of catching a barrage of bullets in the back. "Well watch out then nigga, I'm out of here!" Tyaire said and took off in the direction of Saafie's H-2".

By the time they knew what was happening, Rayon was running up the sidewalk. She had jumped out of the stretched Hummer the same time Tyaire took off from behind the

Cherokee and was screaming for him to stop. "Tyaire!" she screamed, but he kept on running. He didn't know his destiny until it was too late, but Rayon saw it unfolding right before her eyes. She saw when O.D.B. hid behind the car, and she couldn't stop what was already written.

      O.D.B. watched as Tyaire came running right towards him. The embarrassment he felt from nearly being knocked out by him had turned to blind rage, as he clutched his Desert Eagle tighter. The crazy part about it was that everyone in time takes a loss. The feeling of embarrassment would have eventually passed over, but what he was about to do would last forever. Forever in the hearts of Rayon and his family and in the heart of another child who would grow up fatherless in today's mixed up society. "Tyaire!" Rayon screamed again.

      Tyaire heard Rayon calling for him again, but this time it was different. It was as if he could hear the fear and desperation in her voice, so he turned to look. What he saw was Tish and Tasheena restraining her from running towards him, but the gunfire had stopped. Sirens could be heard off in the distance so he knew the police were coming, but why was she still so frantic. He looked across the street and saw Boog getting in his car, but he didn't see O.D.B, that's when his heart dropped. "Tyaire, watch out!" All three of them yelled at the same time.

      Tyaire spun around on his heels and there stood O.D.B. He raised the Desert Eagle and Tyaire turned to run again. "Pow!!" the bullet sounded, as it tore through the back of his thigh, causing Tyaire to fall down.

      "Noooo!" Rayon screamed as she tried to break free of Tish and Tasheena's grasp.

      O.D.B. walked up on Tyaire who was crawling towards the street and kicked him up his ass, making him roll over on his back. He looked up at O.D.B. with pleading eyes and said, "Please man. Please. Don't do this!" as he tried to scoot away on his back. O.D.B. raised the gun again, and the last thing Tyaire saw in his life was a bolt of lightning that flashed through the sky. The bullet hit Tyaire right between the eyes, killing him instantly.

Rayon fell to her knees, hands over her eyes, and cried from deep inside. The cry she cried was from somewhere inside she didn't know existed. It was her soul crying, half of her had just been taken away, she knew it, felt it. Rayon stood to her feet, everything moving in slow motion as she walked to where Tyaire lay lifeless. With every step she took, a deeper sob escaped her chest. Her world couldn't have crashed harder. When she finally reached Tyaire, at that moment she was insane. There wasn't a single thought that passed through her mind that was rational as she sat on the ground and placed his head in her lap. "Baby it's going to be alright. You're going to be fine, ok? Can't you hear the ambulance coming? They're coming for you baby, just hold on." She talked to her lifeless Tyaire as she tried to push his brains back into the back of his head as another boom of thunder, a crackle of lighting, and an increase of heavy rain paraded through the sky. Rayon watched as every hope of a future with Tyaire washed away with his blood, down the drain.

*   *   *   *   *   *   *

Chapter Fourteen

Months had passed since Tish had heard from or seen any of her girls, and the only new friends she had were the players' wives. They had formed a little social circle, and would occasionally hook up, do the town, and run around Atlanta with their heads cut off, while their husbands left town to play away games, but even that was getting old. It was nothing like being around her sista's Rayon and Tasheena. Tish sat on the huge leather sofa in the sitting room, and enjoyed her quiet time. The nanny had taken Tymeere to the store with her, so she was able to flick through the channels on the T.V. and as usual, nothing was on. She walked to the kitchen, grabbed the whole gallon of butter pecan ice cream, the bag of plain chips and a pickle, before going back to her foxhole. She was six months pregnant, so that would make Rayon about due. She wanted to call, but decided against it, and then crushed the plain potato chips up in the gallon of ice cream and dug in.

The day of Tyaire's funeral was the last time she'd seen either one of her sista's, but she always kept the latest updates on them from her mother. No matter what they were going through, Mom Carla was still and would always be their second mom. They always went to check on her at least once a week at her new house. "Y'all need to call one another." She'd always tell Rayon, but Rayon refused. She was still upset with Tish for arguing with her about O.D.B. and Boog's trial, even after she made it clear that she would only implicate O.D.B., but Tish kept insisting that she let that shit go. Tish didn't want her cousin to have a conspiracy to commit murder charge. She knew once O.D.B. was on trial, and realized what kind of evidence and eyewitnesses were against him, he would crack, and they always did in the hood, meaning that both O.D.B. and Boog would go away for a long time. The end result was Rayon not testifying for Tish and Mom Carla's sake, but she hasn't spoken to Tish since. Tasheena on the other hand was a bonafied Muslima. She had as much in common with the streets now, as a priest had with a thief. She had totally given up everything she thought was something, like the clubs, clothes, image, the music, everything. And once she did, she realized she hadn't given up anything. The blessings she was receiving from Allah in bundles, couldn't be compared to anything she'd ever felt, from the marriage to Deon, to her new found pregnancy, life couldn't have been better for Tasheena. And then the phone rang.

*   *   *   *   *   *   *

"Hello." Tish answered the phone, mouth full of ice cream.

"Hey baby, whass'up? Do you miss me?" Trans asked, and Tish couldn't have been happier to hear his voice.

"Yeah I miss you, and can't wait for you to come home." She said.

"I'll be home in the next couple of days ok?" We got a game in Cleveland, then in VH, Philadelphia, and I'll be home. I gotta home game on Christmas against the Nuggets."

"That's only a week away. I wonder if I should…never mind." She said, clearing the thoughts of inviting Rayon and Tasheena down for the holidays, even though she knew Tasheena didn't celebrate.

"What?" Trans asked.

"Nothing." She said, yet her whole voice changed.

"You home sick, ain't you? Or do you miss Rayon and Tasheena?"

"A little bit of both, but I'll be alright." She answered, remembering the eye soaring slums she once called home.

"Alright then. I'll talk to you later alright?" Trans said, and hung up, as he boarded the airplane.

*   *   *   *   *   *   *

Deon had been up since Fajr prayer this morning and that was at 5:57 A.M., and amazed at how much the Deen of Al-Islam had changed his life. Everyday he learned something new, and since he completed his first Ramadan last month, he understood the real meaning of sacrifice. Allah had given him everything he'd ever wanted in life. He gave up the drug dealing soon after Tyaire's death, and everything he earned from it, down to his last dollar to Mom Auntie and got a job. He didn't want anything he earned from the game, because he couldn't make it right. Tasheena was upset at first about his decision, but as long as he was happy, so was she.

Deon had something to prove, not only to himself, but also to Tasheena. He wanted to prove that he could in fact get everything materialistic back, and live comfortable by just believing in Allah, and following the correct Sunnah of the Prophet Muhammad (S.A.W.A.). In the beginning it was a struggle for Deon, but he was a fighter, a hustler to the core. Anyone who could endure what he endured in the streets, and in addiction, and still be sane, could make it anywhere, doing anything. He took his first check from Auto Zone and invested in some wholesale clothes up in New York City, and put a little stand on Market Street. In less than 90 days, with the help from Trans, and a gentleman who knew his mother, the gentleman leased him the property to open a store. "Mom still being mom" the thought crossed his mind; "And she ain't even here" he smiled, at the reality that she got him the property so cheap.

164

Now, six months down the line, Deon a.ka. Yasir, kissed is wife on the cheek, stepped out of his new home, and warmed up his car. It wasn't quite the 745i he had grown accustomed to, but it wasn't a Pinto either. It had heat on this cold December morning, started right up with no problems, and would definitely get him to his new Halaal Meat Market he opened up with Brother Aziz, which only sold Kosher meat. Then as always, he heard the saying in his head, "how many of Allah's blessing's will you deny?"

*   *   *   *   *   *   *

Rayon clutched her stomach and hunched over at the sharp pain, as she breathed in and out three breaths at a time. It was her third contraction in five minutes and she was ready to get to the hospital. Her water hadn't broke yet, but she was beginning to get scared. This was her first time, everything that was happening to her was new, she didn't know what to expect next. "Rayon girl, calm down." She gave herself a pep talk, but it didn't work. Her mind was too busy remembering all the things mothers before her had told her, to be calm.

"Yeah girl, that baby is going to wear your ass out!" One said.

"You think your back hurts now?" Another one said.

"Girl you goin' to need an epidural shot or something, 'cause that baby is going to split you wide open." Another said, now Rayon was past scared, she was horrified. She picked up the phone from her bedside table stand and called Tasheena with the news.

"As-Salaam-Alaikum!" Tasheena answered the phone.

"Wa-laikum-As-Salaam!" Rayon returned the greeting. "Girl what'chu doing?"

"Nothing, why?"

165

"Cause I think its time for real this time. I'm on my way."

"Insha-Allah, drive safe. Can you drive?" Tasheena said.

"Yeah, I should be alright." Rayon said.

"Well come on, I'll be waiting." Tasheena said, this being the third time this month that it was the time, and she prayed it was.

Rayon grabbed her keys, got to the front door and "Oooouch!" she clutched her stomach again. "Come on, make it to Tasheena's, make it to Tasheena's, make it to Tasheena's." She repeated over and over, as she started the Honda, and headed to Tasheena's. She ran red lights, stop signs, and even road the shoulder to get to Tasheena's house before another contraction hit her, but she didn't. They were hitting her almost every two minutes, and as she turned onto Tasheena's block, she felt it: her water broke.

*   *   *   *   *   *   *

Tasheena was already outside when Rayon pulled up. She saw Rayon scooting over the passenger's seat in apparent pain, so she ran to the driver's side, and flopped right down behind the wheel. Rayon was making such a fuss as Tasheena drove, that she didn't notice she was sitting in Rayon's water breakage, until they reached the emergency room and she saw the huge wet spot on the back of her Hijab. "I know that ain't piss!" she asked herself shocked, as she grabbed the material, pulled it, and then turned her body so she could look over her backside. Tasheena watched as the nurses in E.R. placed her sista in a wheelchair, and wheeled her through the doors.

"Come on" Rayon said, looking back over her shoulder, as she entered the hallway, headed to the elevator.

"Girl you know I'm coming!" Tasheena responded, never using the word "Bitch" again, when referring to any of her sista's or any black woman for that matter. It was a word used to frequently to refer to one another, just like the brothers used the word "Nigga", so someone had to break the cycle and who better than her, the one who had the filthiest mouth.

"Ms. Anderson, who is your doctor?" One of the nurses asked, as the elevator stopped and the doors opened up on the maternity ward.

"Doctor Jackson. He's my doctor."

"O.k. Ms. Anderson, we'll call him and let him know you're here. For now you need to get undressed and lay her on this bed." The same nurse said, as the others scurried off, once she was settled in the room.

The nurse, who stayed back, did her regular routine. She clamped the Velcro strapped blood pressure thermometer around her bi-cep, took her temperature and looked in her ears, while she checked her pulse with two fingers then left the room. Tasheena, who wasn't scared at all, because she wasn't on the table, helped her sista out of her clothes.

"When did you get that?" She asked Rayon, as the name Tyaire was neatly signed in ink on her skin, on her back.

"After I got my sanity back and they took me off of the Anti-depressants."

"Oh." Tasheena said.

"Let me see your phone." Rayon asked Tasheena because hers was way across the room in her pocket book on the chair. "Mom, where are you?" She said into the phone as she walked through the door.

"Right here." Ms. Rachael said, with assurance.

"Where's Mom Carla?"

"Parking the car."

"Oh." Rayon said, and for the first time she felt relaxed.

*   *   *   *   *   *   *

Dr. Jackson, a young black man in his mid to late twenties, was fresh off a degree from Temple University and making a strong name for himself. He was good, in fact almost great, at what he did and his list of patients grew rapidly, making his office space shrink sizably. Rayon and Tasheena had their own speculations of why his office stayed so packed, mainly because he was young, very attractive and a single man, who was actually from the hood. He was one who made it out by hard work and educating himself in the public school systems of Baltimore, which earned him a full ride in medicine to the University of Temple.

"Whass'up y'all?" he spoke in his normal slang, as he bopped through the door, just as nonchalantly as he would, as if he were walking through a park.

"Hey Vernon, whass'up?" Tasheena asked her doctor casually the two of them being on first name basis.

"Ain't nuffin" He smiled as he spoke to his other patient, knowing she knew how he felt. "And how are you Ms. Rayon?" He asked with a wink and a smile.

"How do I look?" She waited for an answer, then replied "right, just like I thought."

Vernon Jackson saw her for the first time, six months ago, right after the tragic death of her baby's daddy and reminded himself that he would be patient. "When the time is right." He would tell himself, as he gathered all his inside information from her sister Tasheena. It was love at first sight when he saw Rayon and he felt the feelings were mutual when he starred into her eyes, but the timing was all wrong. "Maybe in the next lifetime" he thought as he often played the song,

and sung along with Erika Badu, even though the song itself
was almost eight years old.

"You look fine and you're going to be fine. You're in
very, very good hands." He assured her, as he went to the sink
to wash off, and slip into his surgical scrubs and gloves.

"I know I am." She flirted along with him. Ms. Rachael
and Mom Carla looked at each other "bug-eyed".

"Mmm-Mmm-Mmm-Mmm-Mmm, you heard that
didn't you?" Mom Carla said leaning towards Ms. Rachael, so
it would be a whisper in her ear, while the doctor's back was
turned, Tasheena smiled and Rayon screamed.

"Calm down, baby girl. You are going to be fine."
Vernon said, and took a look. He then turned to his assistant
and said, "Here, get her into delivery. She's almost 6
centimeters."

They placed each of Rayon's legs into the stir-ups at the
foot of the bed, and begun the delivery the moment she reached
ten centimeters. Rayon cried, strained, relaxed, pushed,
screamed, relaxed, pushed, and squeezed the life out of
Tasheena's hand, while Ms. Rachael and Mom Carla video
recorded the whole delivery, and then they saw the head.

Vernon pulled the baby from Rayon's body, Tasheena
cut the cord, and he sucked fluid from the baby's mouth and
nose with a small vacuum and the little fella cried to life. "It's a
boy!" Vernon said and put the bundle of joy on his mother's
bosom, wrapped in a blanket and completed the delivery by
removing the child afterbirth, and stitching her up.

*   *   *   *   *   *   *

The game against Cleveland last night was an alright
one, but Trans wasn't satisfied. He was leading all the rookies
in minutes played, points scored, assists per game, and was
clearly the choice in for the Rookie of the Year, but his mind

wasn't all the way in the game like he knew it should be. Yes, the team was much more improved from the last year, it was on its way to its first Playoffs in over a decade, but his problem wasn't the Atlanta Hawks, his mind was elsewhere. It hadn't stopped running since the day at the corner store, the night at the Chester High game, the night one of his closest and dearest friend's died. The baby his best friend was having that would be fatherless.

Trans sat in the back of the plane headed to Philadelphia where he would play his favorite player, Allen Iverson, and called his mother. They talked, and she told him that his littler brother was getting too grown, talking back, and she even thought he was smoking weed while his little sister was becoming a woman. "Wow, how much a year, well actually a half year could change a person." He thought, and then called Rayon, she answered on the first ring, but she sounded drowsy and almost out of it.

"Whass' wrong?" he asked, having not heard her voice in months.

"Trans!" she asked, as cheerful as her voice would allow.

"Yeah whass'up? How's my best friend in the whole wide world doing?"

"Sore as hell, your best friend is the mother of a ten pound, three ounce baby and you're the God father!"

"Oh shit! Congratulations!!" Did you tell Tish?" There was silence. "Come on now, I know y'alls beef wasn't that bad." Still silence. "You know what? Hold on." He said, and clicked over on his phone. "Hi baby." Tish answered.

"Hold on." He demanded and clicked back over.

"Hello." He said connecting all three lines.

"Hello." They both said in unison, and then there was a silence again.

"Now are y'all going to talk or not? Enough of the bullshit, y'all are like sisters!" he snapped.

"Rayon is that you?" Tish asked choked up, her heart pounding.

"Yeah, it's me." Rayon said.

"I miss you." Tish said.

"I miss you too." Rayon said.

"I mean it sis, I miss both of my sista's! I'm sorry too, ok? Sorry for the way I acted, I was very selfish." Tish started off.

"It's o.k. And we miss you too." Rayon replied.

"Well bitch, you don't sound like it!" Tish said through a laugh.

"Well maybe it's 'cause I just had a baby bitch!" Rayon managed to chuckle, but it hurt her stomach.

"Bitch get da fuck outta here! When?"

"Earlier today bitch, and we better not let Sista Righteous here us say Bitch 'cause she will snap!

"Who?"

"Sista Righteous, bitch! You don't know? Girl! I'm talking about Tasheena!"

"Bitch stop lying." Then Trans cut in, "I'm hanging up now."

Trans smiled as he disconnected himself from what he knew was about to be a three or more hour gossip session, about absolutely nothing, just the regulars. "Where's he or she at? What is such and such doing?" Nothing major, just talk, but that still didn't make him feel any better. He was angry to the point he couldn't shake it, and didn't understand why." I mean, they were only words. He told himself. "Shit, you got

Tish, y'all married, and have Tymeere and a new born baby on the way, why can't you just let it go?" He continued to ask himself, but he couldn't understand it, he'd never understand it, it was inherited through his bloodline and it was all triggered off by that one little threat.

"Nigga, I'll have dat ass come up missing!"

*   *   *   *   *   *   *

When the plane's wheels touched down at the Philadelphia Int. Airport, it sure looked good. The familiar sights of Philly's city line, and knowing it was only minutes away from home, put a Kool-aid smile on Trans' face. It had been a long six months since he'd been back, traveling from state to state, night in and night out, which never gave him a chance to visit, but tonight he was home. The first thing on his to do list was to go see his mom and dad, go to the hospital to see Rayon, then swing by and check on Deon, on his way out.

Deon had become one of Trans' closest friends since Tyaire's death because he was in fact, Tyaire's best friend. They had met many times before, always feeling Tyaire's presence, which facilitated a bond that only became more brotherly and spiritual since Tyaire's departure. Deon, who changed his name to Yasir legally a couple of months ago, was a Muslim, and a striving one at that. His conduct, his presence, conversation, appearance, his whole aura was strong all the time, and Trans became interested in the Deen. He watched how it changed Deon and Tasheena's lives. He watched Deon give away everything he earned from the game that's why when he asked him to loan him money for the store, and meat market, he didn't hesitate to write the check. The crazy thing about it all was that Yasir had already paid back a fourth of the money, even after Trans told him not to. "I asked to borrow the money brother, so I'm going to pay it back." He would say to Trans, even when he refused to take it, and he would insist. "That's my boy." He said to himself about the most sincere person he'd ever met. Everyone else seemed to always have an agenda, but not Yasir. Trans would seek, and Yasir would guide to the best of his ability, and life's puzzles, seemed simpler to Trans.

Trans disembarked from the plane with the rest of his teammates carrying his gym bag and listening to his Walkman. It was 10:30 P.M., an hour and a half after their flight left Cleveland, and twelve and a half hours away from their 12 o'clock noon tip-off, with the Philadelphia 76ers. They boarded the coach bus, and headed to the hotel as they listened to the same speech by the coach that they heard in every city about curfew times, and staying away from clubs, bars, etc. Then it hit him again, those words, that statement, the look in his eyes when he said it. "Nigga, I'll have dat ass come up missing!" The bus stopped in front of the hotel.

The Double Tree in Center City Philadelphia was minutes away from the Core State Center, and where most professional athlete's, movie stars, singers, rappers, and business executives stayed when in town. The Atlanta Hawks were in town and as usual, so were the groupies. "Hey Trans!" the women screamed to the 19 year old 'Phenom'. "Let's go Hawks!" an odd fan yelled, but like always, they paid them no mind. "Trans!" she screamed again, and he looked. Trans stared closely at the woman, he recognized her but who was she? "Damn whass' her name?" he asked himself, before finally giving up, and just waving to her.

Once Trans disappeared into the hotel lobby without stopping to talk to her, she was more than disappointed. She had been outside the lobby, standing in the cold, for what seemed to be eons, decked out in a full-length fur with a

173

matching hat and gloves, looking more than stunning as he
walked right by her.

"It's cool, I'll get him." Pumpkin told herself.

*   *   *   *   *   *   *

Trans flopped down on the king sized bed in his luxury
suite, kicked off his shoes, and turned on ESPN Sports Center
to watch highlights around the N.B.A. and of their game last
night. It was nothing new to him now, to be lying in a luxury
suite with his feet propped up, compliments of the team. Trans'
body ached and was sore everywhere. The three to four games
a week, night in, night out, were a shock to his system. He was
used to a 15 to 16 game season at the most in high school, but
they'd played twice that already and they hadn't even reached
the All-Star Break yet. Trans stood up slowly, walked over to
his luggage, grabbed a pair of socks, boxers, and a t-shirt with
a Hawks logo then walked into the bathroom to run some bath
water. Taking a bath seemed to be the only thing to sooth the
aches and pains of bumping his body all night long against
grown men chasing a basketball.

Trans turned on the spickets, plugged the tub, and sat
on the toilet to take off the socks, he already had on. He leaned
forward, chest on his knees, and rubbed his feet, picking his
toe jams. "Damn I need a massage badder than a mu'fucka!"
He said aloud, so he could hear himself think. "I need some
pussy too!" He said and couldn't wait until tomorrow night
when the plane left from Philly for his new home in the ATL.
"Shit, I miss my wife!" He continued, but decided not to call,
seeing it was past 11:30 P.M., and she was probably in bed
sleep. Trans stood from the toilet, stripped naked and climbed
in the tub.

*   *   *   *   *   *   *

Pumpkin walked into the lobby of the hotel at 11:30 P.M., the same moment the crowd had disappeared and went home to their normal lives, and not the ones they were living, just moments before, as groupies. She was determined to make it past the security and upstairs to Trans' room, despite the many people who were turned away, she would just have to bribe him. "Hi, uhm, I'm kind of out of the way right now, but my friend is Trans Owens." She said, and waited for a response, there was none. "Well he's kind of like my, uh, you know what I mean?"

"No. What do you mean?" the guard asked, not moved by her antics at all. She was beautiful, yes, but he'd seen better. She wasn't the first one that tried to pull a fast one on him. They came in all shapes, colors, and sizes. Each one with their own story as to why they needed to see this or that celebrity, or athlete, but only one thing got them by, and he was willing to wait, as long as the price was right.

"I mean I'm his friend, a close friend."

"Ok then friend, you'll have to see him tomorrow."

"I need to see him tonight."

"I'm sorry baby girl, specific orders from my boss, and the team staff. No visitors after curfew, which was at eleven."

"Damn brother! You act like you ain't from the hood or some'em!" She scolded, knowing damn well, when this nigga is out of his work clothes, he's straight hood.

"I am from the hood, that's why you should already know what it's hittin' for sista!" He affirmed her statement.

"Well look, here, how about this?" she asked and peeled off two one hundred dollar bills.

"That will be fine." He said and grabbed the money.

"I bet you don't even know the room number, or the floor, do you?"

175

"That's why I paid you."

Pumpkin breathed a sigh of relief, as she stepped on the elevator and headed to room 603. She was tired, tired of Saafie cheating on her, tired of living in the shadows of Tish, and tired of fighting back her obsession. She needed revenge on both Saafie and Tish and would get it at all costs. However, she was motivated by not only revenge, but also a secret and private obsession that only she knew about. It was her desire and it fulfilled her, it had been a secret of hers since she was a child, a nasty one, one no one knew about her. The one she would fulfill at least once a month. The one that felt good yet made her feel dirty inside and out after it was all over. However, her obsession derived from a series of subliminal messages that had been programmed in her mind at a very tender and impressionable age by an unspeakable act: the rape, which claimed her innocence and dignity.

"Here you little bitch! You ain't nothing but a little whore, you and your mommy! Look, she doesn't even care what I do to you, as long as I have the money to pay for you! You'll always be a little whore!" He would say to her, while he raped her, hurting her not only physically, but also emotionally as well. She would try to fight the man that smelled of liquor, but he was too strong. He would cover her mouth when she screamed as he viciously raped her, defiling her body, tearing up her insides and leaving immeasurable physical and psychological scars that would never heal, tormenting her for the rest of her life. Two, three, four times a week it would happen, and then it started to feel good. She had managed to blank out, and become that nasty little whore he wanted her to be. She hated herself and him, yet looked forward to the pain, which hurt so good. He broke her mentally and she began to believe that's really who she was and tonight she felt like one: a nasty little whore. The only difference in this situation was that it would be fulfilling to her obsession of being a whore and revenge to both Saafie and Tish, or so she thought.

Pumpkin got off of the elevator on the sixth floor and slid into a janitorial closet in the hallway. She hung her mink up on a buffer, took her Chanel boots off, and stripped down butt-naked. Once she stood in the dark, nude, she put back on her mink and boots, and then placed her clothes in her large Chanel bag, and just like that she was a dirty little whore.

*　　*　　*　　*　　*　　*　　*

Trans was awakened by a knock on the door; he jumped up and was puzzled to find that he was in the bathtub asleep. "Damn how long have I been sleep?" he asked himself wrapping a towel around his waist as he stepped out of the tub. He felt like he'd been sleep for hours, but when he looked at his phone he realized it had only been twenty-five minutes. "Who is it?" He asked as he went to answer the door, in only a towel.

"Pumpkin."

"Who?" He asked and looked out of the peephole before asking himself. "Damn how she do dat?" referring to how she got past the security guards.

"Pumpkin." She said again, and then he remembered as he studied her face through the peephole.

"Oh shit! Yeah, I remember her now that's Saafie's girl!" He said to himself bewildered as she stood at his door. Trans opened it up, peeked his head out the door, and looked both ways, up and down the hallway, before stepping to the side and letting her in. "It's cool, ain't nobody with me or following me. I roll solo!" She said bluntly.

"I heard dat." He replied then asked, "How'd you get up here?"

"A lil charm, a lil class, a lil persuasiveness, and don't forget a whole lot of good looks." She smiled and was speaking the truth about her looks.

"That's all it took? Well we need better security then!" He joked and chained the door. "So whass'up? What brings you here?"

"The Phenomenal, or should I say the Phenom, that is you right?

"You can call me Trans, Trans is good."

"Well Trans, I see you're modest. I guess you didn't let the money go to your head, huh?

"Its only paper, some'em I learned from brother Yasir."

"Oh so you know Deon too huh?"

"Yeah, that's my boy. Can I get you some'em to drink?" He asked going towards the portable refrigerator, which was packed with beverages.

"No, I'm fine." Then there was an awkward moment.

"So what brings you here tonight?" He asked the same question, trying to break the silence.

"Just thought you'd need some company, I figured you were probably traveling by yourself, plus I thought, that well maybe we need to get to know each other better, feel-me?" She asked in a deep, naughty voice, as she switched positions in her seat, as the words "dirty little whore" echoed between her ears.

"Do we?" Trans asked.

"Don't we." She said, matter of factly, batting her eyes, and then licking her lips, sending a feeling of guilt through his mind. He hadn't even done anything to this woman and already felt like he cheated. "Why?" he asked himself, but already knew the answer. He should have never let her in; never opened the door and now her perfume lingered

178

seductively in the room. The smell was erotic, almost devilish, giving his man hood a semi-erection, and then he remembered he was only wearing a towel.

"Pumpkin saw the print of his dick poking from the towel, and got even more aroused. "Lil whore!" the words reverberating through her eardrums as if someone was whispering in her ear simultaneously moistening her softness. When he sat down to hide the bulge underneath the towel, she smiled because it only exposed him more. Pumpkin could see right through the towel to the thing she loved so much and his, well, his was blessed. She got excited.

"Why'd you sit down? I already saw it." She picked.

"Saw what?" the embarrassment was evident.

"Your dick, it was getting hard. Must mean, well can only mean one thing." She said and stood up. "One thing." She repeated.

Trans' mouth dropped wide open, as Pumpkin stood up and moved her body like a belly dancer. She was beautiful. She waved her body from side to side like a snake; slowly unzipping her mink coat, and then stopping, keeping Trans on edge. She walked a little closer to him, perfume getting stronger, and placed her hands on his knees, as he sat on the edge of the bed. Pumpkin leaned down, stared him in the face, and watched as he squirmed beneath her power. She loved the power, the power she had over men, now it was her turn, her turn to rape him.

Pumpkin pulled at the towel, but he was sitting on it, so she settled for just opening it up. Trans was still semi-erect, but she was going to change that, as she smiled a devilish grin and stepped away from him. Pumpkin started again, her belly dance, but this time let the mink drop to the floor. She stood stark naked, in a pair of high heel Chanel boots that came up to her knees, revealing a set of perfectly shaven legs and thighs. Her pussy lips looked puffy, like dinner rolls turned vertically and her titties were small yet palmable with huge brown nipples the size of green grapes. Trans' dick shot straight to the ceiling, as hard as Chinese Arithmetic and she loved it. "Dirty lil whore!" She heard sinisterly singing in her ear.

Trans watched intensely as she stood up from the chair, because when she stood up, it looked like she was butt-naked underneath the mink, and he secretly wanted her to be. He felt guilty. He had been thinking about pussy all night long and was glad the road stretch was coming to an end because tomorrow he'd be in the arms of his wife. Right now though, he was in the company of Pumpkin, the girl of his archenemy, the one who made his blood boil to rage. The one whose threat stayed stuck in his head nearly everyday. "Nigga, I'll have that ass come up missing!" However, now was his chance he thought, his chance to get back at that pussy ass nigga with all that mouth. The one who was the real reason why Tyaire wasn't here now, but then there was Tish, his wife, who was at home pregnant and eagerly awaiting his return. He couldn't do it.

Trans tried his best to fight back his lustful desires, but Pumpkin was doing everything in her power to edge him on. She danced in front of him, made erotic noises, and faces, and her body was flawless, everything was in place.

"Does the 'Phenom' like Pumpkin Pie? It's real sweet." She asked, tasting her fingers, after they left her slice. He didn't answer. He couldn't answer. He was too tongue tied by her antics, as she traced her finger around her navel piercing. Trans couldn't hold back any longer, she was just too much to resist. His dick got hard and there was no way to hide it, he was exposed. She smiled.

Pumpkin dropped to her hands and knees where she stood and crawled across the floor towards Trans, who was lost in lust. She started at his toes, licking, sucking, and feeling him squirm beneath her power. "Dirty lil whore!" the words grew louder in her ears. She worked her way up his legs, and then to his inner thighs sucking lightly, not hard enough to bruise, but hard enough to feel the pressure. Her tongue twirled in circles, flickering in and out like a Cobra's, leaving moist spots on his body that she blew softly, sending chills up his body. "Dirty lil whore!" the words sounded again. Pumpkin ran her freshly manicured nails down the sides of Trans' body hard enough for them not to tickle and let her hands rest on his dick. She toyed with it at first, then gently placed it in her mouth and worked like a pro. "Dirty lil whore!"

Trans closed his eyes and moaned softly at the job Pumpkin was doing. It felt good for a moment, but guilt wouldn't let him enjoy it because his heart and his mind belonged to Tish. He sat up.

"Whass' wrong?" she asked, staring in his eyes, while his dick went limp in her hands.

"As much as I want to, I can't do it." He told her pushing her away.

"What? What'chu mean you can't do it?" Pumpkin said getting pissed.

"I'm married and like I said, I can't do it. I love my wife."

"Fuck dat bitch! I don't like her ass anyway!" Pumpkin snapped, and Trans saw her agenda for the first time since she'd been in his room. She wanted some get back, and he was glad he didn't fall into her trap.

"Nah, baby girl, fuck you! And you can get the fuck out of my room" He said standing up.

Trans walked over, picked up her mink, and threw it over her head and said, "See ya!!" as he banished Pumpkin from his room.

*   *   *   *   *   *   *

Chapter Fifteen

Rayon awakened to one of the most unbelievable scenes she had ever experienced in her life. Her entire room had been decorated with flowers and balloons and she was taken a back by the display. "Who would do this?" She asked herself, hands covering her mouth with surprise. "Who would spend this type of money on flowers and balloons?"

"Good morning. How are you feeling today?" A nurse asked as she propped up Rayon's pillow.

"I'm fine, can I see my baby?" Rayon said with urgency and excitement.

"Yes, of course you can. It's time to feed anyway. That's why I'm here; I was coming to wake you up."

"Who brought all these flowers and balloons?" Rayon asked.

"I don't know, but someone thinks you're real special, maybe the baby's father, huh?" the nurse suggested.

"No." Rayon said. "The father died."

"I'm so sorry." The nurse said.

"Don't be." Rayon said.

"Let me go get the baby." The nurse tried to smile, but was obviously upset about asking the question.

"Ain't nobody do this shit, but Tish and Trans." Rayon said to herself, as the nurse left the room. "They ain't got nuffin' else better to do with their millions except waste it on some shit like this." She smiled and then grabbed the card from the plant at her side. "Congratulations on motherhood" was on the outside of the card, while the inside read, "On your first born!" There was also a little scribble on the inside that read, "I hope you enjoy the flowers. I did my best at trying to find something for you that was as beautiful as you. I hope you like them." There was a smiley face in the card, but no signature, which baffled Rayon.

"Say, hi mommy!" The nurse said cheerfully as she came back into the room carrying baby Tyaire. She placed him in Rayon's arms as smiled a smile of completeness. She felt whole again. Baby Tyaire had filled the gap of losing Tyaire and she knew now that she could start putting her life back together. The pain would always be there, but looking at her baby let her know that Tyaire was always with them because he was the spitting image of his father. Rayon removed her breast, placed it in the baby's mouth, and then saw that nasty scar, which reminded her of the day at the hospital when Tyaire came in the room nervous about her injury. She smiled.

*   *   *   *   *   *   *

Trans boarded the bus with the rest of the team, as they left the Core State Center. The Philadelphia 76ers had just proved to them why they were number one in the Eastern Conference division by handing them their worst loss of the season. There wasn't any booing from the hometown fans that came to see Trans play, they were just happy to see him. He did however dazzle the crowd with a few no-look passes and two rim shattering dunks, but that was it. He shot five for twenty-two from the field, while the league's leading scorer, and Trans' favorite player, A.I., scorched them with a season high of 49 points.

The bus arrived at the airport at its scheduled time, 5:00 P.M., which was thirty minutes before the team's plane was scheduled to depart. Trans would miss the flight though, and take a later one out of Philadelphia to Atlanta, so he could stop by and see his peoples. He pulled the cell phone from his sweat pant's pocket and dialed Yasir's number.

"As-Salaam-Alaikum!" he answered with zeal.

"Wa-laikum-Salaam!" Trans answered, as best he could. "How's the brother?"

"The brother is Tahid, Al-Humdu-Allah. How about yourself?"

"I'm good." Trans said.

"Al-humdu-allah."

"What are you doing? Are you busy right now?" Trans asked.

"No, I'm not busy. Why whass'up?"

"I need you to come scoop me, take me by the hospital to see Rayon and the baby, and then I want to spend a little time with you and Tasheena. Can I do that brother?"

"Sure you can brother, Insha-Allah. Where are you at?"

"I'm at the airport with the team." Trans said.

"Well, Insha-Allah, I'll be there in a little while."

"Ok brother Deon, I mean brother Yasir." Trans said.

"Ok brother, As-Salaam-Alaikum!"

"Wa-laikum-Salaam." Trans said.

Deon made it to the airport in less than twenty minutes and had the luxury of meeting the entire team before they left for Atlanta. Trans introduced him as his brother in-law, Yasir; due to the brother/sister relationship he had with his wife, and saw that Deon enjoyed it. The players did too, and some even inquired about his religion and as usual he came prepared and handed them whatever literature he had with him. Trans smiled. He remembered the Deon before he became Yasir, but as he looked at him now he couldn't find a single trace of that person at all. Deon had made a complete one hundred and eighty degree turn around.

"Islam is the way!" Deon said reading Trans' mind.

185

"I heard that." Trans said, not knowing he was that obvious in thought as they approached Delta Airlines reservation department. Trans reserved a seat in first class, for tonight's departure at 10:47 P.M. from gate 12, to Hartsfield-Jackson International Airport arriving at 1:07 am, and then they left the airport.

*   *   *   *   *   *   *

Dr. Vernon Jackson, Obstetrician, was in big bold print on the front of his office door, and whenever he saw it, a strong feeling of accomplishment overcame him. He, at the ripe age of 2 years old, had accomplished everything he sat out to do as a teenager, except get married and settle down. He knew growing up in Baltimore's notorious Murphy Homes Projects, in the United States murder capital that life had to be better, than the small two-bedroom efficiency he grew up in. He, like many of the other kids in the projects, set out goals that few met, but he was determined. His wasn't as far fetched as the others were; his was attainable with hard work, and a little bit of self-discipline. No wanting to be like Mike or Magic for Vernon. No trying to rap his way out of the hood like Run DMC. He wanted to be a doctor, and a doctor was what he was going to be.

In the beginning, Vernon almost didn't reach his goals either. He, like eight out of ten young males that grew up in the projects, had been sidetracked by the glitter and gold of the game. Nino Brown and Scarface (Al Pacino) had become hood idols, and seeing them be successful in the game only made the young and hungry project kids believe that they too could be hood rich. So Vernon dabbled in the game. He sold nickels and dimes of Heroin in capsules on 9th street in the heart of Baltimore, now famous for the H.B.O. series "The Wire", during high school, but he knew that wasn't the life he wanted

186

to live, especially since his best friend was gunned down right in front of him. At that point, Vernon's life changed forever. He hit the books with a vengeance his tenth grade year, something nearly unheard of in the hood, by males anyway. It was usually the sista's who were determined to make it out of the slums, but Vernon was going to try and change that scenario. By the time he reached the twelfth grade, he had academic scholarships almost everywhere, but decided to attend Temple University because it was close to home.

Dr. Vernon Jackson and his medical assistant, Angela Bowman, closed the office doors at 5:00 P.M., after a very hectic eight-hour day. Two deliveries, over twenty patients, and three new patients, had exhausted them and 4 o'clock couldn't have come any quicker. It took a whole hour to go over paperwork and prepare for the next day before they could leave, but it was finally over.

"I'll see you tomorrow, Angie." Vernon said, turning the key on his Porsche 911.

"Ok doc," she replied getting into her new Volvo, and then the two pulled away.

"I wonder what Rayon thought of her flowers and balloons?" he asked himself, then re-routed his direction from home towards the hospital to see Rayon.

*   *   *   *   *   *   *

The joys of motherhood had Rayon on a natural high. It was an indescribable feeling and if you were not fortunate to have a child, if you tried hard enough, you could almost imagine it. The feelings were divine and to anyone who didn't believe in God before, they definitely would after giving birth. Just knowing that there was a living, growing, human being inside of your body, and watching it as it came out of your body, was enough to bring anyone closer to the Creator. God had chosen Rayon for this test, the hardest one of her life, and she vowed not to fail.

Rayon gave baby Tyaire to Tasheena so she could eat the plate Tasheena brought her from home; stuffed fish, fried potatoes, and baked beans. The hospital food they tried to feed her earlier was horrible, so she didn't eat it at all, but now she was starving.

"Girl, I was going to refuse dinner too." She said, stuffing her face with fish, as she flicked through the channels on television, stopping at the news.

"Well what did they try to feed you for lunch?" Tasheena asked.

"Mystery meat and some soup." Rayon said jokingly.

"Eeww, I wouldn't have eaten that mess either!" Tasheena said, and then continued, "Now who you say brought all these flowers and balloons?"

"Girl, I don't know? I thought it was probably Tish and Trans."

"You sure it wasn't them?"

"Mmm-Hmm, 'cause they would have at least signed the card."

"What did the card say?"

"Nuffin' really. Just some'em about how beautiful I am and how they hope I enjoy the flowers and balloons."

"It wasn't signed?" Tasheena asked.

"Nope, it just had a smiley face on it." Rayon said.

"Get out of here!" Tasheena said.

"Seriously."

"Mmm, who could that be?" Tasheena asked but already, had an idea. "It can't be nobody else except Vern." She said to herself, growing a wide smile.

"What'chu smiling at?" Rayon asked smiling, thinking the same thing.

*   *   *   *   *   *   *

Dr. Vernon Jackson walked through the hospital doors tired but rejuvenated at the thought of seeing Rayon. He liked her from the day she walked through his office doors, three months pregnant. She was deeply in love then. She talked about her baby's father all the time, and the more he listened, the more he envied the brother that was so lucky to have a woman so dedicated. See, because in his own private life, he couldn't seem to find anyone sincere, everyone always seemed to end up having an agenda and he wasn't about to fall for the banana in the tailpipe later on down the road. He had a couple of friends who he kept relations with, as far as the sex life went, but nothing serious. He always had in his mind that he'd be a bachelor for life, but then it all changed.

Rayon came into his office one day, and never spoke another word about him, her baby's father. She just up and stopped talking about him, and he knew something was wrong. He would ask her little questions about him, but she would never respond, then she came to him about the medicine, and how it would affect her baby. That's the day when she broke down and told him everything, that was almost six months ago. He knew from that day forward, he would wait, wait until the time was right to grab his woman, and what better time than now?

Vernon spoke to familiar faces, as he stepped off of the elevator on the maternity ward floor. The sounds he heard when he stepped off were music to his ears, but to someone else, it would probably be annoying. Women screaming, babies crying, and doctors coaching mothers along as they brought life into the world. It was such a beautiful song. He walked

through the room door unannounced, dressed in his usual
attire, a pair of Roc-A-Wear jeans, a button-up shirt, a fitted
hat, and the S. Dot's on his feet.

"Hey! Whass' up?" He said, seeing Tasheena in the
chair, and Rayon lying in the bed. "How are my two favorite
patients?" Rayon, who had been sleeping off and on all day
long, ducked her head under the covers with embarrassment.

"Eeewww, get out! Don't you know how to knock?" she
asked, hiding her face and hair, which was all over her head.

"Whass'up Vern?" Tasheena replied.

"Nuffin', just coming to check on the new mother." He
said and tugged on Rayon's blanket at the foot of the bed. "I
ain't thinking about what you look like, I'm here to see how
you feel."

"I feel alright." she replied, easing her head from
beneath the covers. "I'm just ready to go home. I think these
people trying to kill me with this food."

"You'll be able to leave tomorrow." He said.

"Well whass'up wit'chu doc? Where you coming
from?" Tasheena asked.

"My office. I'm tired as hell, I had a long day."

"You look like it."

"Oooo, look y'all!!" Rayon blurted out. "Here goes
Trans on sports highlights!" she said as they all focused on the
television.

"Yo, ain't he here from Delaware. I mean ain't he from
Delaware?"

"Yeah." They said in unison.

"I like his game. He's a beast. He's going to be around
the league for a long time." Vernon said, then continued,
"I'mma try to get some tickets for the Wizard's game in two
weeks."

"I can get those for you." Rayon said flatly, like they were nothing to get.

"How you going to do that? He sells out all the games he plays; he's the 'Phenom'. Vernon said.

"We can get them." Tasheena added.

"How?" Vernon asked.

"Don't you remember I told you about my other sister Tish?" Rayon waited for an answer.

"Well, that's Tish's husband," Tasheena finished.

"Yeah?" he asked and before he could say another word, Trans and Deon walked through the door.

"Hey big head! Whass'up dirty Tasheena?" Trans greeted them playfully.

"Baby, I know you ain't going to let him talk to me like that, are you?" Tasheena asked her husband.

"Watch your mouth cousin!" Deon checked Trans with a grin on his face.

"Whass'up brother? Whass' your name and who are you first of all?" Trans gave Vern the third degree playfully, but with a twist of seriousness behind it.

"Boy stop! Don't do that." Rayon said, "That's my doctor."

"Oh shit, my fault cousin. I just can never be so sure when it comes to my lil sis, you know?" Trans apologized with an open hand.

"No need to explain, I know exactly what you're talking about, I have three of them." Vern said, taking his hand.

"Damn baby girl." Trans said, directing his attention back to Rayon. "Who bought all these flowers?"

"I don't know, I thought maybe you did at first." Rayon said.

"A flower maybe, but all these, hell no! You ain't my wife!" He teased.

"Bump you!" and just like that, every person in the room turned to Vernon. "What better time than now?" he asked himself before saying, "Yeah, I bought 'em. I bought them for somebody very, very special. I hope you like them Rayon." He finished, and Trans bagged up laughing.

"Damn doc. That was mushy as a mutha'fucka." He said getting his last chuckle out.

"Forget him Vern." Tasheena said.

"Yes I like 'em Vernon, and they are beautiful." Rayon assured him.

"Doc, I wasn't laughing like that cousin. You just caught me off guard, that's all." Trans said, feeling a little bad about his outburst.

"No harm was taken," Vernon replied, remembering he was six to seven years their seniors, except for Deon, who was one year younger, but of course he didn't know that. Deon just acted more mature.

The five of them sat and talked for at least another hour, while they passed baby Tyaire around like a hot potato. Trans called Tish like he promised he would when he got to the hospital and she joined in the conversation. She, Tasheena, and Rayon talked in code that often broke out into laughter, while Trans took down all of Vernon's information, so he could send him some tickets to the games nearby, and then they all left, leaving the doctor alone with Rayon.

192

Chapter Sixteen

Trans stepped off the plane at Hartsfield-Jackson International Airport at 1:15 A.M. pulling his luggage on the wheels, he walked into the parking garage and walked straight towards his Phantom Rolls Royce and got in. When the engine purred to life, he found his favorite radio station; Atlanta's 97.1. Their motto was: "From the 80'ies, to the 90'ies, to now! We play the best music." And for the most part, they were right.

Trans pulled out of the parking garage and headed to Old National Rd. in College Park, by way of I-285, and for the first time, he really got to test his car. The interstate was never empty, so he smashed the gas pedal. In no time, he was doing 120 mph. but he thought he was only doing 75. The metal machine was worth every bit of the hundreds of thousands he spent for it, so he didn't mind, as he slowed to get off the exit on Riverdale Rd.

When Trans pulled up to his home, the grass was freshly manicured, the tree's perfectly trimmed, and the lights along side of the driveway were lit up like a landing pad. The house was beautiful, and to sum it all up in three little words, it was Drop Dead Gorgeous. Trans stopped at the huge iron gate, with the letters (T.N.T) on the entrance, which surrounded his house, and pressed a code, as the huge doors to the gate swung open. The minute he drove up the driveway, he saw the front door open up, and smiled at his wife, who was waiting up for him. He didn't even pull into the garage, or grab his bags, he just wanted to get into the arms of his baby, and hope it would take away his feeling of guilt.

"Hey mommy, did you miss me?" he asked as he held her in his arms and kissed her softly before she could answer.

"Mmmm." She said, "Maybe I need to get you away more often, especially if you going to act like this when you ain't seen me in a week." She answered as Trans made their welcome almost too warm. "What'chu done did?"

"What'chu mean, what did I do?" Trans asked defensively.

"Just what I said." Tish replied.

"I ain't do nothing." He lied, or did he. That's what bothered him the most, the fact that he didn't know if he did or didn't do anything wrong. He knew he ain't fuck, so that had to count for some'em, but he'd never tell, even though he did put the bitch out.

"Well you sure don't act like you didn't do nothing." She said more curious than before.

"Why you say that?" Trans asked.

"Because you act like you're trying to apologize for some'em."

"Baby, why is you buggin'?"

"Never mind." Tish said.

"Nah, for real, why is you buggin?" Trans asked.

"Because, I'm all fat now, and you're this big star, and you're around beautiful women everyday when you're on the road, and I'm all pregnant. You don't even tell me I'm pretty anymore and then you come home acting all different, how am I supposed to think?" she asked, upset, and on the brink of crying.

"Baby don't do that. Why are you doing that? You know damn well you're sexy, ain't none of these bitches got nuffin' on you." He said and even though her mind was made up, she felt better.

Trans walked in behind his wife a proud man. He didn't feel inferior to her past with Saafie anymore, because he was the man now, the real man. He showered her with gifts, gave her a $8,000 dollar a month limit on her credit cards, and filled her bank account with one hundred thousand dollars for general purposes. Their house was something out of a fairy tale book, and life couldn't have been better for them. There was talk of the "Rookie of the Year" award being spread around more and more, and the city of Atlanta embraced him with open arms. He was to the hardwood, what Michael Vick was to the football field and they loved it. Trans walked up behind his wife and grabbed her from behind, letting his arms rest upon her belly, and he whispered in her ear; "Thanks for making me a daddy, baby. I love you, hear?" and Tish started crying.

"Why are you crying baby?" he asked her, but she didn't answer and the guilt hit harder. "But, I ain't do nuffin', he said to himself.

Tish wasn't crying about anything Trans had done, she was crying because that's how grateful she was to have Trans in her life. Just last year this time, she was struggling to get Christmas presents for her family and her son, now there wasn't a worry in the world. Just last year at this time, it seemed like the projects would have a hold on her forever, now she lived in a 1.5 million dollar home. Just last year this time, she didn't know what love felt like, now she was submerged in it with her husband. Just last year, she would sit around and share her dreams with her sisters Rayon and Tasheena, now she missed them dearly, but that would change. Tish would invite them all down for the holidays, everybody from Mom Carla, to Mom Rachael, from Carron, to baby Tyaire, and even this Vernon guy Tish wanted to meet, would all be here, Tish thought as she gave the house a once over. She saw the fireplace lit up and the Christmas tree in the corner, beautifully decorated. She envisioned the mistle toes hanging oddly, their parents trying to run shit, and everyone generally having a good time. She was looking forward to this event because she missed Tasheena and Rayon. Tish turned around to face her husband, looked him square in the eyes and said; "No baby, I love you. You can't begin to imagine." Then kissed him, kissed him with everything she felt inside and they made love right there, right in the middle of the living room floor.

*   *   *   *   *   *   *

Trans woke up the next morning drained. The seven game road trip that lasted for more than a week, had wore him out, but the love Tish gave him last night was what kept him under the covers way past his wake up time.

"Good morning baby, are you hungry?" Tish asked then continued; "Cause if you are, I left you a plate on the stove downstairs."

"Where you going at?" he asked, noticing the keys in her hand.

"Downtown with Laura, remember her? She's one of the players wife, uhm, whass' his name?"

"I know who you're talking about, I'm trying to figure out where you're going."

"I said downtown. We'll probably go to Lenox Square too, so I'll probably be out for a while."

"What's a while? I thought we were going to lie up in bed for these three days I'm off." He stated, trying to make her feel some type way.

"What? You don't want me to go? 'Cause I can call her and say never mind."

"Nah, go ahead. Do you."

"I ain't going if you going to act like that."

"Why? You better go, 'cause I'mma bout to leave too."

"Where you going?"

"With Ooo-Wee and Junior."

"Mmmm." She said. "Well I know what you'll be doing."

"Whass that supposed to mean?"

"Ooo-Wee is too slick. He swears he's a pimp."

"No he don't. Ooo-Wee is just Ooo-Wee, you won't meet another mutha-fucka like him nowhere in America. That's my nigga! Him and cool ass Junior!" he said, energized the more he talked about his new homies.

"Well what time you coming back?"

"Later on. I ain't going to be long though."

"Ok then. Why don't we both be back at 7:00 P.M.?"

"Yeah, you be here by seven, I'mma call you." He said and she left the room.

After Trans called Ooo-Wee and set up a time and place to meet, he jumped in the shower. Deon's people Jo-Jo had introduced Trans to Ooo-Wee and Junior the first time him and Tish visited Atlanta and they kept in touch ever since. Ooo-Wee was the out spoken one, flamboyant in his own way, but was a genuinely good person. He'd give you the coat off his back if need be, plus he was rich. Ooo-Wee had a saying too, he said it nearly everyday. "I don't like that nigga 50 Cent, but I respect dat nigga! Dat nigga said one got damn thing I'm always goin' to respect! Nigga, get rich! Or die mutha-fuckin trying! I don't care how you get it nigga! Rob a bitch, sell some drugs, nigga rob a bank! If you get killed my nigga, you know what I'mma say? I'mma say dat nigga died tryin' to get some mutha-fuckin money! Get money nigga!

Junior on the other hand was laid back. He didn't talk too much, wasn't too flashy, but his body language and gestures spoke volumes. That nigga stayed serious all the time, but Trans loved them both and they loved him, and he knew today, like always would be an adventure.

*   *   *   *   *   *   *

They met at the strip mall off of Old National Rd., where Ooo-Wee and Junior had a storefront. It really wasn't anything to do this early in the evening but Trans wanted to get out of the house. In the six months he'd been down in Atlanta, he barely knew his way around so whenever he could, he loved to get out, especially with Ooo-Wee. When he pulled up in his Dodge F-150, with the 26-inch spinners on it, there was Ooo-Wee as usual, in a females face.

"Let her breathe nigga!" Trans yelled from the truck.

"Hey my nigga! Whass' happening folk?" he shouted a little too loud, but that's how they talked in the south.

"Ain't shit." Trans said, hopping down out of the truck and then playfully saying, "Are you alright baby girl?"

"Nigga, what'chu mean is she alright? Dis my hoe nigga! Tell 'em hoe who yo' daddy is!"

"You my daddy, pimpin." The woman answered proudly.

"I heard that." Trans said then Ooo-Wee pulled her to the side.

"Aye folk. Go on inside with Junior and nem." He said.

"I'll be right back, I'mma walk my baby to da car my nigga!"

Trans stepped in the strip mall, and shook a couple of hands, and then grabbed the ball from one of the little boys standing around.

"Take it, and I'll give you five dollars." Trans said, and about ten of them tried to steal it at the same time. He dribbled in and out of his legs, through their legs, and behind their backs, keeping the ball away from them, until they wore him down and eventually stole it, as a crowd formed to watch the 'Phenom'. Trans reached in his pocket and got some change from Junior for his fifty-dollar bill, and handed a 5-dollar bill to each of the kids.

"Go on now! He ain't here to be signing no autographs and shit." Junior said to the people who stood around to watch with their pencils and pens out.

"They alright," he told Junior, and then addressed the little mob of people. "Look, I'mma sign as many as I can ok? But I'm leaving soon. I didn't come here to be doing this, but I will for a little while alright?" Trans said to the people's approval. He signed pieces of paper, shirts, old lottery tickets, and hats: whatever. It didn't matter what it was that they handed him, as long as it put a smile on their faces after he signed it.

Ooo-Wee came through the door, and broke up the little gathering in front of his store, and started complaining about his business just to relieve Trans from the mob. He knew that this happened to him whenever he went out, it didn't matter what city, or town, but Ooo-Wee wanted him to be able to relax when he was with him. He just wanted him to feel regular, like he wasn't confined to his own celebrity status.

"Ok my nigga, come on! Go ahead and sign that last autograph so we can go. I gotta go meet my hoe somewhere folk." Ooo-Wee said, as Trans signed the last autograph.

"Alright nigga, here I come." Trans replied. Trans left his truck and keys at the strip mall with Junior, so the dude could wash it with the bucket outside in the parking lot. He jumped in Ooo-Wee's S.U.V. and the two headed downtown to Phillips Arena, so Trans could see his trainer and team doctor. He wanted to make sure that the pull he felt in his calf was nothing major because the big Christmas day game on ABC was just three days away.

"My nigga, I hope you got my tickets for that game on Christmas. I promised one of my hoes that I was going to take her to see the 'Phenom!' Ooo-Wee said, and put his hand out for some dap.

"Nigga, you know damn well I got'chu. I'mma put y'all right behind the bench so she can really see the 'Phenom'" Trans said, playing one of Ooo-Wee's games.

"My nigga, you can have da hoe! We ain't even gotta wait till the game my nigga! In fact, I'll call dat hoe right now folk!" Ooo-Wee said, pulling out his cell phone. "Shit, dats more stress off Ooo-Wee's shoulders."

"I was only bullshittin' man." Trans said and then continued, "You know damn well I love my wife."

"Me too my nigga! Me too!" Ooo-Wee teased, as they pulled into the arena.

*   *   *   *   *   *   *

Trans was in and out of the examination room in less than a half hour. The pull he felt in his calf was nothing more than a minor muscle strain. The doctor said that the three days off was plenty of time to heal it for the Christmas day dame, so he should rest up. Trans thanked the doctor, took the heating pad and muscle rub, and then left the office. "Damn, that's all I needed." Trans told himself relieved, after hearing the good news about the strain. It would have crushed him to find out anything other than "it's nothing." He wouldn't have been able to take sitting out the Christmas day game because this would be his chance to get back at the Nuggets, who embarrassed them earlier in the season. Carmelo Anthony, his hometown's next door neighbor, had blazed them for 37 points, 12 rebounds, and 13 assists, while their defense held him below double figures. Trans had the rematch marked down on his calendar and it was only three days away.

Ooo-Wee was in the gym shooting jumpers on the Phillips arena floor when Trans came walking down the tunnel. Playing by himself, he tried to re-live his glory days by shooting jumpers, fade-aways, and lay-ups like he had defense in his face.

"Nigga, you washed up!" Trans said from the sidelines.

"I'll still give you 10 points on any night!" Ooo-Wee shot back.

"You won't even score nigga! I'll beat dat ass 32 to nothing bum!"

"Yeah right."

"Not right now though, the doctors told me to rest up, but as soon as I'm ready, I got'chu alright? Now come on, let's go."

They left the arena and rode out by way of Peachtree St. but stopped on Mitchell St. so Trans could get a haircut from his boy Amir at Kurt's loft. By the time Trans got out of the chair it was five of seven, and him and Ooo-Wee hadn't even really done anything yet. He knew when he called his wife at seven, she'd probably want him to come home, because he'd been out on the road almost two weeks, but he enjoyed the couple of hours out of the house with his boy, Ooo-Wee.

At seven o'clock on the dot, Tish was calling Trans' phone. She trusted her husband with all her heart, but when he was with Ooo-Wee, anything could happen; he was a man. Trans answered the phone on the third ring, after fumbling with it for a second and she began.

"What'chu doing? Why it take you so long to answer the phone? Who you wit? You ain't all in some bitch's faces are you? You probably are, hanging wit Ooo-Wee.

"Damn, why is you buggin'? Yo, that shit is really startin' to get on my nerves, seriously." Trans said.

"Oh, so I'm getting on your nerves? Well, I won't call at all then!" Tish said out of anger.

"Fuck you mean you ain't going to call?" Trans said, pissed.

"Who are you showin' off in front of?" Tish asked.

"I ain't showin' off in front of nobody."

"Then why the fuck are you talking to me like that?"

"Cause you trippin'?

"Mmmm."

"Mmmm, shit. I'll…yo, I'll see you when I get home." He said and hung up the phone. The second the line went clear, he turned to Ooo-Wee who was driving and said;

"Cousin, take me back to the strip mall, so I can get my car. I'm about to go in."

"What, the wife acting crazy?"

"Yeah man, she's trippin'"

"Man don't worry about that shit, my nigga! She just acting a fool now folk 'cause she knocked up. Dats how they get my nigga! Start thinking they ain't sexy no more and shit." Ooo-Wee assured him.

"Man, that's just what she said."

"Nigga I know! You need to start listening to Ooo-Wee sometime nigga, with yo' young ass." Ooo-Wee laughed, before going on. "What'chu really need right now is to let Ooo-Wee put one of these old hoe's on you, let 'em fuck you real good, feed yo lil ass, and then burp you nigga! I bet that'll make yo lil ass feel god." Ooo-Wee said as they pulled back up to the mall.

*   *   *   *   *   *   *

Tish knew he would say "Yes" before she even asked him, because he missed them as much as she did. Their phone bill proved that. Christmas was only three days away, so she had to move fast if she wanted everything to go smoothly. She had already met with the interior decorators and the light specialists while she was out at the mall, so that part was handled. The house would look like the North Pole by tomorrow night. What she had to do next was book eleven first class, round trip tickets from Philadelphia to Atlanta to arrive before Christmas, and that was nearly impossible to do, on such a short notice, especially for the most popular holiday of the year. The first call was to American Airlines, but to no surprise, they were all booked up. She then called U.S. Airways, same thing. Finally, after calling Delta Airlines, she managed to book all eleven seats in first class, landing first thing in the morning, Christmas Eve, and smiled a smile of relief when she hung up the phone. "Damn it's funny what money will do." She said to herself, remembering when there was none.

　　　Tish lay back, and stretched out across her favorite couch, then started calling everyone up. She started by calling her mother, and then she called Mom Carmen and Mr. Carl, Mom Rachael and Rayon, Mom Judy, Tasheena and Deon, and informing them all about the surprise Christmas gathering. "Girl, you are crazy!" they said to Tish, about springing surprises on them with such short notice, but they still all agreed. She told everyone to clean out from under their tree' and bring that along too, she would pay the cargo, and then Trans walked through the door, while she was hanging up.

　　　"Who was dat? Why you hang up when I came through the door? You swear you slick don't you?" Trans said, giving her some of her own medicine.

"What'chu mean being slick? I was already hanging up before you came through the door. Why is you buggin?"

"I ain't buggin. I'm just showing you how that dumb shit feel. You don't like that shit do you?" he asked; "Well I don't either."

"Well I'm sorry, I didn't know it made you feel like that."

"Well it does."

"I said I'm sorry." Tish said.

"Yeah, alright." Trans said nonchalantly.

"I am." She said undoubtedly and then thought; "Let me let him calm down first, before I tell him what I did." Tish said, as she watched Trans walk off into the kitchen. When he came back carrying the big bag of potato chips, and a bottle of water, she didn't hesitate she went right into it.

"Baby, guess what I did?"

"What?"

"I invited everyone down so we can all have Christmas together."

"Who's everybody?"

"Your mom, dad, brother, and sister, Rayon, Ms. Rachael, and that doctor who likes Rayon, my mom, Ms. Judy, and Tasheena and Deon. Plus I want to see the baby, and they miss Meere-Meere!"

"Are they all going to come, 'cause I know Deon and Tasheena don't play that Christmas stuff?"

"They said they were. They said they're just coming to see us, and that it's no holiday for them. They'll all be here Christmas Eve morning."

"That's whass'up. I want to see everybody anyway, especially Carron. My mom said he's fucking up, said he's smokin' weed and everything. I might have to beat his lil ass, feel me? My pop ain't going to do nuffin', he's too soft, and my mom can't hurt him, he's too big, you know?"

"Carron?" she asked surprised.

"Yeah, Carron."

"I can't believe that."

"Well I can, 'cause she ain't going to lie. I know he better come correct, or I'mma bust his ass, word!" Trans said getting more worked up the more he talked.

"Baby calm down, it's probably nothing. Let's just be thankful that we'll be with family and friends for the holidays." Tish said happy that she was able to pull it all together in so little time.

*   *   *   *   *   *   *

Chapter Seventeen

Delta Airline's first flight out of Philadelphia to Atlanta arrived promptly at its scheduled time. The whole clan, from Mom Carla and Mom Carmen, all the way to baby Tyaire was present and anxious to see Tish and Trans. Rayon, Tasheena, Deon and Vernon had already seen Trans just a couple of days ago, but no one had seen Tish in over six months so she was the one who everyone wanted to see, her and Meere-Meere. The clan piled off the plane behind the rest of the travelers headed into the airport, and stood in an endless line at luggage claim. The men, Mr. Carl, Deon and Vernon left the women, and went to claim all the boxes of presents from cargo and were to meet back up with everyone once the task was completed.

Rayon, Tasheena, and lil Kiesha, Trans' sister, sat in one of the many chairs spread throughout the huge airport. The holiday crowd of people moving around frantically was ridiculously overwhelming and they were just glad to be seated and not involved with all the hustle and bustle.

"Girl, it is too many damn people in here!" Rayon said, as she looked around aimlessly at nothing in particular, trying to feel out her new environment.

"Mmm-Hmph! All these people caught up in Ol' Saint Nick! It don't make no sense at all, especially now that I know the truth." Tasheena said.

"Well what's the truth then, girl?" Rayon said, wanting to get her girl started.

"The truth is that these white people, not all white people, but the one's who run this Westernized society got us poor people, black people, who are already in bondage, debt, and everything else, running out to get in deeper debt with them, by spending what little we do have on some toys that will be broke next week, so some jolly fat white man, with rosy red cheeks can get all the credit. But you know what the stupidest part of it all is?" Tasheena paused, to catch her breath. "We don't even have damn chimneys in da hood!!" Rayon fell out laughing and so did lil Kiesha, but the truth was the truth.

"Girl, you is crazy as shit!" Rayon said, still laughing but opened herself up for what came next.

"Not crazy as you are though, 'cause see, I still got some money this year, and will have some when the New Year kicks in, how about you?" Tasheena asked.

"Forget you!" Rayon said.

"Merry Christmas, Ho! Ho! Ho!" Tasheena said, but this time she fell out laughing.

"Oh my God, girl look!" Rayon said "No she don't got that on!"

"What?" Tasheena asked.

"Look." Rayon said, nodding her head in the direction of what she was talking about.

"Girl you are crazy! I ain't messing with you!" Tasheena said, when she saw what Rayon was talking about, a woman with some Capri's on and some ran down jellies.

"She know she look a sight! Kiesha, girl, don't ever do no shit like that, you hear?" Rayon said.

"You don't gotta worry about that." She answered rocking baby Tyaire in her arms.

"Kiesha, whass' wrong with Carron?" Tasheena asked, as she noticed how he isolated himself away from everybody, every since they met up at the airport in Philly this morning.

"He thinks he's grown. He be smoking weed and everything! I even heard he be selling drugs, that's probably why he didn't want to come, so he could be home selling drugs with his friends."

207

"Get out of here! Are you for real?"

"Yeah I'm for real, ask my mom. That's why she made him come. At first she was going to let him stay, but Trans said no because he wants to see him."

"Carron!" Rayon called, "Come here boy!" She finished, more than disappointed. She couldn't stand drugs no more, or anyone involved in them. She didn't even smoke her weed no more. Tyaire's death was too much, gave her a nervous breakdown and she wasn't about to let what happened to him, happen to Carron.

"Whass'up?" He asked when he got there.

"You tell me whass'up? What's this I hear about you selling drugs?"

"What?" he asked and then turned to his sister; "Damn Kiesha, why you always in my business? You get on my nerves wit dat shit! I should get somebody to punch you in the face!"

"Watch your mouth!" Rayon demanded.

"Go get 'em!" Kiesha replied.

"Hold up! Hold up!" Tasheena snapped; "Are y'all brother and sister or some strangers in the street?"

"Brother and sister." They answered on cue.

"Then what's all that shit about?" Tasheena asked, about what just happened between the two of them.

"Nuffin' she just always in my business, that's all." Carron said, and stepped off when he saw his dad, Deon, and Vernon coming towards them with all the boxes of presents. Tasheena wanted to call him back but decided against it. She knew by the way Carron bobbed off with his pants sagging and arms swinging, that everything Kiesha said was true. She had seen it too many times, in fact, when she was all caught up in the Dunna, the street life, and the same characteristics Carron was displaying was what she looked for in a man. He was

208

caught up, and it was going to take more than a speech to bring him back to reality.

"Boy come here, ain't nobody done talking to you!" Rayon said.

"Let him go girl, he'll learn the hard way." Tasheena said.

Mom Carla led the way with Mom Carmen, mom Judy, and Mom Rachael on her heels, as they pulled luggage through the airport. With Carla talking on her cell phone, and the other three talking amongst themselves, as they headed to the meeting point, they looked identical to Angela, Whitney, Lela, and Loretta Devine, the four women who starred in the movie *Waiting to Exhale*.

"Girls, it's been almost twenty years since I got away." Judy said, relieved that the wait was finally over.

"Me too girl. I haven't been no where since Rayon's father died." Rachael said, staring into space remembering the times.

"Girl and I was too busy being a wife and raising those three kids that I ain't ever think I'd get away." Carmen said, with a chuckle.

"I heard that girlfriend!" they responded in unison, then turned their attention to Carla when she hung up her phone.

"That was Tish." Carla answered the unasked question.

"What she want?" Carmen asked the question for all of them.

"Wanted to know if everybody made it down here, and what's taking us so long to get outside to the limo, if our plane landed on time because the driver keeps calling and asking about our whereabouts."

"Oh, so, the driver is outside already?" Judy asked.

"Yeah, he's outside."

"Good, 'cause my damn feet hurt! We were standing in line for almost an hour." Judy replied.

"Tell me about it girl, now all we gotta do is pray that Carl, Deon, and Vernon are ready too." Carmen added, as they approached the meeting spot.

"I know 'cause their line looked longer than ours." Rachael said, but was relieved when she saw them already there with Rayon and the rest of crew.

*   *   *   *   *   *   *

The limousine pulled up to the iron gate with the initials "T-N-T" on the entrance and stopped. Inside its perimeter sat Tish and Trans' home, a huge, two-story, eight bedroom Victorian, surrounded by two acres of beautifully landscaped grass, trees, and hedges dressed for the holidays. A giant replica sled with Santa Claus's reindeers tied to it sat parked in the front yard with bags of toys on the back of it, while a blow up Santa Claus was tied down to the roof, near the chimney. The color light bulbs that hung around the house and on the hedges weren't on, but they were visible to the eye, so were the clear bulbs that were spread all across the lawn. The driver, a heavyset black man with graying edges growing around his partially shaped-up afro, got out and pressed the buttons on the gate's numbered keypad, and the gate swung open. He then walked back to the driver's seat of the car, and waited until the gate fully opened before driving up the driveway.

"Girl look at this shit!" Rayon said to Tasheena in her ear, over excited, as the limo made its way onto the premises. "They know they need to stop!" she added, in a good way.

"Damn!" was the only reply Tasheena could give as the house did to her, and everyone else in the car, what it did to

210

everyone who saw it for the first ten times, it took her breath
away.

Tish was in the kitchen preparing tomorrow's
Christmas day dinner when she heard the buzzer to open the
gate ring. She turned the fire burners down to a simmer, wiped
her hands off on a dishcloth, and went to buzz them in. They
were finally there; her mother and her extended family, and
she didn't know what to do with herself. Her hair was tied up
in a scarf and she was in sweat pants and a tee shirt looking a
mess, but so what, they knew she could get sharp, besides she
was trying to get everything ready for them. She turned the
doorknob to the front door and stood beyond its' glass screen
door, as she watched the limousine drive up the long, snake
like driveway. When its wheels came to a stop, she bolted out
the doorway like a sprinter in the Penn relays. Rayon and
Tasheena screamed, and followed up with; "As-Salaam-
Alaikum!" as she ran to the outstretched arms of her best
friend, equal only to Rayon.

"Heeeey Girrrrl! Look at you, looking like a ninja!" she
joked, with no harm intended, and none was taken, it was
more of a compliment than anything else.

"And look at you!" she said to Rayon.

"What'chu mean look at me? I know you ain't talking
about this?" Rayon asked, and pinched her gut.

"No bitch, I'm talking about this!" Tish said and
smacked her on the hips. Bitch I told you after you have a
baby, them mutha'fucka's was going to spread out."

"Yes you did," Rayon replied and swung them hard.

"And why do y'all got all those hot ass clothes on?"

"Cause everyone don't live in the "ATL" like you, that's
why. It's winter time where we live at."

211

"Oh, that's right." She teased; "It don't stay fifty to sixty degrees all year round, I mean, all winter long up there."

"Oh, they all you see, huh?" You can't come give your big brother a hug?" Deon asked, playing like he was mad.

"Heeey brother! Look at you and this beard!" She said.

"Yeah, it's my Sunni, you like it?"

"Yeah, it looks good on you too." Tish answered, and then saw her mother, mother-in-law, mom Judy, and Mom Rachael getting out of the car, with Mom Rachael carrying the baby. "Oooo! Let me see the baby!" Tish whined with her arms out, and spoke when she had him. "Hey y'all, whass'up mom?"

"Hey baby." Mom Carla answered and that sense of pride overcame her again, as she watched he child stand proudly in front of her home. "How have you been, and where's my grandbaby?"

"Yeah, where's my grandson at?" Mom Carmen asked also.

"In there sleep, I had to spank his butt."

"For what?" they asked surprised, like he wasn't the baddest two year old around.

"Because he was going crazy, while I was trying to cook."

"Well he's only a baby, what do you expect him to do?"

"Sit his behind down when I tell him to." She answered, and then said; "That must be Vernon, huh?" She asked her mom and them, as him and Carron pulled luggage from the car.

"Yeah, that's him." They answered in unison.

Tish handed baby Tyaire back to Mom Rachael and walked over to the car to introduce herself to Vernon, while everyone else walked inside the house. The closer she got to

him and Carron, the more intense her observation of him
became, as she talked to herself in her head. "Nice" she
thought of his shoes. "Nice hair cut too and he's clean shaven
with a nice trimmed mustache. I love his casual look, nice
build, nice complexion, now all he has to have is good teeth,
and a good personality." She said to herself, as she prayed he
wasn't the 'Wayne Brady' type. "Hi. You must be Vernon, I'm
Tish."

     "Hey whass'up cousin? I heard so much about you"
was his response, and a big fat "Yes!!" went off inside her
head. He wasn't some stuck up brother who thought he was
white, or one who had lost his blackness by being away in
school for so many years; Vernon was still hood, a major plus.
She was tired of the so-called stereotype her black brothers
held, as being 'Thugs' or 'Crooks' and she spoke to herself
about it. "Shit, you ain't gotta be a thug or drug dealer to
quote on quote 'be real'. You could be a doctor, corporate
executive, anything, and still have your 'street edge', feel me?"
She asked herself, answering the question she already knew by
looking at Vernon.

     "Ain't nuffin, whass'up wit'chu?" She asked. "Did you
enjoy your trip?"

     "Yeah, I enjoyed it, but not as much as I'm enjoying
meeting Ms. Tish." He answered.

     "Cut that out, I'm from the hood too, just like you so
you ain't gotta front!" She said about his response, and they
fell out laughing. "Good, he even has a sense of humor." She
thought, and knew right then and there he was the one for her
sister.

*   *   *   *   *   *   *

     Trans left the house that morning, the same time their
plane landed in Atlanta. He wanted to stay and wait for them

to get there, but his coach had called an early practice. Their
usually scheduled practice time would have given Trans plenty
of time to see his family, before going in, but it was the
holidays, so coach wanted to get it done and over with. He
wanted to give the entire team and coaching staff the
opportunity to spend time at home, with family, since they all
had to work tomorrow.

The practice itself began like always, in the film room
studying film. The assistant coach had put together, and edited
their last game against the Sixers and their first game against
the Nuggets in which both games they loss. His focus was on
turnovers, rebounding, and helping one another out on double
teams, which they did so little of in both losses. As the film
rolled, he passed it, pointed out mistakes, and rolled it again,
and that went on for almost the entire two-hour segment. He
wanted to make sure it sunk in to his team's heads, which were
on the verge of making the Playoffs for the first time in more
than a decade.

Trans was focused. He listened and watched intensely,
never taking his eyes off himself as the film rolled, and the
coach taught. He wasn't boxing out, calling out picks, or
making wide-open shots. Instead, he stood around and
watched the game. He was more into watching his opponents,
Carmelo Anthony and Allen Iverson, play their game, than he
was at playing his own, and it cost the team. "Damn!" he told
himself, "I gotta start playing my game, fuck everybody else. I
gotta get my team more involved, and in position to win," then
the film stopped, and the lights came on.

When Trans took his last jump shot of the day, it
finished up the second half of practice on the court, and he
headed for the showers. He didn't participate in the walk
through with the rest of the team, he ran sprints and suicides

trying to test his muscle pull, and the team doctor was right, his legs felt fresh. He couldn't wait till tomorrow. Trans stood under the hot water, and couldn't believe how much his life had turned around in the last six months. He was the 'Phenom' a nickname given to him by the sports world, short for 'Phenomenal'. He was rich. He was happily married to his wife. He was about to be a father. He was one of the most talked about athletes' in the world, and he was only nineteen year old. Life couldn't have been any better.

*   *   *   *   *   *   *

Chapter Eighteen

Silent night, Holy night
All is calm, all is bright
Silent Night
The Temptations

Christmas Eve, the night before the most celebrated holiday of the year, was a time to spend surrounded by family. For the Christians, it was a time to celebrate the birth of their Lord and Savior, Jesus Christ, and to welcome a jolly fat man in a red suite into your home to eat milk and cookies, after he left his gift, if you believed in the myth. Tish ran back and forth, in and out of the kitchen, playing host to her family and friends, as they sat around in the living room catching up on past times. The stereo played softly, but loudly, the remake of 'Silent Night' by the Temptations played behind the murmurs of their conversations, as they laughed and drowned down glasses of eggnog. This was the first time since Trans was drafted into the N.B.A that they all had been together again, and Tish loved it. It was something about being surrounded by family and friends that she yearned for, but was still in search of an answer, to a mysteriously lingering question.

Maybe it was because her father, who left to live another life with the adulteress, the ugly woman who had stolen her father away from her mother and made a family with him, abandoned her. Maybe it was because every time she went over his house to spend weekends with her half brothers and sisters, she never actually felt a part of that family. Maybe it was because when she spent time over Trans' parents house, she saw how family really functioned and she wanted that. Or maybe it was because she was afraid of being alone, and being sad all the time, like her mother was. Whatever the case, she reasoned, "I'mma always have my family and friends around me." She thought as she carried the third refill of glasses of eggnog on a silver platter.

"Girl, ain't it crazy that this is our first time seeing each other in over six months?" Tish asked, sitting the tray down, and taking baby Tyaire from Rayon.

"Mmm-Hmm." Rayon answered through her nose, as she sipped the eggnog.

"And look at you!! I still can't believe you." Tish said talking to Tasheena, who was in full Hijab. "Do you keep your face covered too?"

"Mmm-Hmm, when I'm outside."

"Well when did you become a Muslim all the way? Because, I remember before me and Trans moved down here, you only had your head wrapped up."

"Like a couple weeks after y'all left."

"What made you go ahead and do it?"

"At first, it was Deon, I mean Yasir, but then I started reading the Koran and Hadith, and whatever other literature Yasir would give me. Then all of a sudden, everything in life started to become clearer to me. I started understanding why I did this, or why I did that, before and after I did it. It was like a light clicked on in my head and said, Tasheena girl, what are you going to do? Are you going to keep playing games with your life and in this and world? Or are you going to live for Allah and try to make it to paradise? I mean, well, what I'm trying to say is, I believed in God, but I didn't fear him, I wasn't afraid to do any wrong, but now I'm petrified of him. Girl, Allah is everywhere but you can't see him, that's what made it even scarier for me, because you can't see the air. Or a breeze, but you know when it's there. Feel me? Look girl, let me shut up 'cause I can go on for days, and still can't say enough about my God!"

"Mmm Hmm, I know that's right!" Rayon said playfully.

"Bump you girl!" Tasheena said and all three of them cracked up laughing.

*   *   *   *   *   *   *

Trans sat in a huddle with the men, Deon, Vernon, his dad, and Carron, answering questions about the players around the league. There really wasn't much he could say about them, except what he learned about them on the court, but he did tell them there was a lot of shit talking going on during the games.

"Does A.I. talk shit?" Deon asked.

"Damn right he talks shit! He talks cash shit! Man A.I. is like one of us, you feel me? He from the hood, and no matter what they say about him, how many times they put focus on him, he ain't going to cross over for David Stern, or nobody else. That's my mans, and he real as shit."

"Whass'up wit Carmelo?" Vernon asked of his hometown hero.

"He's another one who talks cash shit! The first time we played them, and loss, he told our coach to call a time out because he was killing our forward. He yelled over to our bench and said, "You better call time out coach, because he can't guard me!" after he dropped his six straight bucket.

"Well, who talks the most shit of 'em all?" Mr. Carl asked.

"Gary Payton!" Trans answered, and got up to leave when his mom called him. "I'll be back." He said.

Ms. Carmen knew it was the holidays and she knew
Trans was enjoying himself so spoiling his evening by telling
him about Carron was the last thing on her mind, but she had
to. Carron was getting out of hand to the point where she
couldn't control him anymore. He was smokin' weed, staying
out till two, three in the morning, and he was always coming in
the house with bags and bags of shit, and they ain't gave him
no money, so he had to be selling drugs, she concluded.

"Whass'up mom?" he asked, following her off into the
kitchen away from everyone else so they'd have some privacy.

"Before we leave here to go home the day after
tomorrow, I need you to talk to your brother." She paused, like
she was having problems getting the rest out. "Trans he's
getting way too out of control."

"What'chu mean, mom?"

"He's staying out all times of the night. He's coming in
smelling like cigars and reefer mixed all together. The boy
keep brand new boots and sneakers on his feet, not to mention
clothes on his back, and neither me nor your dad ain't gave
him no money, so I'm afraid of what he might be doing. And
shit, our little city is becoming a war zone for young black men.
It's just too crazy! Baby I'm so glad you stuck to what you
loved to do, and stayed away from all that mess, I don't know
what to do. Did I ever say how proud of you I am?"

"Yeah mom, more than enough times, and I don't
believe you anymore this time, than I did the first time you told
me."

"Ok. Baby, but please, talk to your little brother
because I would go crazy if something happened to him, he's
only sixteen years old. He hasn't even begun to live, and
neither have you."

"I know mom, I got'em ok?

"Yeah baby, I know you do." She said looking up to her first born, who was towering overtop of her just like Terrance, Trans' father, used to, and looking more and more like him everyday. "I know you do." She said and they embraced.

When they got back out to the living room, everyone was standing near the front door putting on their coats and jackets, like they were about to leave.

"Why are y'all putting on y'alls coats? Where y'all going?" Trans asked.

"We going outside to look at the lights!" Mom Carla, Joyce, and Rachael exclaimed at the same time.

"Well we ain't." Tasheena said, standing next to Deon.

"Why not?" Mom Rachael asked and the whole living room stared at Tasheena waiting on an answer.

"Because we're not here to participate in any reindeer games, we're here to spend time with our family, and we're all family here, but don't let us not going out, stop y'all."

"Stop who? Shit, I'm going to see them lights light up around the house, and yard, and I don't give a damn who coming!" Mom Joyce said, a little too animated for her daughter, but everyone else got a laugh out of it.

"See mom, that's why I don't like it when you drink, 'cause you start acting like you crazy." Tasheena said, embarrassed by her mother's behavior.

"Well I must be crazy too, cause Joyce baby, I'm wit'chu home girl!" Mom Carla said, and slapped Mom Joyce a high five, not seeing anything wrong with the way Joyce was acting, and they really started laughing.

"Ok y'all, that's enough now." Ms. Carmen said and then turned to ask Tasheena, "What harm can it do to y'all for coming to see the house lit up outside? You just said, with your mouth Tasheena that we all family, so why we can't do this together as a family? I know y'all don't celebrate, but it's only a bunch of lights."

Tasheena looked at Deon, whose eyes said he didn't see it as much of a problem and then back to Mom Carmen and said, "It ain't really no problem, I just think it's stupid now, that's all."

"You ain't used to think it was stupid!" Mom Joyce butted in.

"That's 'cause I ain't know no better, but now I do. I just think it's totally stupid to be wasting all your money, hard earned money, on some old stupid fantasy every year, but if it means that much to y'all, we'll come too."

"Keep your thoughts to yourself 'cause we don't think it's stupid." Mom Joyce said.

"Well, that's all we wanted Tasheena, that's all we wanted." Mom Carmen hurried up and responded to stop their going back and forth. "Now come on everybody, let's go see the lights."

Trans waited until everyone got in their positions in the driveway, and turned towards the house before he started his count. "Ten! Nine! Eight! Seven!" he began, everyone joining in at seven. "Five! Four! Three! Two! One!" they yelled, and he hit the switch. Everyone, including Tasheena, took a huge gasp of air, at the sight of the house. It was beautiful. The plain white bulbs spread throughout the front lawn made it look like they were surrounded by snow, and the house looked like a gigantic, lit up, Ginger Bread house with Santa on the chimney, and his reindeer in the front yard. The spectrum of colors was absolutely breathtaking.

*   *   *   *   *   *   *

Phillips Arena was sold out again, which was nothing new since Trans became the number one pick, it just marked a

record setting day. It marked the breaking of the longest home
game sell out attendance record the Hawks held, since playing
in the Omni Arena and since it was Christmas Day, the front
office staff had a huge half-time show set up for the fans.
Usher, Lil Jon and Ludacris would be performing the number
one song in the country "Yeah!"

The buzzer sounded, bringing a close to the first half of
another close and exciting game between the home team
Hawks and the visiting Denver Nuggets. Trans was on fire and
had a game high 26 points at the half, bringing the fans to their
feet with a few rim rocking dunks, and Harlem Globetrotters
type passes on the break. The atmosphere was Playoff like,
sorta indescribable, you would have had to be there to get the
real feeling of the game, but you can imagine over 20,000
people screaming and cheering their team on. Trans walked off
the court after being interviewed by Michelle Tafoya, and
waved at his family and friends, and then blew a kiss to his
wife, as he headed down the tunnel to the locker room.

Tish, Rayon, Kiesha, and Tasheena thought they were
in Hollywood, or at least at a music awards show, not a
basketball game, but they were. Atlanta was known for
bringing out the stars and celebrities, but they came out in
droves today. Everywhere they turned, they saw someone
famous enjoying themselves just like they were. Janet Jackson
and Jermaine Dupree, Chris Tucker, Outkast, Jimmy Jam and
Terry Lewis, Gerald Levert, Evander Holyfield, Michael Vick,
India Arie, Beyonce and Kelly, no Jay-Z, and even Demi
Moore and Sandra Bullock showed up for the game and that's
only naming a few.

"And girl there goes Jada Pinkett and Will Smith!"
Rayon said excitedly.

"Where?" Tish asked, just as excited.

"Right there!"

"Oh, I see 'em." Tish replied, and then said, "They got their shit together. You don't ever here nothing negative about them, do you?"

"That's because they don't put their business out in the open." Tasheena stated.

"Mmm-Hmm, and that's why they going to be together for ever, watch! Because they don't let the outside play a third party in their relationship and cause them to go at each other. I know they fight and shit, every couple does, but we or nobody else will hear about it because whenever they come out into the public, they're either arm and arm or hand in hand, and smiling like Cupid shoots them in the ass everyday! That's how me and Trans going to be." Tish spoke, and made a great point, as the lights dimmed in the arena, and quieted the crowd.

Vernon was hyped up like never before. Trans was awesome and now he really realized, after seeing him live and up close, why they called him the Phenom. He couldn't wait to get back and brag to his boys, who are all Phenom fans, about how he knows him personally and how his new girl is his wife's sister. Not to mention he stayed with the family for the holidays and has a camera full of film to prove it, but he wouldn't have to, would he? The whole world knew now after seeing Mom Carmen, Trans' mom, being interviewed by the same lady, Michelle Tafoya, who just interviewed Trans.

"Yes, and this is my family." She said, and introduced everyone from Mom Joyce, to himself, as family early in the second quarter.

Mr. Carl, Carron, and Deon went to the concession stands to grab up a few things to eat, while they watched the half-time show, but Deon changed his mind when he got there.

"These mutha-fucka's got to be absolutely out of their got damn minds!" He thought to himself, but said, "Mr. Carl, check out these prices! They got to be crazy!"

"Yeah, that's how they do it at these games, it don't make sense! I see I'mma have to change my taste buds and fix them on some'em else, huh?" He said, and they laughed after seeing the price of the hamburger he wanted. "Looks like I'mma have to get some of those nacho's." He finished, tallying up the difference. "Hamburgers, $6.75 plus tax, nacho's, $3.50 plus tax."

"Go ahead and get the burger dad, I got it." Carron said, pulling out a little knot.

"Where you keep getting money from?" Mr. Carl asked.

"I have been saving up all my allowances, that's all." He shot back; "And I just feel like treating, dats all."

But Deon new that was bullshit. He was about to say something about it, but he let it ride. He did, however, make a mental note to holla at Trans later on today about the situation, because he heard a few things in the street about Carron too.

"Alright then, I guess it's your treat." Mr. Carl said and ordered his hamburger.

"You want some'em too Deon, I mean brother Yasir?" Carron asked.

"Naw, I'm straight. I wouldn't even do that to you, young brother. If I won't spend my money in this place, why do you think I'd spend yours?"

"I heard that." He said, and paid for him and his father's food, and then they headed back to their seats to catch the half-time show.

Mom Carmen, Carla, Joyce, and Rachael were having the time of their lives cheering, laughing, and booing during the basketball game. They didn't know it could be this much fun. This was their first time ever being live at a basketball game, except for Carmen, who either comes or goes all the time, but it wouldn't be their last. They were having just as much fun as, if not more than, Tish, Rayon, Kiesha, and Tasheena who were pointing out the stars.

"Damn girl, that mutha-fucka is sharp!" Joyce said, talking about Gerald Levert, who was only a few seats away from her.

"Well say some'em to him girlfriend, you might get lucky!" Carla said.

"Me and him both might get lucky girl, 'cause I ain't goin' to be no more lucky to get a piece of him, than if he was to get a piece of me! You know what I'm sayin' girlfriend?" She said and gave Carla a high five, as they chuckled.

"Girl, if they don't look just like Tish and Tasheena sitting there." Carmen said to Rachael who was busy giving this guy eye conversation.

"Huh girl, I ain't hear you."

"I said, don't them two look just like their daughters?" and the lights dimmed to start the half-time show.

"Damn! Just when I was a about to say some'em to him!" Joyce said as Usher's voice exploded at the same time: "Yeah!!" the crowd's screams were deafening.

*   *   *   *   *   *   *

225

Chapter Nineteen

Guess who's Bzack, it's the Boah B-Mzack!
a.k.a. Mr. Crack Bitch!
Turn a whole one from a half of brick,
See I master this,
You can smell it once the plastic rips!!
Guess Who's Back
Jay Z featuring Beanie Segal

Carron drove the H-2 back to Saafie's house, after
picking up a bag of money from the West side. The throwback
Jay-Z song had his mind in a whole other world, as he bobbed
his head to the bass in the song. "Man dat nigga must have
been crazy." He thought to himself, about the conversation he
and his brother had over three months ago, as he looked over
at the bag of money on the passenger's seat. "What? Dat nigga
expect me to keep asking him for shit? I'mma grown ass man,
I ain't going to be asking another man for shit. What dat nigga
need to do is let me flip some of that change he got!" He said to
himself as he turned into Saafie's driveway, and parked behind
Pumpkin's car.

Despite what people had told him about Saafie, he
stayed with him anyway. He didn't care that people said he set
his boy Tyaire up to be killed so he could get his money, or that
he was the real father to his nephew Tymeere, he looked past
that. Saafie was good peoples to him and his boy Lil Tone and
he wasn't going to let a few rumors discourage him from doing
what he needed to do: Get money. Carron pulled the screen
door to the side of the house open and was about to knock,
when Pumpkin snatched the big door open. His eyes grew as

226

wide as fifty-cent pieces as she stood in the doorway in just a towel.

"Oops!" she said and let her towel drop to the floor on purpose. "Let me get this." She said and knelt down to pick it up. When she stood back up, she was stark naked and in no rush to hide herself from him. She took her time wrapping her body back up, but only after she was sure he got an eye full. "Dirty lil whore!" the words began to echo again, as she smiled a devilish grin.

"Umm, is S-S-Saafie here?" Carron stuttered like he did something wrong by seeing her naked.

"Uh-uh-uhm, no he's not." She teased. "But you can come in and wait for him if you want.

"Alright." He said.

Carron followed Pumpkin through the laundry room and down the hallway into the living room. "Mmm, Mmm, Mmm." He thought to himself as he watched her ass shake loosely through the towel. "Damn I know Saafie wearing dat ass out!"

"What'chu say?" She asked.

"Huh?" He asked shocked, realizing that he wasn't talking to himself.

"Don't huh me, when you know you heard me. I said what you say?"

"What did I say?" He replied, thinking that maybe she really didn't hear him.

"Never mind, don't worry about it, but just to let you know, I thought it was cute. I took is as a compliment, lets me know I still got it when a young boah like you see me as attractive! How old are you again?"

"Seventeen. I just turned seventeen last month." He answered, not knowing where this conversation was heading.

"Boy you still a baby. I'll catch a charge if I gave you some of this pussy." And right then, he knew where she was going with the small talk. "Why'd you get so quiet? I know you ain't get scared of a lil pussy did you?" She instigated as the words dirty lil whore were ringing in her ears.

"No I ain't scared. I'm just sayin' Saafie is my peoples and I don't think it would be cool, feel me?"

"Boy please! How the hell Saafie going to find out if you don't tell him? I bet that mutha'fucka would fuck your girl!" She stated matter of factly.

"I don't know about that one." He said.

"Boy you better wake up! Do you know what type of game you playin' in? This is the drug game, hustlers ain't shit and neither are their women and I'mma be the first to tell you. I want you to listen to me Carron and listen good." She said taking his face into her hands and staring into his eyes. "Listen baby, a drug dealer will cheat on his woman, just as fast as the other bitch can make his dick hard. The bitches don't give a fuck if he's got a woman or not. Those bitches are tryin' to see what they can get out of whoever it is their fucking. To hell if that nigga got a family or not. Those bitches have an agenda and they'll do whatever it takes to get what they want, especially after they fucked him, knowing he has a wifey at home. Those bitches will lie, blackmail, and disrespect his wifey, whatever, until she gets, at any cost, what she came to get in the first place. Now the drug dealer woman, or these so-called drug dealer wifey's out here will do the same thing the niggas will do. Yeah, they will have a man, a drug dealer man, a mutha'fucka who loves the ground the bitch walks on, but that nigga will only have a little bit of some'em feel me? A little apartment, a Honda Accord or some'em, and the first time that bitch get a chance to fuck the nigga with the Benz, she'll

jump right on it. But you know what's crazy? Her man, the
one with the Honda, will, nine times out of ten, have more than
the nigga with the Benz. See 'cause, the Benz will be leased
and the nigga probably will still live at home with his mom.
And that's where the bitch fucks up at, 'cause the nigga with
the Honda will find out and cut her dumb ass off, and then
she's stuck." She said almost out of breath. "Baby this is a
dirty game, so if you going to play it, play it! You have to be as
cold as a December morning." She finished, and let go of his
face.

"Ok, so after telling me all of that, what's the point?"
He asked.

"The point is that the game you're playing in is dirty, so
you need to get dirty too."

"So ok, what's next?" He asked.

Carron couldn't believe he just said that. The last thing
in the world he wanted to do was cross Saafie, but his dick told
him otherwise. Pumpkin was sexy as hell, and as she stood
before him with drops of water from the shower still present
across her shoulders, and the cold air causing her nipples to
press through the towel like they wanted to escape, his dick got
hard as a brick. Pumpkin walked up to Carron and stood right
in his face. His heart was pounding, as he felt her breath blow
softly across his lips, but he stood firm.

"Gimmie a kiss," She said, and slid her tongue in
between his lips, and grabbed a handful of his dick. "Dirty lil
whore!" She thought to herself.

Pumpkin stroked his love muscle through his jeans and
twirled her tongue around in his mouth wildly, almost
animalistically. She shuttered with excitement as he followed
her lead, running his hands all over her body. Pumpkin placed
both her arms around his neck, and let the towel fall to the

floor as his fingers found the inside of her. "Mmm" she
moaned as Carron ran his middle finger in and out of her body
until she soaked his hand with secretions.

"Come on" She said, after giving his bottom lip one last
suck. "Let's go over here." She suggested grabbing both his
hands and walking him to the couch.

Pumpkin sat down on the couch while Carron stood
before her and unbuttoned his pants. He couldn't believe what
was happening to him, as she slid his pants down around his
ankles, and took his manhood in her hand. Just like that, in a
few swift motions, Pumpkin had placed his dick in and out of
her mouth, and was standing to her feet when he was fully
erect.

"Your not worthy of that yet." She said and continued,
"Let me see how you do in this good pussy first." She finished,
and placed one leg up on the couch, and bent over to grab her
ankles. "Dirty lil whore!" those words echoed louder, in that
same raspy voice. With her left leg up on the couch, and her
bending over to grab her ankles, she reached back with her left
hand and grabbed Carron's dick and placed it gently up to her
softness and then grabbed her ankle again.

"Are you going to work or do I gotta do everything?"
She teased, knowing he was scared. "Shit, you make me want
to go strap on my dildo and fuck you!"

"Fuck who?" He said.

"I don't see no owls up in here, do you?" She answered
and then he went to work.

Carron grabbed her around her tiny waist, right at her
hips where they spread out like a heart and pounded away.

"Oooo Yeah! Oooo Yeah! Do your shit young boy, do
your shit!" She shouted, only making Carron go harder. "Yeah
right there! Oooo baby! Oooo! Squeeze ya ass baby, squeeze ya

ass!" She coached him on, and within minutes her body was tingling all over and she shook uncontrollably. "Oooo baby, I'm cummin!" She shouted, but Carron wasn't done. He stood her straight up and then laid her down on the couch.

"Put your legs up here" He said as he tapped the back of the couch. Carron climbed on top of her, and pounded away until she felt him jerk and explode inside of her, and right then, at that very moment, Carron didn't think he'd ever be able to look Saafie straight in the eyes ever again.

"Was it good?" Pumpkin asked, wiping her sweat soaked hair from her eyes.

"Mmm-Hmm" He moaned out of breath, and then they heard the car door shut.

"Oh shit! That's Saafie! Get up, hurry up and put your shit on! Pumpkin panicked.

"I am!" Carron replied, ten steps ahead of her.

"Grab the remote, act like your watching T.V." She said and darted up the stairs.

"Alright" Carron said and grabbed the remote from the coffee table, and flopped down on the couch. No sooner than the T.V. picture came in, Saafie's keys were in the door.

"Hey baby boy, how long you been here?" Saafie asked as he stepped in the door.

"Not long, I just got here about ten minutes ago." He answered.

"Did you grab that change?" Saafie asked.

"Yeah, I grabbed it, plus dropped that thing off to the boy."

"What thing?"

"That bird." Carron said.

"Oh, oh, yeah, that's right. What the boy on the Eastside wanted, right?"

"Yeah, so when you count the money, that's where that extra twenty three came from.

"Alright. Was all the other change there?"

"Yeah."

"Where's Pumpkin at?"

"She went upstairs."

"Hold on, I'll be right back" Saafie said and headed up the stairs.

Carron breathed a sigh of relief, when Saafie disappeared up the steps. He thought for sure that Saafie suspected something because he felt the look on his face would surely give him up, but it didn't. "Damn" He said to himself relieved, "That was close." He thought, as he remembered what happened just minutes ago. Just remembering the feeling of her throwing that pussy at him had him fucked up. Pumpkin had the best shot he'd ever had in his young life, and probably the best he'd ever get, he thought. "Our secret is safe with me," He said as if she could hear him and then thought about that song by Alicia Keys.

Pumpkin was sitting on the edge of the bed in a pair of his boxers and a white t-shirt when he came through the door.

"Hi baby." She said, just as innocent as a child.

"Hey baby" He replied instantly sensing something was wrong. "Whass wrong with you?"

"Nuffin' why you say that?" She answered and swallowed hard.

"Never mind." He said, and stepped towards the closet. "Did anybody call for me?" He asked and opened the safe up.

"No." Pumpkin said.

*   *   *   *   *   *   *

When Saafie finished counting the money Carron just bought to him, not a single dollar was off. That was the way it always was whenever Saafie sent Carron to handle a collection. His other workers and runners would always peel off a couple hundred, and sometimes more, from the money he sent them to collect depending on how much they were grabbing. They figured it was usually so much that he'd never notice it, but he always did, but not Carron. He never peeled off or came up short on money from a package he had given him, or from a collection. Everything was always right, and Saafie loved him for that, but that one reason wasn't enough to stop what he had in store for the young boy. Carron was his pawn, his way of getting back at Trans for the way he felt each and everyday about not having Tish or his son Tymeere in his life. He was determined to get back at Trans and there was no better way than to use his little brother he thought.

"Since I can't make him come up missing, I'mma make his brother disappear" ran through his mind, but then he thought that maybe that was too harsh. Then the thought of getting him knocked off with a couple keys of cocaine seemed a little better. "Yeah, then maybe the Feds would implicate Trans like they did Jamal Lewis of the Baltimore Ravens" he thought wishfully, hoping the Feds would think that Trans was supplying money for his brother to run a drug ring. Either form of revenge was good, he just hadn't decided on one yet. The day for Trans to pay would come up one day in the near future, but for now he was just plotting.

After Saafie counted the last of the money, he looked at Carron and asked, "Whass up cousin. You alright?"

"Yeah I'm aight. Why you ask me that?" Carron answered as best he could.

"Cause you don't seem like yourself today." Saafie said.

"Nah, maybe it's because I been thinking real hard lately. Thinking about how I'mma start investing some of this money into some legal shit!" He replied.

"I heard dat! Well here's some more to think about investing." Saafie said, and threw him a knot worth five thousand.

"Good looking." Carron said, and put the money in his pocket, but the money was nuffin to him, 'cause his mind was stuck on Pumpkin.

*   *   *   *   *   *   *

"Whass up Deon, I mean, Brother Yasir?" Trans said into the phone's receiver. He still had trouble with calling Deon by his Muslim name, because he had been calling him Deon for so long, but he was getting better.

"As-Salaam-Alaikum brother Trans. I was just about to call you."

"Call me for what? Why whass going on?"

"To let you know I mailed off the rest of the money you loaned me to open up the store. You should be receiving a check in the next few days."

"Didn't I tell you when you sent me the last check that you didn't owe me anything?"

"Yes you did good brother, but a loan is a loan."

"Yeah, I guess you're right." He said then asked, "Brother D-Yasir" he caught himself, "Are your ears still close to the street."

"Not as close as they used to be, but it ain't too much in the hood that I don't know about."

"Well whass up wit Carron? My mom said that since y'all left from down here around the holidays that nigga ain't do nuffin' but get worst." Trans said almost out of breath.

234

Deon tried to think fast. Think of an easier way to let
Trans know that his mother wasn't lying, but he couldn't; the
cold-blooded truth was the only way it could be told. Carron
was gone. He was a full-fledged hustler in Saafies's little
organization. Deon knew what he was about to tell Trans
would hurt him to his very essence because that's the kind of
love he had for his brother, but he had to know. Carron was
dealing with a slimy dude, a dude who Deon himself
introduced to the game, so he knew better than anybody what
Saafie was capable of. Saafie held onto grudges. Revenge was
his motto and Deon feared for Carron. He just had an eerie
feeling that Saafie was using him as a pawn to get back at
Trans.

"Yo man Carron is gone cousin. That lil nigga is on
some real nut type time. All that nigga do is smoke weed and
sell coke, but that ain't the crazy part. The crazy part is that he
hustles for Saafie."

"Who?" Trans cut him off.

"Saafie cousin! I tried to tell him to stay away from that
nigga, but he won't listen. I just got a real bad feeling about
the whole thing."

"Like what?" Trans asked, with worry in his voice.

"Like dat nigga is using Carron to get back at you for
marrying Tish." Trans' heart dropped to his stomach as he
recalled those cryptic words, the words that kept him up
occasionally at night. "Nigga I'll make dat ass come up
missing!"

"Oh yeah? Well we'll see about that." Trans said and
that uncontrollable anger rushed through his body causing his
blood to boil, and him to break out in a sweat. "Man I'mma
kill that nigga." He said to himself realizing that that was the

only way to stop those words, those nightmares, and probably save his brothers life.

"Man, just don't do nuffin crazy." Deon said feeling the negativity in Trans' words.

"I ain't cousin, I ain't that dumb," He said with a chuckle, but his mind was made up. Saafie was going to die.

Trans hung up the phone and paced the floor frantically. Here he was all the way in Atlanta, thirteen hours away from home by car, two and a half hours away by plane, and what seemed like an eternity away from saving his little brother's life and his mom the grief of burying one of her children.

"Damn dat lil nigga is hard headed!" Trans repeatedly told himself as he went from one end of the hall to the other. "Dat lil nigga don't have to want for nuffin. All he gotta do is ask me, but he too mu'fuckin stubborn." Trans said to himself as he remembered their conversation. From the first word he said to his brother, he knew Carron wasn't trying to hear it. His whole demeanor spoke rejection as Trans tried to make since of his words. "I got 90 million dollars plus Carron! There's no need for you to be hustling."

"Like you just said, you got yo 90 Million, not me! I'm a grown ass man just like you, so why would I want to keep asking you for shit?" Carron shot back.

"Grown man? Nigga you only sixteen!"

"Like I said, grown man!" and right then Trans let the whole conversation go. He just hoped that his words would somehow seep through his armor eventually.

*   *   *   *   *   *   *

Carron read the fifth text message on his phone in the last five minutes and shook his head.

"This broad is crazy!" he said to himself as the words in all capital letters read: "I'M YOUR DIRTY LIL WHORE!"

Pumpkin had been leaving these types of messages in his phone for the past few weeks now, but they were all becoming too rapidly now. Each message said something different. Some were directions to meeting places where they would fuck each other to death, and some were just to say hi or I miss you. All in all, at the rate Pumpkin was going, she was sure to get them caught up. Carron pressed the speed dial to Pumpkin's number and she answered on the first ring. "Hi baby!" she said gingerly.

"Hey whass'up baby girl" Carron asked, she loved it when he called her that.

"Nuffin. Sitting here thinking about you."

"Where you at?"

"At my desk about to go on lunch. Why where you at?"

"I'm around." Carron said.

"Does that mean close to me?" Pumpkin said.

"It can mean that."

"Depending on what?" Pumpkin asked.

"Depending on you." Carron said.

"Well meet me at McDonald's on New Castle Ave. in ten minutes."

"Ten minutes?"

"Yeah, ten minutes in the ladies room." She said and the phone went dead.

Carron made a u-turn on Gov. Printz Blvd and shot past Gander Hill Prison to get on I-495 South to meet Pumpkin. In what seemed to be only seconds, he was getting off at Terminal Ave. and getting on New Castle Ave. headed to McDonald's.

"Imma tell her we gotta fall back for a minute because we getting too sloppy" He said to himself and those were his intentions until he walked into that ladies room.

Pumpkin heard the door squeak open and spun on her heels in the direction of the door. "Dirty lil whore!" those words echoed the minute she saw Carron. Without a single word, Pumpkin lifted the skirt to her Chanel suite and hopped on the sink panty-less. Gapping her legs wide open, she ran two fingers over her clit and moaned. "Come on baby, fuck your pussy!" before putting them in her mouth.

Carrons' dick got hard as Chinese Algebra as he fumbled with the lock on the door. Once it was secured, his pants dropped to his ankles and there they were again, at each other's flesh like two savage beasts. Carron pounded, as Pumpkin's moans grew louder. So loud that Carron reached over and pressed the hand-drying machine to kill the sounds bouncing off the walls of the tiny restroom and just like that, they were holding each other so close and tight, they felt they could be one.

"Carron, you know what?"

"What?"

"I love you"

"You do?" Carron said, shocked.

"Yeah, lets take all the money and go! Go out west and live happily, forever. Every penny is in my bank account, and the loose money lying around the house is in the safe. Come on baby, tell me you'll go."

"Let me think about it baby girl."

"I already thought about it." Pumpkin said adamantly.

" I see. Give me a few days O.k.?"

"O.k. but that's it, a few days." She said and they began fixing their clothes back up. Once they were dressed and ready to leave, Pumpkin gave him a soft kiss on the lips and told him to go, while she stayed back giving him time to disappear.

Carron was at a total loss for words as he drove his Crown Victorian out of the McDonald's parking lot. "Yo, she really is crazy." He thought, but what she said sounded good to him. He loved her too and their creeping and sneaking was beginning to wear on him, so why not leave? It was only one of the many questions he had to ask himself over the next few days, but it was just as important as any of them.

*   *   *   *   *   *   *

When Saafie pulled up to the stash house on West 30th street, as usual Carron was already there sitting on the trunk of his Crown Vic. Saafie pulled up right behind him in his Jag, and got out to greet him with his right hand extended. Carron slid down off his trunk where he had been sitting for the last fifteen minutes watching the youngin's ball in 30th street Park, and reached out to grab Saafie's hand. When they grasped one another's hand in greeting they followed it up with a half hug.

"Nah this can't be." Saafie said to himself and as they released from each other's grasp, as he got one more whiff and his worst fear was confirmed. Carron's clothes were drenched in the smell of Pumpkin's perfume and he became infuriated, but he kept his composure.

"Got damn baby boy! Where you coming from smelling all good and shit? Saafie asked, as normal as he could. He didn't want Carron to sense that anything was wrong.

"From out to my young babe's crib" he answered on cue.

"Damn she got a nose for perfume. If I didn't know no better nigga, I would a sworn you just left my Pumpkin, nigga." Saafie said and saw the guilt flush over Carron's face.

"Man imagine that. Imagine Pumpkin even looking my way." Carron responded, but Saafie already knew and Carron felt it. Carron knew their little charade was over. No more creeping here and there, no more messages over the phone, and no more lovemaking. The thought of what Saafie might do to him was almost unimaginable. Carron almost panicked and then he remembered the conversation with Pumpkin earlier that day and his mind was made up. He was moving out west.

Saafie listened to the bullshit response, but watched the look on his face and the two didn't mix. It took all the humility he had in his body not to go up side the young boy's head with the butt of his 40 cal., which was hoisted in the small of his back, but he managed. He had to manage, or he would have caught a case right there. The more he thought about Pumpkin and this little nigga fucking, her sucking his dick, the easier it was for him to make a decision about what do with Carron. "This nigga going to come up missing." With that decision freshly made in his head he knew that not only would he be getting back at Trans, he would also be getting back at the ungrateful young boy. "Yeah, that's what imma do. Imma knock his ass off tonight." Saafie confirmed to himself and then continued on with what they came there to do in the first place, which was grab up a couple kilos and drop them off.

Chapter Twenty

Saafie couldn't wait. The anxiety was almost driving him crazy. It seemed as though the sun just wouldn't go down, so the sky would turn pitch black, and he could follow through with his plan. Carron had already been set up for the kill, now he was just waiting for the night to approach. Saafie had explained to Carron earlier that day at the stash house that a large package was coming that night around one o'clock in the morning.

"I need you to meet me here cousin" He said, and then continued, "Cause you know I don't trust none of those other nigga's, feel me?" and Carron fell for the bait like a fish about to be caught on a hook. He knew that Saafie only trusted him because he said it on more than one occasion, so he hadn't got the slightest inclination that something was wrong.

"I need to find something to do to kill some of this time," Saafie told himself as he glanced down at his Techno Marine watch that read 6:00 PM.

Saafie turned the radio on in the Jaguar and let the car take him where it wanted to. He didn't have any particular destination. He just drove. When the Jaguar broke through the Pennsylvania state line and was heading to Philly, Saafie for the hundredth time played out the night's scenario in his head. He knew Carron would be at the house promptly, so he gave him a key to the house.

"Mmm-Hmm and I'mma already be in there waiting on that lil nigga to walk through the door and bang! His brains will be all over the living room floor" his smile revealing evil intentions. The same one he had when he watched his fish devour the rats in the tank that afternoon.

*   *   *   *   *   *   *

241

Carron called Pumpkin the minute he and Saafie went their separate ways. He explained in detail to her, play by play, everything that happened from the time he pulled up to the time he smelled her perfume all over his clothes.

"What he say when he smelled it?" She asked thinking it was cute.

"He ain't say nuffin he just asked me where I been and then he said, if I ain't know no better, I would have sworn you was with my Pumpkin." Carron said and she panicked.

"He knows baby!" She said.

"He don't know" Carron responded.

"I'm telling you baby, he knows. What did he say after that?"

"Nothing, just that we need to meet at the stash house tonight around one."

"In the morning?" Pumpkin asked.

"Yeah." Carron said.

"Baby don't go! Please. Look let me call you back in about fifteen minutes, ok?"

"Ok, and baby girl, guess what?" Carron said.

"What?" Pumpkin asked.

"Let's go out west."

"I knew you would, love you baby."

"Love you too," he said and she hung up the phone.

Carron was uneasy now, as he slid his Nextel back into the holder. He thought back on earlier that day to see if he let anything pass him by and sure enough he did. He was so busy trying to cover up his lie that he didn't even notice that Saafie was acting a little bit too calmly. Like he was trying to hide something or keep it to himself. "Maybe she's right" Carron

thought about what Pumpkin just said. "If she is" He
continued, "I'mma get that nigga first" and his phone rang.
"Hello."
"Hi baby, look. I just tried to call Saafie's phone and
he's not answering. That's not like him he always answers my
calls. I don't care what he's doing; he stops to answer my calls.
Baby he knows, I'm telling you. Please don't go over there
tonight" She pleaded.
"Baby girl, ain't you the one who told me it's a dirty
game?"
"Yes."
"Then I'mma play one, you heard? Since that nigga
trying to get me, I'mma get him first, word I am!" He said and
Pumpkin blushed. For the first time in her entire life, she felt
genuinely loved by someone.
"Just be careful baby, Ok?" She said.
"Ok. Don't worry about nothing" He said and blew a
kiss in the phone. "Damn!" He said not knowing which move
to make next. He always knew that eventually the shit would
one day hit the fan, but he wasn't expecting it to hit so soon.
He wanted to call his boy 'Lil Tone' and let him know what he
was planning to do, but quickly decided against it. "I don't
need no co-defendants" He said to himself and then headed
home to grab his burner.
*   *   *   *   *   *   *

The Atlanta Hawks boarded the airplane bound for
New Jersey at six o'clock sharp in College Park. Hartsfield-
Jackson International Airport was bursting at the seams with
fans there to wish their home team a good road trip. Actually,
this was the first time since the high-flying Dominique Wilkins
was a Hawk that the Hawks were even a contender in the
playoff race, but to the fans that supported them; it was well

243

worth the wait. Trans dressed in his usual 'Phenom' apparel by Reebok walked up the stairs to the airplane with his bag draped over his shoulder, and his earphones jammed in his ears. When he reached the top step, he turned around threw both arms in the air and pumped his fists to the fans, and chants of "Phenom! Phenom!" erupted in the air. Trans then blew a kiss through his hands at his three number one fans, his wife Tish, stepson Tymeere, and their newborn daughter Kenya, named after the beautiful African country.

Trans boarded the plane and sat in the back as usual. Throwing his bag in the overhead storage compartment top of the seat, he settled in and got comfortable. "I'mma have dat ass come up missing!" those words echoed again, but he tried to relax. He reached in his pocket and grabbed two Extra Strength Advil's, and chased them down with a ginger ale soda, because he felt a migraine headache coming on. "Why?" he asked himself again was the question he had no answer for. He just could not make sense out of it all. He tried a psychologist on the low and that didn't work. He tried a prescription drug designed to ease the thinking pattern, but that didn't work, it only made him sleepy and he tried talking to his mother. The only clear answer he got from her was, "You know what? Your daddy couldn't let things go either and he could not get over a threat!" She would always say before finishing. "I always said you had his temper!"

"But fuck that" Trans thought "That nigga ain't have nothing to loose" and he was right in a sense. "Yeah, my dad had a newborn son, and a woman to stay home for, not to mention his freedom, but I got all of that and more!" He talked to himself, trying to make himself see things a little clearer. "I got a wife, kids, millions of dollars, fans all over the globe, and good sense, but I just can't let this ride. Now the nigga even got

the nerve to have my lil brother selling drugs for him! I know
dat nigga done bumped his head." Trans rambled on before
saying." I just hope Boog be there when I get off this plane in
Jersey, 'cause I'mma handle my business. The only way I'mma
make it stop is to get rid of this nigga, so guess what? I'mma
peel his cap!" Trans finished and took out his wallet. He looked
at he picture of Tymeere holding Kenya and Tish holding him
as she stood behind them and hoped like hell what he was
about to do wouldn't take him away from his family, like it did
his father, but it was a risk he was going to take.

*   *   *   *   *   *   *

When the Jaguar bent smoothly around the Concord
Pike exit ramp, Saafie's adrenaline was already pumped. He
hadn't felt this way in a long time. It was almost like he was in
a blind rage, except he was well aware of how he felt, and
conscience of what he was about to do. He headed northbound
on Concord Pike towards his two-story duplex in Brandywine,
and pressed the no button on his cell phone, rejecting
Pumpkin's call for the fiftieth time. The last thing he wanted
to do was talk to her. She had betrayed him and he knew it.
He didn't have to catch them together to know they were
creeping because he smelled the perfume. He bought that
perfume for her because it was what he liked. Besides, nobody
was spending nearly $200.00 on the smallest bottle in the store
except if they were rich, so the case was closed. There was
nothing that Pumpkin or Carron could do or say that was
going to stop what was about to go down. The only thing Saafie
was unsure of was whether or not he should put two in
Pumpkin's dome as well.

"Just one more hour!" He said to himself as the clock
struck twelve. "Just one more hour!" He repeated as he pulled

into the driveway. "I'mma go in here, grab my pistol, throw my black on, and head to the stash house to pop this nigga's top, and then I might pop this dumb bitch's as well!" He talked to himself, as he exited the car, but then felt as if someone was watching him.

*   *   *   *   *   *   *

Carron was parked in the 7-eleven parking lot next to the charcoal pit on Concord Pike in the rental car he rented earlier today. The road, Concord Pike, was nearly empty this time of night except for a few cars and trucks that occupied its pavement every five to ten minutes, but he was patient. He knew Saafie's routine, and when Pumpkin said he hadn't been home, he knew he had to go there because he didn't ride dirty. He knew he would have to go home first to grab his gun before going to the stash house. Carron looked at the clock and saw that it was a quarter to twelve, and knew he'd be passing by any minute.

"Baby are you alright?" Pumpkin asked when his silence on the other end of the phone became loud in her ear.

"Yeah, I'm fine baby girl. I'm just thinking," He answered.

"Are you scared? Because if you are, I can just grab this change in here and we can go now" She said.

"Nah, we ain't goin' to do that 'cause then we'll always be running, feel me? I'm goin' to handle this business and then we'll handle whatever else as it comes along, alright?" He stated.

"Alright." She said and they both got silent again.

Carron's heart was pounding with fear, but not because he was afraid of Saafie. Carron was afraid of the unknown. He was afraid of you of how things were going to turn out and then the Jaguar shot by.

"Baby I gotta go!" he said all of a sudden.

"Why?"

"He just rode by." Carron said and then he pulled out to follow him.

When the phone went dead, Pumpkin's heart went straight to her throat. She could feel the beat in her ears. She was afraid, unsure, and felt uneasy about what was about to go down because she still loved Saafie. In fact, she loved him with all of her heart once upon a time, but that love faded away over the years. The cheating, the mental gymnastics, and the trust that was lost made her literally hate the man. But she wasn't sure if she wanted him dead. After all, he was her best friend, and he did provide for her. She knew that he loved her, but her love was lost and would never be found. Her heart had become hardened towards him and the more she thought about all the shit he did, the more she didn't care one way or another what happened to him. She just wanted it all to end well, so she could move on with her young boy Carron.

*   *   *   *   *   *   *

The airplane's wheels came to a screeching halt in New Jersey's International airport at ten o'clock sharp. Trans' heart was pounding the moment the pilot told everyone to strap on the seatbelts for the landing, and also because he was hoping that Boog was waiting on him so that he could handle his business. He called Boog three days ago to let him know what he needed from him and what he planned to do and then he called again before he left Atlanta to make sure he remembered.

"You dead serious, huh cousin?" Boog asked.

"Yeah I'm serious nigga! You just have to promise me that you'll never say another word about this ever again in life." Trans said and then continued, "I'mma make sure you don't ever need for anything ever again, feel me?"

"Man I don't want none of your money cousin. You're my favorite cousin's husband dog! I don't want shit. My main concern is making sure I get you in and out of there safely, that's all. But if I ever need you, I know you got me." Boog said.

"So are you going to be there?"   Trans asked.

"Think I ain't cousin? Ten o'clock sharp!"

"That's whass'up."

"Awight."

"See you when I get there."

"Ok. 'Phenom.'"

"Yeah nigga the one and only" He replied and they laughed together before hanging up the phones.

Once the plane was completely at a stand still, the hydraulic door opened up, and the cool evening March air breezed through the plane letting everyone know that this was definitely not the warm Atlanta air they were used to. The entire team, all except their star player and team leader, was on the same page. They were focused on the four game lead that Jersey had on them for first place in the East, and the two game lead Philadelphia had on them for second place. Trans however, was focused on getting rid of the headaches and nightmares he suffered from every single night and day, because of this one nigga.

Trans stepped off the plane, walked into the airport and the first person he saw was Boog.

"Hey cousin!" Trans said, and greeted him with a hug.

"Hey cousin" Boog responded.

"Listen, I have to ride to the hotel with the team so follow the bus. As soon as I put my shit up, I'mma slide out of the doors unnoticed. The most important thing about this whole plan is I gotta stay unnoticed. You have to get me there and get me back, feel me?"

"I got you" Boog guaranteed.

"Alright then, let's go."

*   *   *   *   *   *   *

It took less time than Boog thought because Trans was walking out of the hotel like three minutes after he got parked good.

"Damn!" He said, when he saw him. Trans, dressed in all black sweats with a hoody, hopped in the car and said, "Let's do this!"

"Well grab yo' shit from under the seat, and let's go" Boog said as Trans retrieved the bag from under the seat. A black mask, a chrome 40 cal. with a marble grip and a pair of latex gloves was what he needed to end the dreams, and Boog had the medicine all in the bag.

When Boog and Trans finally got to Delaware it was a quarter to twelve, on a Monday night, so where else could the nigga Saafie be, but in the house. Boog crept through the quiet neighborhood slowly, with his foot off the brake and pointed out the house to Trans.

"Are you sure that's it?" Trans asked.

"There goes his Hummer right there."

"Oh ok. I see it. Look, let me out, park right around the corner right there and don't move until I get back here ok? Trans asked.

"Ok." Boog responded and pulled off.

249

Trans crept up on the side of the house and was easing up to knock on the door when he saw headlights pulling up. It was Saafie in the Jaguar, so he fell back into the shadows of the bushes right next to the front door. Trans watched as Saafie exited the car but as soon as he hit the car alarm, shots rang out.

"Pop! Pop! Pop!" was the sound that caught Trans by surprise. He definitely wasn't expecting for this to go down, but he had to finish the job. He watched attentively as Saafie ran towards him and then as an unknown gunman appeared behind Saafie still firing shots.

*   *   *   *   *   *   *

The first shot hit the door causing Saafie's awareness to shoot sky high. He ducked down behind the car first, his heart pounding as his eyes were searching for an escape route. "Oh shit!" he panicked as he flashed back to the night he lost Tyaire. "I have to make it to the crib" he thought as another shot rang out.

*   *   *   *   *   *   *

Carron was on his ass the minute he stepped out of the car. "Pop! Pop! Pop!" went his nine-millimeter as he fired shots at Saafie. With each squeeze of the trigger, he gritted his teeth with cruel intentions. He wanted the nigga to die. He knew as soon as Saafie was gone and out of the picture everything the nigga owned down to his woman would be his, as greed fueled his madness. He squeezed again.

*   *   *   *   *   *   *

Trans was waiting on him to come in point blank range, so he could splat his brains into fragments. Saafie was only a few steps away from him, when the gunman in all black stopped firing.

"He must be re-loading" Trans thought and knew now was the time. Trans never even had to come from behind the bushes as Saafie fumbled with his keys in the door. The only thing he did was extended his arm, pistol in hand, as the barrel sat just a few inches from his head. "Pow!" Trans' gun went off and sent Saafie's soul to another place, as his body and brains lay splattered at his doorway. Trans held the smoking gun.

As Saafie's body laid lifeless on the welcome mat, Trans stepped from behind the bushes and for good measures, he dumped two more into the corpse. Instantly he felt relieved. He knew the dreams and headaches would never come again, he took one last look at his worst nightmare and then disappeared around the corner.

"Come on, let's go" Trans said and then Boog mashed the gas. "Since we're so close, stop at my moms crib, I still got a key." He said and tossed the latex gloves out the window. After he did that, he pulled off his mask, and put it and the gun back into the bag.

"Park right here." Trans said and disappeared up the side of the house, his mom's car was there as well as his pop's truck, but all the lights were out. He slowly eased his key into the lock, opened the door and eased into the house. Tip-toeing down the hallway, he crept down to the basement and pushed the bag up under and behind the hot water tank and left the house headed back to Jersey.

*   *   *   *   *   *   *

Carron was fucked up when he saw the other masked gunman. He didn't know what was going on, all he knew was that whoever it was behind the mask, was a cold blood murderer. He watched it all, the entire thing, from the point blank range temple shot, to the two that went into the lifeless body on the ground before he himself ran off into the night.

"Why did you do that?" Carron asked Pumpkin through the phone when he got back to his car.

"Do what?" She asked honestly not knowing what he was talking about.

"Have somebody else kill him. What? You ain't think I could do it?" He asked upset.

"No baby, I really don't know what you're talking about." He heard the sincerity in her voice.

"Then who was that?" He asked, but wasn't looking for an answer.

"I don't know," She said and a tear fell from her eye. "He really is gone," and she cried.

*   *   *   *   *   *   *

Chapter Twenty-One

For the third year in a row, the Atlanta Hawk's were eliminated from the Playoffs in the second round. The 'Phenom' couldn't do it by himself. He needed some help. Since his contract ended this season, he was definitely going to let them know he needed some help while they negotiated. He knew that whichever way the ball bounced he wanted to stay a Hawk, because he fell in love with the city of Atlanta. There was no other place on God's green earth he'd rather be. He was going to make some demands. The first one would be for the G.M. to get him a good center and power forward so they could take it to the next level, the NBA finals. Then he and his agent would demand a contract that would keep him a Hawk his entire career. Lastly, it had to be a blockbuster deal in the hundred million dollar range, because he knew his credentials proved him worthy of a check that large. He was rookie of the year his first season. He led the league in assists and became an all-star the next season, and this year he led the league in scoring: not bad for a 20 year old.

Trans walked out back into his huge backyard to soak up some sun. As he carried Kenya in his arms, he was followed by his two lil man's his son Tymeere and nephew, baby Tyaire who was huge for his four years. This was his favorite part of the year, the off-season, when he could spend time with family. Just the other day, Rayon and Tasheena flew in with their kids little Tyaire and baby Ali, which Tasheena and Deon just had. Trans sat down in his swinging lawn chair and rocked as the sound of the sprinkler watering the lawn put his mind at ease. He was at total piece for the first time in a long time. The best part about it all was that he hadn't been bothered by a single nightmare or headache in the past three years.

*   *   *   *   *   *   *

Tish stood at the kitchen sink staring out the bay window into the backyard at her knight in shining armor: Trans. Her life felt like a fairytale that had came true. She thanked God everyday for sending Trans to her and rescuing her from the projects and prayed that the rest of her days would be filled with as much joy as they were that day. Tish reached down and rubbed her stomach and a smile overcame her face. She was pregnant with her third child and her husband's second. She made a vow to herself that as long as Trans could keep making her pregnant, she would keep having babies. She knew how it felt to be an only child and she never wanted any of her children to feel that type of loneliness. This way, by having baby after baby, and when Tish and Trans passed away, they would still have each other.

"Girl, what'chu out here doin'? Rayon asked when she walked into the kitchen.

"Nothing girl, just thinking about some shit, that's all." Tish answered and Rayon stood next to her.

"Girl ain't it crazy?" Rayon asked.

"What?" Tish asked not fully understanding the question.

"Just look. If that ain't Tyaire and Saafie all over again." Rayon said emotionally, before going on. "I miss him Tish, he was my baby."

"I know you do girl. The crazy part is, I kind of wish Saafie was still alive, at least so Meere-Meere could know his real father, I just guess it wasn't a part of God's plan."

"Did they ever find out who killed him?" Rayon asked.

"Nope." Tish said.

"That's a shame." Rayon said.

254

"Oh well, that's just how shit goes sometimes." Tish said and let the conversation drop.

"I guess you're right." Rayon said and they left the kitchen and went into the living room to see what Tasheena was bickering about.

"Girl, please come get this little boy!" Tasheena pleaded, holding baby Ali out towards Tish.

"His little ass will not stop crying! I'm about to throw his little behind across the room." She said laughing as Tish took him from her.

"Yeah bitch. You finally met your match!" Rayon said.

"What did I tell y'all along time ago about that bitch word?"

"Oh shit! We forgot Sista Soulja!" Tish and Rayon said in unison and all three of them fell out laughing.

*　　*　　*　　*　　*　　*　　*

The door flew off the hinges around five o'clock in the morning and the house quickly became filled with men and women dressed in all black. Some were unmasked and others wore masks to hide their identity, but everyone who saw them knew who they were because of the big bold yellow letters, which read FBI.

Carron and Pumpkin thought it was a nightmare as they were awakened to the sight of gun barrels staring them in the face.

"Whass'going on?" Pumpkin asked, but was ignored as they snatched Carron from the bed.

"Yo man! What da fuck?" Carron snapped, as he hit the floor.

"Shut up punk!" the man on his back said, and Carron knew from his voice that he was some big husky white boy that wouldn't hesitate to fuck him up, so he chilled.

255

The Feds placed them both in handcuffs and took them downstairs to the sight of about twenty other officers who were busy flipping furniture, rummaging through drawers and searching aimlessly for anything illegal. The house was clean, but they detained Carron anyway and hit every other house they knew he had connections with, but he was sure they wouldn't find anything. He always kept his back door covered.

What he didn't know was that for the past six months he had been buying kilos of cocaine from a Federal agent that knocked off his original connection. The agent was Dominican, and was posing as a cousin of the original supplier, so not only was Carron going down, but also countless others from Philly, Jersey, and Baltimore that were caught up in the multi-city drug sting.

"Bingo!" one of the agents said, during the last raid, at Carron's mother's house. "Looky here!" he said, pulling the bag from behind the hot water tank and holding up the chrome 40 cal. and mask. "Looks like at least another five years mandatory for good old Carron." He joked with the other agents, but didn't know how wrong he was. What he held in his hand was the end to a very special person's prominent career.

*　　*　　*　　*　　*　　*　　*

The news was still hard to believe, but it was true. The 40 cal. handgun found behind the water tank at the Owens' residence was a murder weapon, however the prints found on the gun were not Carron Owens: they belonged to Trans 'Phenom' Owens. No one in the entire Bureau could make any sense of the discovery or the act; to them it was senseless. Why would someone of his stature risk everything that he worked so hard? It was a question to them where no answer would suffice as an explanation. Saafie was a low life in the eyes of the law, and if only Trans could have waited for maybe six months, the Feds probably could have executed the warrant they were building up against him, but Trans decided to seal him and Saafie's fate. It was too late for the Feds to do their job and take Saafie off of the streets and put him in prison where he belonged because Saafie was dead, and Trans was the number one suspect. The three-year-old cold case had been ignited by a huge firestorm so sensational that no one would be able to predict the repercussions. The lead detective of the case grabbed a warrant, and he and his team headed to Atlanta.

*   *   *   *   *   *   *

     Trans knew the day would come when the cops would bust his little brother. He told him over and over, time and time again, to stop selling drugs, but he was too far-gone. In fact, the money he was making surprised Trans, so he couldn't blame him for not wanting to stop, he was just concerned. Trans placed the receiver down on the phone and was exhausted. That was the fifth lawyer he talked to that day about Carron's case, but they all said the same thing. "We'll try and get the best plea agreement we can for him." and Trans understood. The evidence they had against him was just too incriminating.

     "Oh my God! No!" Trans heard Tish scream and then heard her, Rayon and Tasheena burst out into heavy sobs. He jumped up from the bed, heart pounding and raced down the steps, only to be met by three men in blue suits and displaying badges.

     "Trans Owens?" the first one asked?

     "Yes" Trans responded.

257

"I'm detective Mahoney, and you have the right to remain silent." He began with the Miranda rights. When he was finished, Trans asked, "Why am I being arrested?"

"For the 2004 murder of Saafie White." Trans knew then that they had the gun. He had been meaning to grab that gun and throw it in the river on more than one occasion, now all of the missed opportunities and the could of, would of and should of's in the world couldn't change what happened. Detective Mahoney told Trans to turn around and place his arms behind his back, as he slapped the cold metal bracelets on his wrist.

Tish and Rayon were still crying hysterically, as they watched the detectives cuff Trans. They were going so crazy in disbelief that they were beginning to scare the kids and before you knew it, they were crying too. The only one who was calm, cool, and collected was Tasheena. She shed a few drops because of the situation and the pain she knew Tish was suffering, but then she reverted back to her calm demeanor. Her belief in Allah wouldn't allow her to crumble because she knew whole heartedly that what ever happened in life was simply the colors of Allah. It was what he, the most high originated. "Ooo-tho-be-la-he-men-a-shay-tan-a-rah-zheen!" she said out of her mouth, as they brought Trans down the steps. Those words meaning: "I seek refuge in you Allah, from the accused Satin."

"Tasheena." Trans called out to her. "Hold it down for me baby. Tish ain't going to be able to handle this shit emotionally. I need you to get me a lawyer and everything, ok? He said and then turned to his wife. "Baby, I'm sorry and I love you more than life itself!" He said, and then she cried harder.

258

"I got you brother." Tasheena assured him as they escorted him out the door.

*   *   *   *   *   *   *

Trans hired the best attorneys money could buy and they fought with everything they had to exonerate him of the charges he faced. They hit great points in all of their arguments and used Saafie's criminal background against him to conjure the notion of reasonable doubt in the jury's minds. Now the moment of truth arrived as the foreman of the jury stood in the box and read off the verdict to a silent courtroom.

"As for the case against Trans D. Owens, we the jury find him guilty of second degree murder." And for Trans the moment was bittersweet. He was informed by his attorneys before the trial even started that it was likely that the state could get a second degree conviction, and if so, he wouldn't do more than twelve years in prison, eight at the least, so he was pleased with the decision. However, what had he done to his family, his team, and his fans? He would miss his children growing up, his parent's growing older and his career was over. After the commotion in the courtroom settled down, and the few outbursts from Saafie's family members ceased, he stood to his feet. He looked back into the crowd at his wife Tish, as she managed a funny looking smile, but he understood this was new to the both of them. The bailiff walked over and the guards followed him to place Trans back in handcuffs and that's when Tish fell apart. She couldn't hold back the tears.

"I got her." He read from Tasheena's lips and he responded with a, "Thank you." as he was led from the courtroom.

Downstairs he was piled on a court van, from the prison, with twelve other inmates. Some of their cases were as serious as his was, some as minor as jaywalking, either way,

259

they were all headed the same place, Delaware Correctional Center. Trans watched as the big steel gate slid open and didn't feel anything. For this being his first time ever being in trouble, it felt as though he'd been here before. He didn't know why, but it did. "Probably inherited this bullshit from my pop too!" he said disgusted, mad at the man for handing him down all his genes. Then it settled in and hit him like a ton of bricks. He was gone from his family. He wouldn't be able to hold his Kenya, or see the new baby born, let alone cuddle into the comfortable arms of his wife, and he realized he was human, as a single tear stained his cheek.

The guards came out of the building and escorted the inmates into booking and receiving. They fingerprinted them, stripped them naked, made them bend over and cough, and took their pictures for prison identification cards, and then dressed them in white, and handed them cardboard boxes. Inside were three pairs of socks, boxers, and t-shirts. Also, there were two sheets, one towel, one washcloth, one blanket, one toothbrush, a tube of toothpaste, a small toothcomb and a bar of Viola soap. "Damn, they got me living like this." He thought, as he noticed nothing new in the box except the soap, toothbrush, and toothpaste. "Damn, I even gotta wear another nigga's boxers!" He said. "I bet Carron ain't gotta go through this shit in the Feds." He said as he thought about his little brother who was doing a seven year sentence.

After being giving his cell number and building letter of the place he would be housed, he grabbed his box, clipped his prison I.D. on his shirt and headed out to the compound. Carrying his box out in front of him, he stepped into a new world, a place he never thought he'd be. As he walked out onto the pound or yard as they called it in jail, he saw a softball game going on, and as he neared his building he saw them playing basketball in the yard. "Man fuck a basketball." he thought for the first time in his life as he entered the fence, and headed inside the building. The whole time he was walking, he didn't even notice that everybody on the compound came to a complete stop. They couldn't believe it was actually him, the 'Phenom' in their house with them to live, but it was. The initial shock would be over in a few days and the prison would be normal again, but at that moment the atmosphere was different. For now, it was exciting to actually see someone famous.

"Whass'up cousin!" he heard a voice yell from the basketball court. When he turned to look he smiled and said, "Whass'up nigga!" when he saw who it was. It was his boy Darrell from high school that he hung with everyday. "Damn, so this is where you been huh?" He asked, as they both became embarrassed at their encounter. "I told you to stop selling that shit cousin." Trans said.

"Yeah and I told you to stop loving them bitches so much?" He shot back, and for the first time in months Trans had a laugh.

"Fuck you nigga!" He said, and then he saw him, that man who his mom brought him to see when he was sixteen. Yes, he knew it was his dad, but what was he supposed to do, he barely even knew him.

"Hi son" his dad said, as he approached him.

"Hi" Trans answered and the man embarrassed him, holding him tightly, repeating the words, "I'm sorry" over and over again.

"For what? Why are you sorry?" Trans asked.

"For not being there for you and your mom," Trans' dad answered.

"Look dad, don't ever be sorry for anything you did in life. You did it because you thought that was the best way to handle the situation. I have no regrets. You blessed me physically, gave me the natural ability to become who I am, and who I will always be, regardless of what may have happened to me... you know? I can't do nothing but thank God that he made you my father 'cause in all reality, I wouldn't even be here if it wasn't for you." Trans said and there was an uncomfortable silence.

"Thank you son, thanks for not holding any grudges against me."

"I guess it's true about what they say huh?" Trans asked.

"What's that?" He asked.

"The apple doesn't fall far from the tree."

*   *   *   *   *   *   *

Tish was at home in Atlanta, accompanied by her two best friends, sisters as they called themselves, Rayon and Tasheena, and all four of their kids. They watched as little Tyaire played with Tymeere. They watched as Kenya tried to kiss and pat the back of baby Ali, as he lay on a blanket on the couch and they just enjoyed being in one another's company.

"You know what bitch?" Rayon said to Tish.

"What?" Tish asked.

"You need a mutha-fuckin blunt!" She blurted out and couldn't have been more correct.

"You ain't lying!" Tish responded.

"Whass'up with you Tasheena? You wit us?"

"I'm Muslim y'all and Muslims don't get high," She answered.

"I respect dat, but bitch we about to get it in!" Rayon said to Tish and pulled out a dutchie and a bag of haze.

262

Tish and Rayon stepped out on the back deck, while Tasheena stayed in and sat with the kids. Rayon passed Tish the blunt and the Bic lighter and she put it in the air. The first pull nearly choked her, but she eased the smoke out of her lungs. "Damn! I ain't smoked in so long I almost choked." Tish said and took another pull.

"Bitch I don't care if you smoked everyday. That shit right there goin' to make you cough." Rayon said.

"I heard dat." Tish responded as smoke escaped her mouth.

Tish was floating by the time Rayon plucked the blunt roach out into the grass. She was feeling a feeling she hadn't felt in a long time and it felt good. All the pain, agony, and stress over the past months felt as if they had been lifted from her shoulders and 'Oh what a relief it was' like the old Alka-Seltzer commercials said. Tish followed Rayon into the house and into the living room, only after she stopped and grabbed a soda from the refrigerator to kill her dry mouth.

Tish flopped down on the couch, pulled her feet up under herself and for the third time, she read the newspaper. The article read as so: "Fans all around the world were stunned today when the verdict was handed down in the murder trial of Trans 'The Phenom' Owens. It took three whole days of deliberation from the jury before they came up with a second-degree murder conviction. The sentencing date was scheduled for later this month. Inside sources say he will receive a twelve year sentence, suspended after eight." and then Tish didn't read anymore.

Tish stopped reading right there at the eight year part every time because the tears that fell from her eyes blurred her vision to the point where she didn't want to try to complete the article. She had read enough. Just knowing that she would be away from her husband for eight years drove her crazy inside, as her silent sobs became loud cries.

"See Rayon, I knew y'all shouldn't have smoked that weed." Tasheena said, as they watched their friend fall apart. There was nothing they could say or do that would change what happened to her husband, or the way that she felt, and they knew it. She would have to mourn for a while, but they vowed to be there by her side for as long as she needed them to be.

Tish wiped her eyes, threw the newspaper to the middle of the floor, and looked around at her surroundings and at that moment, finally grappled her reality, "Damn! It's just me and my girls."

THE END!
"So real you think you lived it!"

Next Books to be released:

Bloody Money 2

From Ashy, To Nasty, To Classy: The Tommy Good Story...

Street Knowledge Publishing
Order Form
Street Knowledge Publishing
P.O. Box 345, Wilmington, Delaware 19801
Email: jj@streetknowledgepublishing.com
Website: www.streetknowledgepublishing.com

Also by the Author:

Bloody Money
ISBN # 0-9746199-0-6 $15.00
Shipping/ Handling
Via U.S. Priority Mail $3.85
Total $18.85

Me & My Girls
ISBN # 0-9746199-1-4 $15.00
Shipping/ Handling
Via U.S. Priority Mail $3.85
Total $18.85

Bloody Money 2
ISBN # 0-9-746199-2-2 $15.00
Shipping/ Handling
Via U.S. Priority Mail $3.85
Total $18.85

The Tommy Good Story
ISBN # 0-9746199-3-0 $15.00
Shipping/ Handling
Via U.S. Priority Mail $3.85
Total $18.85

Purchaser Information

Name: _____

Address: _____

City: _____ State: ___ Zip Code: _____

Bloody Money ___

Me & My Girls ___

Bloody Money 2 ___

The Tommy Good Story ___

Quantity Of Books? _____

Make checks/money orders payable too:
Street Knowledge Publishing